Crow Creek

CROW CREEK

A Bettendorf Tale Book 2

Matthew Speak

CONTENTS

For Michelle

BRIEF SUMMARY
OF CHARACTERS
AND RELATED
EVENTS

Jack Davies – A sixteen-year-old from Bettendorf, Iowa, who has lived his whole life haunted by ghosts. Discovers that he is a peregrinator—a person with the power to travel between dimensions. Rescues the mysterious girl Ava from a pit in Sunnycrest Park. While at a Halloween party, Jack is kidnapped by Brother Jones and the Sunset Circle cult, who offer him to the Devils of the Glen. During the Devils Rite, the devils led by Surgat, attempt to use his power to open the gates to a hell dimension. Before the gates can be fully opened, Jack and his friends are rescued by the wolf spirits, Opus and Maximus.

The Devils of the Glen – Surgat, Bukavac, and Onoskelis—three ancient demons long ago imprisoned in a cave in Devils Glen Park. Surgat is the greatest of them and their leader. During the Devils Rite, they are released from their prison through a spell cast by the Sunset Circle cult. They attempt to use Jack Davies' power to open the gates to a hell dimension and call forth their powerful master. Before they succeed, they are killed by the wolf spirits, Opus and Maximus.

Brother Billy Jones – A malicious figure who comes to Bettendorf disguised as a preacher. Has the ability to turn the dead into monsters. He assists the Devils of the Glen in finding the peregrinator, Jack Davies. Kidnaps Stephanie Caine, Jimmy Vance, Emily Scott and Lara Fanning, turning them into vampires. At his church on Devils Glen Road, Brother Jones conducts a series of services in which he kills congregants by touching them with his right hand. He brainwashes his congregation into sacrificing themselves and their loved ones in order raises an army of undead. Brother Jones directs his army to attack Bettendorf on Halloween night as a distraction from the Devils Rite. Kidnaps Jack Davies and brings him to the Bennett mansion. Brother Jones escapes when the devils are killed by Opus and Maximus.

Randy Wall – Jack's best friend. During the Devils Rite, Surgat injures Randy's arm by grabbing it and digging his nails into the boy's flesh.

Johnny Raynis – "Imaginary" childhood friend of Jack Davies until the age of four. At first, Johnny protects Jack from the constant hauntings, but something changes in him and he turns evil. He betrays Jack by offering him to the malevolent wraith, Griselda Bennett. Johnny is eventually banished from the physical world by the ghost of Anne Davies.

Anne Davies – Jack's twin sister who died during birth. Summoned back to the physical world as a ghost by Jack Davies. Protects him from the ghosts and demons drawn to his power. As a result of the Devils Rite, Anne appears to have been resurrected as a living teenage girl.

Lara Fanning – A seventeen-year-old high school girl. Sees visions of a blue aura whenever Jack Davies is around. While babysitting, she is kidnapped by Brother Jones and turned into a vampire along with her friends Emily Scott and Stephanie Caine. However, unlike her friends, she does not turn to evil but remains good. Attempts to help Jack Davies during the Devils Rite. With the help of Jennifer Warren, travels into the alternate dimension Bettendorf to help find Jennifer's husband, Mark. When they are attacked by Griselda Bennett, Lara saves Jennifer by grabbing Griselda and flying into the sky.

Mark Warren – An officer with the Bettendorf Police Department. After the death of his wife, Mark suspects something isn't right in the town of Bettendorf. Begins his own personal investigation of the Sunset Circle neighborhood, which leads him to suspect even the Bettendorf Police Department. Before he can discover the truth about the cult, he is killed by

Brother Jones at the Fenno Cemetery. Wakes up in the guest house of the Bennett estate in the alternate dimension Bettendorf. Meets the ghost of Genevieve Bennett, mother of William Bennett III, who directs him to find a pair of gates hidden deep in a maze of tunnels below the Bennett Estate. With the help of his wife, he keeps the gates to the hell dimension closed during the Devils Rite.

Ava – A mysterious spirit drawn to Bettendorf. Ava appears as a teenage girl, though she claims to be many centuries older. She is kidnapped by the Sunset Circle cult, through the power of the young witch, Bettie Stone. Jack Davies rescues her, and she is immediately attracted to the power she perceives in him. Though her true nature and motives remain unclear, Ava becomes romantically drawn to Jack. She decides to help him and his friends during the Devils Rite.

Leo Lourogen – "Extremely large rider of motorcycles" and Randy Wall's cousin. Assumed by most Bettendorf citizens to be mentally challenged—and possibly dangerous. Helps Jack and his friends during the Devils Rite. Appears to know much about the supernatural forces invading their town. Highly skilled in combat and swordplay. Rescues Shaun Porter and Joe Lampert when Brother Jones's undead army attacks on Halloween night.

Griselda Bennett – The long-dead wife of city founder William Bennett III. Appears in the physical world as an old wraith with no eyes and a mouth that hangs open. Griselda haunts the grounds of the Bennett mansion, both in the physical world and in the Bettendorf of the alternate dimension.

Genevieve Bennett – Mother of William Bennett III. Now lives as a spirit in the alternate dimension guest house of the Bennett estate. Helps Officer Mark Warren to locate the gates below the Bennett estate and tells him to do what he can to keep them closed. Her spirit fades from the alternate dimension Bettendorf. She leaves the guest house and all her possessions in the care of the Warrens.

Bettie Stone – A powerful twelve year old witch. Was used as a pawn by her own parents, both of whom were members of the Sunset Circle cult. Her drawings of mysterious figures and symbols were part of an elaborate spell to unlock the Devils of the Glen from their prison. During the Devils Rite, she has a change of heart and decides to help Jack and his friends. She forces Griselda Bennett back into her crypt, banishing her from the physical world.

Jennifer Warren – Wife of Officer Mark Warren. While working at the private school in the Bennett mansion, Jennifer comes into contact with the ghost of Griselda Bennett who proceeds to possess her. Driven mad, she is sent to a mental hospital for three years. Eventually, she escapes long enough to deliver a message to her husband, "Seek the gates, and save the boy." She kills herself with a knife in the middle of Sunset Circle. She awakens in the alternate dimension Bettendorf, where she is captured and enslaved by Griselda. During the Devils Rite, Jennifer escapes Griselda and brings Lara Fanning back with her to the alternate dimension to find her husband and defeat Griselda. Eventually, Jennifer makes it to the gates where she assists Mark in keeping the gates closed.

Shaun Porter – Friend of Jack and Randy. Is eating ice cream at Whitey's with Joe Lambert when Brother Jones's undead army attacks. One of the undead, a girl, seems drawn to him. He and Joe are rescued by Leo Lourogen, who drives away with them on his motorcycle. Leo drops the boys off at a crossroads, telling them to wait for him.

Joe Lambert – Friend of Jack and Randy. Is eating ice cream at Whitey's with Shaun Porter when Brother Jones's undead army attacks. Is rescued by Leo Lourogen and dropped off at crossroads.

Jimmy Vance – Teenager and town bully. Recruited by Brother Jones to assist with his preparation for the Devils Rite. Jones turned him into a half-vampire. Was nearly killed by Randy Wall and Leo Lourogen, but managed to escape while they were distracted.

Lucy Doyle – A teenage girl suffering from emotional disturbance. Her parents sacrifice her to Brother Jones during a sermon at Valley Baptist Church. Brother Jones kills her by touching her forehead with this hand. Later, she is resurrected along with other members of the congregation, to serve as a soldier in Jones's undead army. On Halloween night, Lucy, along with several hundred undead, attacks the Whitey's Ice Cream Shop on Devils Glen Road. While eating the brains of a server, she sees Shaun Porter and appears to be mesmerized by him.

Opus and Maximus – Wolf spirits who were trapped in our world and forced to serve Griselda Bennett and a mysterious shadow man. They are set free by a young Jack Davies. In thanks, they pledge to help him whenever he needs it; all he must do is call their names in a time of great need. Jack summons them during the Devils Rite, and they arrive just in time to kill the Devils of the Glen along with several of the Sunset Circle cult, disrupting the ceremony in the process. Jack pledges to return the favor whenever they need his help. The wolves reluctantly accept his pledge and return to their own dimension.

1

PROLOGUE: OF THINGS THAT MADE IT THROUGH

1.

"It's late," said Lindsey Meeks, as she wiggled herself out from under her boyfriend.

"Baby, we've got all the time in the world. It's Halloween." Trey Washington grabbed her by the waist and rolled onto his back so that Lindsey wound up half-straddling him. "Just relax."

"If my dad finds us on the couch, you're dead, and you know it." Lindsey managed to pull herself away to sit on the coffee table facing him.

"Your dad's a racist."

"My dad's a *dad*," Lindsey said. "No man wants to come home to find his daughter grinding on the couch with a boy, white or black."

"Boy, huh?"

Lindsey rolled her eyes, crossing her arms over her chest.

"I'm kidding! But come on, now. You know being *male* ain't the only thing your dad has against me. It's cool. Just tellin' it like it is; that's all."

Trey reached out, pulled her to him, giving her a long slow kiss. Lindsey felt her defenses begin to waver.

"Telling it like it is and telling it like you see it? Those are two different things," she said between kisses.

"Mmhmm."

Lindsey pulled back and held his hands in front of her.

"Seriously, I know he's cold with you, but you have to believe me. He's like that with every boy. I know my dad, and I've never heard him say a racist thing in his life. He votes Democrat every election."

"Girl, that doesn't mean a damn thing. I'm telling you it's ok. Everyone's got a little racist in him. Don't matter who you're talking to. We *all* do."

"Oh, is that right?"

Trey winked.

"I just gotta win him over. Show him I'm a good guy. Might take a while, but it's worth it."

"It is?" Lindsey asked, a small flutter tickling her insides. They'd only been seeing each other a couple of weeks—their best friends were the only other kids who even knew about their relationship. And here, right now, was the first time he'd let on that maybe he *liked* her—as in a girlfriend. *No!* She wouldn't let herself get caught up in those thoughts. She'd stay calm and let it play out—that was her plan.

"Of course, it's worth it. *You* are worth it! Why do you think I've been coming over here so much? I want this to work, like, for real," Trey said.

Now, a flock of butterflies shot through Lindsey's stomach in a rush that almost made her dizzy. She became embarrassingly aware that she wasn't hiding her feelings very well. Small tears formed just at the corner of her eyes—not enough to come dripping out, not yet, but if she didn't wipe them soon, one of them would soon emerge and give her away.

She shivered. Grabbing an elastic band from the coffee table, she tied her hair back into a ponytail and stood. She shook her head, walked to the kitchen, and leaned on the counter with a sigh, keeping her back to him. Tw0 tears had already escaped down her cheeks, and she knew there would be more if she didn't get control of herself. *Shit*, she thought as she heard him quietly step behind her. A moment later, his hands slid around her waist—not in a sexual way but with care.

"Look," he whispered. "You know I'm not some player. When have you ever seen me acting like those other guys—chasing after every girl who passes by? When have you seen me do that?"

"Never," she answered, knowing it was true. Trey was focused for a teenager—he had always been that way. For Trey, life was football, grades, and that was it. And when he committed to something, he gave everything he had to it.

"See? If I'm saying I want this, I mean it. And I'll do what I have to do to make it work—I promise you that."

"What about next year?" She turned to face him, crossing her arms again.

"What about it?"

"You're going to the University of Iowa."

"Yeah, so are you."

"But *you're* going there to be a big football star. I'm going there to be a teacher."

"No, I'm going there for medical school. I'll just *happen* to be playing football too," he said, crossing his arms to mirror hers.

"I know, but you'll *also* be a star football player. Athletes are like celebrities at U of I! How many girls will be lined up to do—*whatever* you want them to do? I'm just me, OK? That's all I'm ever gonna be." She knew she would regret this later, but right now, she had no choice.

Trey paused. "You know what? You're right. If things go as well for me as the coaches say, it's gonna be intense. A lot of attention, no doubt about it, but so what? Look, there are no guarantees no matter who you are. You want to date some other guy? Someone you think has a future that's safer? Go ahead, but you won't know that relationship is going to work either. Nothing's guaranteed. All I know is I'm faithful—that's me; that's who I am. And I wanna be with you."

Lindsey smiled and wiped her eyes then laughed a little.

"You're dumb," she said, behind her hand.

Trey stepped into her, wrapping his arms around her, placing his chin on her shoulder. The two stood there like that for a few minutes. Lindsey peered over his arm to see the time was 12:40 when she noticed the lights flicker. Trey pulled her face in front of his own and gave her the most loving kiss she'd ever had.

"Be my girlfriend?" he asked.

The old-fashioned-ness of it made her want to giggle, but she stopped herself. "Yes, of course—"

Her answer was interrupted by a sound, sudden and loud. They jumped away from each other. Then, nothing. Silence. The noise was unlike anything she'd ever heard, almost as if the very air had exploded. It had come from the direction of the bedrooms, down the hall off the kitchen.

"What the hell was that?" Trey asked.

"I don't know," she said, and they both turned to look toward the hall. From where they stood, they could only see a few feet down it.

"You sure no one's here? Your brother?"

"No, Ricky's at a sleepover with some of his fifth-grade friends. No one's here."

Trey thought for a moment. "Where's the sleepover?"

"At the Golieb's house. A couple blocks away."

"Ah ha!" Trey exclaimed.

Lindsey thought for a second, and then it dawned on her. She laughed and whispered, "You don't think he and his friends are *spying* on us? Trying to scare us?"

"It *is* Halloween, ya know?"

"Of course! That little shit," Lindsey said as she stormed down the creaky wood-floored hall. Trey followed to the doorway, chuckling as he watched Lindsey check each room. She looked under every bed, opened every closet, and rifled through hanging clothes, but found no evidence that her brother and his friends were in the house.

Finally, after she searched the last room at the end of the hall, she emerged and slowly walked back toward Trey. "That's weird," she said. "I wonder what could have made that sound. I mean if no one is here—"

She stopped speaking when she saw Trey's face. His eyes had gone wide, and his mouth was hanging open like he was trying to call out to her, but no sound was coming out. Oddly, he was not looking at her, but staring over her shoulder at something behind her.

"Trey," she said weakly.

Lindsey sensed a presence. The skin on the back of her neck tightened and her eyes widened. Someone was behind her, close to her back. Cool breath brushed against her blond ponytail. The flesh on her arms stood in a million tiny bumps, and her eyes widened. The sound of raspy breathing grew louder as the floorboards groaned at her heels.

"Baby, get over here. Now!" Trey said, his voice cracking. But she could barely hear his words.

Suddenly, she felt a tightness in her back—*or was it her chest? Both?* Yes, she felt tightness in her back and in her chest. It was like steel. And when she looked down, she saw the strangest sight. A shiny object, metallic and sharp, protruded from between her breasts straight through a hole in her shirt.

How odd. That hole wasn't there before. Was it?

It was a familiar thing jutting out from her chest, an everyday item—one she had seen every day of her life—but for some reason, she couldn't quite place it. What was it? It was on the tip of her tongue.

A knife! That's what it is, she remembered. *It's the tip of a knife. But how bizarre! Why is the point of a knife sticking out of my chest? That doesn't make sense at all.*

Looking up to ask Trey what was happening, she saw him bent

over at the end of the hall, the veins in his forehead popping out. He seemed to be screaming at someone behind her, but not making a sound.

Why does he look so upset? Did I do something wrong? And why is everything silent?

Then she felt herself jerking violently back and forth, and a moment later, a cold hand gripped her forehead, pulling her head back, until she stared up at the hallway ceiling. Cold metal sliced along her throat, followed by a rush of fluid down her neck. Oddly, it didn't hurt. In fact, Lindsey wondered if she was dreaming the whole thing. The warm liquid ran across her chest, soaking in the padding of her bra, as her remaining energy slowly faded. She fell to her knees for a few brief seconds then slumped onto her hip, steadying herself with one hand while the other gingerly touched the growing red spot on her shirt.

This will stain, I think. Oh my god, how embarrassing.

She reached out her hand to her new boyfriend, the boy of her dreams—Trey Washington, star running back for the perennial powerhouse Bettendorf Bulldogs—who will soon be a star Iowa Hawkeye, lighting up scoreboards on Saturday afternoons. And Lindsey, his faithful girlfriend, will be cheering for him from the student section of Kinnick Stadium, her face painted black and gold. She called out to him, but her mouth refused to form words as a flood of thick blood rose in her throat.

Trey looked at her once more with shock frozen on his face as Lindsey felt the cold metal piercing her back again and again. She shook back and forth with each blow, like an old rag doll. Finally, Trey said something to her, turned, and ran back through the kitchen toward the front door. It seemed to Lindsey almost as if he was moving in slow motion—as if the whole world had slowed to a dead crawl. She finally slumped to the floor, her cheek resting on the cool wood slats.

Then she watched as one large boot stepped over her head and onto the floor in front of her. She looked up to see the enormous figure of a man, dressed in a dark black overcoat that hung down to the tops of his heavy work boots. The back of his bald head was covered in burns and scars. She watched him methodically stride down the hall, he too in slow motion until the world went black, and Lindsey Meeks gave up the last moments of her young life.

Seconds later, Lindsey's parents pulled their Land Rover into the driveway right as Trey Washington burst through the ornately designed glass of their front storm door. They stared in wonder as he sprinted away down Crow Creek Road, screaming at the top of his lungs for help.

2.

Allison Murphy and Chad Howard stood on the shore of the old quarry that sat in a small wooded area behind Crow Creek Park. Chad had talked her into skipping Jen Graver's party and meeting up with some friends at the park instead. Though she was never a big fan of Jen Graver, Allison wished they had at least made an appearance. The other kids who had joined them were more Chad's friends than her own, except for Tatsu, the Japanese foreign exchange student who was staying with Allison's family for the year.

Dan "Danimal" Hammon and Sherry Watts were both juniors, like Allison and Chad. Eddie Simonian, Chad's best friend since kindergarten, came along, hoping to get a chance to talk to Tatsu. Eddie wasn't the brightest bulb in the chandelier, but he was a nice guy, nonetheless. Tatsu had pale, almost translucent skin and shiny black hair, cut into an adorable bob. She was taller than Allison, at least 5'10", with a gorgeous figure. Allison told her every day that she should stay in the States and become a model, but Tatsu only laughed, saying she could never do something like that. Her goals involved medical school. Though she had only been in the United States for a couple of months, her English was better than most of the kids born in Bettendorf. In addition to smarts, Tatsu was opinionated, sassy, and full of personality. Allison had liked her immediately.

She could tell by the girl's body language that Tatsu wasn't particularly interested in Eddie, but she seemed happy enough to have something to do on a Saturday night, and she loved talking to people. She was not too familiar with Halloween, so she had thousands of questions. And of course, she found great fun in the cosplay aspect of it.

Chad and Dan were typical Iowa boys—white, stocky, and seemingly unable to leave the house without putting on a cheap farm utility baseball cap, which they both wore absent an ounce of hipster irony. Eddie was half Armenian, with black hair and deep brown eyes. He played linebacker on the BHS football team, though he tended to be hurt on the sideline more than playing on the field.

Sherry spent ninety percent of her time staring into a phone, taking selfies, or texting her friends. She was never present in any situation. Several sighs and rolling of the eyes made it evident that Sherry would rather have been at Jen's party than chugging beers at Crow Creek Park.

They had all parked their cars a mile away on a residential street off Crow Creek Road and walked to the park. Somehow, they had awkwardly carried a picnic basket full of snacks and a pony keg without being spotted by any Bettendorf police officers. And it wasn't long before they had tapped the keg on the far side of the park, behind a merry-go-round shaped like half an eggshell.

After much drinking and a few rounds of truth-or-dare—which Tatsu won quite comfortably by singing a Katie Perry song in her underwear while balancing on top of the playground monkey bars—Chad had sidled up next to Allison on the grass while the other couples talked. She agreed to take a walk with him through the trees at the far end of the park and to the quarry, though her defenses were on high alert for any clumsy moves he might be planning to put on her.

And so, by 12:40 am, Chad and Allison were standing on the shore of the Crow Creek quarry, staring at the smooth water. At first, Chad had been doing his best to creep Allison out, but now *he* was the one glancing behind them every few seconds.

Suddenly, in the distance, they heard a popping sound ring out through the night sky.

"What was that?" Chad asked.

"I don't know," Allison said. "Fireworks?"

"For Halloween?"

"Maybe someone has some leftovers from fourth of July."

"Yeah, maybe," Chad said. They stood there for a while, listening to the popping sounds continue sporadically. "Did you know there's a huge crane at the bottom of this quarry? They decided it wasn't worth it to try to bring it back up before they flooded the place."

"Everyone's heard that." Allison rolled her eyes and looked back in the direction of the park. The popping sounds had stopped.

"Well, do you know the legend?"

She glanced at him with an incredulous frown. "What legend?"

"About the crane worker—the legend of the crane worker."

"What 'legend of the crane worker?'" Allison asked, even though she was almost sure she would regret taking his bait.

"Well, ya' see, this dude who worked the crane down there was all broken up because the mining company was closing the quarry and he was gonna lose his job. The night before they flooded the place, he went down there with a case of beer and climbed into the crane. He, like, got shit-faced and passed out. So, when they flooded the place the next morning, he was still in the crane—dead asleep. I guess the guys up top saw him struggling to get out of the thing, but by then, it was too late—the water was already flowing too fast. By the time they shut off the water, it was already ten feet above the roof. There was nothing they could do. People say he roams these woods at night, looking for revenge!" Chad stepped closer and tried his best to put on a Vincent Price *Thriller* voice for that last part.

"Oh, that's B.S. Like they wouldn't check and double-check the whole area before they flooded it with a gazillion gallons of water," she said, rolling her eyes, and looked back toward the park. "What do you think the other guys are doing?"

"I don't know. Eddie was working his mojo with Tatsu. They're all probably having fun," Chad said, putting his arm around her tentatively.

Allison still wasn't sure if she was interested in Chad, but she was feeling a little chilly, and he was warm, so she didn't rebuff his modest advance. "I suppose we should probably get going soon. If I'm not home by one, my dad won't be happy."

"Yeah, I guess you're right. But, just one thing. . ."

Allison tensed up involuntarily. She had an idea just what this *just one thing* was going to be—an offer to have dinner or a movie. If he were a more aggressive guy, he might have asked her to come back his house—sneak her in the basement door. However, for all his goofiness, Chad proved to be something of a gentleman.

"I just want to say I had a good time tonight, and I, you know, would like to do it again sometime. That's all."

Relief rushed through her. Chad wasn't trying to pin her down to anything specific. *Thank God!*

"Yeah, that would be fun," she said. "Let's talk about it on Monday."

"It's just that—"

Before he could finish the sentence, a scream rang out into the night, echoing across the park and through the trees, followed by yelling, cursing, and cries for help.

"What the hell was that?" Allison asked as she stepped back from the shore.

"I don't know. I think it came from the park. Come on," Chad said, and he grabbed her by the hand, pulling her away from the quarry.

Allison glanced back. For a moment, she thought she saw a man standing on the opposite side of the water, next to the rotting trunk of the dead pine. From that distance, it was hard to make out much, but he looked somewhat husky, wearing a wet pair of old overalls. But before Allison could get a good look, the road took a turn, and a line of trees blocked her view.

Screams echoed from the park along with cries for help. Those were their friends' voices. The path was lined on either side by dozens of old oaks and maples whose bare branches arched over it, creating a kind of woodsy tunnel. Allison found that it looked a little too much like the path you would avoid if you came upon it at a fork in the road. Earlier, on their way to the quarry, she swore she could see glowing eyes looking out at her from the underbrush and wailing ravens staring down from their perches. Now, the Crow Creek woods were deserted.

Suddenly, Chad stopped in his tracks as an enormous explosion shook the earth, illuminating the trees in front of them. A small mushroom cloud of fire and smoke rose at least a hundred feet into the sky, lurching over the tops of the trees. Allison stared at the plume of smoke for several moments, frozen with fear and confusion.

Finally, she came to her senses. She grabbed Chad by the hand and yanked him behind her, yelling, "Come on!"

When they finally broke into the open expanse of the park, they saw what looked like a battlefield a hundred and fifty yards away, right where they and their friends had been chugging beers only twenty minutes before. A dozen small fires burned all around the playground equipment, but they saw no movement. As they drew closer, the smell of charred flesh overwhelmed them. Chad stopped to cover his face with his hands, retching into a nearby trash can. But Allison, panic-stricken, ignored the stench and continued to run all the way to the playground. Once there, she searched for their friends in the ashes.

"Oh, my God," she cried, now covering her mouth and nose with the top of her blouse. "I think they're dead. These are Dan's shoes—I remember the weird buckles. And I think that's Eddie over there by the slide, maybe? But other people are here, too. Like five or six other people."

The bodies were blackened and burned so badly it was impossible to recognize anything. In fact, it looked like the blaze had burned so intensely, so quickly that some of the bodies appeared melted together. A massive blaze roared a dozen feet away as some of the nearby weeds and shrubs caught fire.

"What?" Chad called to her, still bent over the garbage can. "Who are they?"

"I don't know," she said. "I don't recognize any of them. They're all badly burned. But they don't look like people we know. I don't get it."

Eventually, Chad joined her at the playground, covering his mouth with his hand and pinching his nose closed with his fingers. He looked like he might heave all over the ground at any moment. "What's that?" he choked out finally, pointing toward the swings.

Allison saw that someone was crawling next to the plastic pirate ship, struggling to move away from the fires. It looked like a girl, half-naked and injured. She approached the girl, asking, "Tatsu? Is that you?"

"Allison?"

Allison rushed over to her and took the girl in her arms. "Yes. Yes, it's me. What happened here?"

Tatsu lay in her arms, weeping for several minutes before she could speak. When she finally did, she spoke in Japanese, repeating the same phrases over and over.

"I'm sorry, Tatsu. I don't understand," Allison cried. "What are you saying?"

Tatsu looked up at her with tears flowing down the sides of her face. Finally, she lifted her head and screamed, "I killed them! Oh, help me. I killed them all!"

2

AFTERMATH

1.

Shaun Porter and Joe Lambert crouched behind a row of bushes at the crossroads of Crow Creek and Middle Roads, still in their Beatles Halloween costumes, though both boys were now covered in dirt and blood spatter. The mop top wigs had flown off their heads almost immediately after hopping onto the back of Leo's motorcycle.

Crow Creek was nothing but gravel and dirt on the west side of Middle but newly paved on the east, where it led to a new Pleasant Valley housing development. On the northwest corner stood Dale Morgan's farm, most of which had been sold off to build various housing developments over the years. The past few years, he was only planting about twenty to thirty acres, though it didn't matter. Each year, he made a bundle selling off the land to one housing development after the other, so now, farming amounted to little more than a hobby—granted, it was a *hobby* that still managed to take up a good portion of his time during the spring, summer, and fall.

Leo had dropped off the boys, instructing them to hide in the brush until he got back, but that had been three hours ago. They had texted him repeatedly, along with all their other friends, but received no replies. Whatever had drawn Leo away was obviously not letting go quickly, so they stayed hidden, anxiously listening to the distant screams and sporadic gunfire ringing out from the direction of Whitey's Ice Cream. At one point, a massive explosion had sounded from somewhere behind them, off toward Crow Creek Park, and they saw a towering mushroom cloud of fire and smoke rise into the air. Then there was the bizarre light in the sky that made it look like daylight had come early. Though all of that had ended hours ago, the boys remained on anxious alert.

"Something's moving over there," Shaun whispered, nodding his head in the direction of the cornfield across the road.

"Think it's one of those zombies?" Joe asked.

Shaun shook his head no, but that was a lie. Shaun knew who was moving in that field, and he couldn't shake her from his thoughts—the dead girl they had seen at Whitey's earlier. She had looked at him like she knew him—like she wanted him—and thoughts of her had invaded his mind ever since.

Joe asked, "Think we should get moving?"

"I guess. I don't know what else to do."

"Leo said something about a church out there on Forest Grove Road or something," Joe said.

Shaun thought about it. "I parked with Kelly Tramer out there once, I think. I remember a church out that way." Shaun rose to a crouch and peered over the brush to check out the area. "I think that's Mr. Morgan's farm over there across the road. Let's see if he's home first but quietly. He's got a huge shotgun, and I don't want to get my head blown off if he's looking for zombies. If he's gone, we'll duck into the cornrows and head for the church. Might be best to stay off the main roads."

"Yeah, good idea," Joe said.

The boys jogged across the road and made their way onto the Morgan property. As they passed the farmhouse, they peeked through the dark windows but could see no movement inside.

Shaun and Joe continued past the house, crossing between a pair of barns right to the edge of a massive yellowed field. The wind whistled through the stalks, rustling the long blades. Dry leaves flapped up and down, and long tassels swayed back and forth in the night breeze.

"Shit," Shaun said. "I hate cornfields at night."

"Me too. *Children of the* damn *Corn* ruined them for me. That frigging red-headed kid gave me the creeps. So how are we gonna stay headed in the right direction? We can't see over these stalks."

Shaun thought about it for a moment and then looked up into the northern sky. Suddenly, he had an idea. "That church is just north of here, right?"

"Yeah."

"Well, look up there in the sky ahead of us. I think that bright star just above this row is the North Star. Let's keep it in our sights, and we'll head in that direction. We should at least come out of this field and hit somewhere on Forest Grove Road—from there, we can find the church, I think."

"Ok, let's get going. I keep hearing things behind us."

Shaun and Joe quietly took off down the cornrow, while following a flickering heavenly body they mistakenly believed to be the North Star.

Behind them, a girl who was not quite living and not entirely dead emerged from a grassy ditch at the corner of Middle and Crow Creek, sniffing the air. She was only hours into her new life—if *life* is what you could call this strange existence—and her senses were sharper than they'd ever been. Her eyes darted quickly across the landscape, searching.

She sensed movement behind her. Two undead men in bloody business suits climbed from the ditch and stood behind her, waiting, their vacant eyes staring only at her. A hierarchy had already formed, subconsciously, and the men were keenly aware of who was in charge. They communicated their subservience telepathically to their newly appointed queen.

Lucy, they had called her in their thoughts, and the name, though half-forgotten, seemed right. *Yes—Lucy I am and will be.*

Lucy scanned the horizon. The fat one on the motorcycle had roared past her only a few hours ago, but Lucy hid in the ditch to avoid detection. She did not fear the fat man, though she sensed a peculiar power in him. But he was not the one she wanted. It was the boy—the boy from the ice cream shop, the boy who had stared at her—*he* was the one. He was hers.

Of course, this was not the task assigned to her—not what her creator had ordered her to do–no, it was not. The preacher had given her different instructions, but she suddenly found herself not wanting to follow that man's orders—he stank of lies and weakness. And Lucy was strong, ever since she had met the man in the suit. What had he said to her? He had asked her a question that changed everything. What was it?

Do you want to ascend? Yes, that was the question. And she had nodded and received his gift.

Just then, she sensed movement. Her eyes fixed themselves on the cornfield across the gravel road. She sensed a slight disturbance in the corn. And she smelled something—a familiar scent. A grotesque smile lifted the corners of Lucy's black lips ever so slightly. She moved across the road and onto the property of a farm. The house smelled empty. She passed it without care and continued to the cornfield, followed closely by her faithful servants. She glanced back at them.

I'll need more like these, she told herself. *Once I have that boy—when we are as one—we will need more like these. Many, many more.*

2.

"We have to find her, Mark," Jennifer Warren pleaded, as her husband stood in the front window in the parlor of the old Bennett guest house, their new home. He still wore his police uniform, with his service revolver strapped to his side. "She saved our lives."

"What are we supposed to do?" Mark asked. "Griselda is still out there somewhere, most likely waiting for us to leave this house. You want to run into her again?"

"Of course, I don't! You have no idea just how awful that woman was to me—even if I could find the strength to tell you, I don't think I could ever describe it in words, which is why, even though I would rather do anything than leave this house, I still say we have to go find Lara." Jennifer walked over to her husband and slowly wrapped her arms around his chest, pressing her forehead against his back as she fought back the tears.

"Why would you want to risk that kind of torment again?" he asked. "We have a chance to be happy here, *together*. If this is the afterlife, I'm good with it so long as you're here with me."

Mark's resistance was cracking; she could hear it. He was a good man, right to his core. He would never deny help to someone in need. She watched his eyes roll back and forth across the room, no doubt following his racing thoughts. She gently took him by the arm and spoke softly. "You *know* it's the right thing to do."

Mark exhaled slowly. "Ok, fine, but on one condition."

"If your condition is that I stay here, no way. You're crazy."

"You must."

"I will not. Lara saved *my* life too, Mark. It's *my* duty."

"Then no deal." Mark broke away from her and crossed into the formal dining room, putting the large oak table between them. "I won't do it unless you agree to stay here. I won't risk losing you again."

"Then I'll go by myself," she said. "And you can follow me if you like, but you're not leaving me behind. That would be the cruelest thing you could do. Besides, you don't know your way around the woods—I do. There are dark places in this world, places even *Griselda* avoided—things she refused to speak of—creatures she hid from when they passed."

Mark stared at her silently, a slight furrow growing on his forehead. "How do I know you're not just saying that to make me change my mind?"

"Because I will never lie to you, Mark. I don't know if I ever lied to you before; that life seems so long ago to me now, but I promise I'll never tell you anything but the truth from now until whatever end comes to us." Jennifer approached the table, putting her hands on the back of the closest chair. "Lara doesn't belong here; she belongs to the world of the living. I'm the only reason she's here. I couldn't live through eternity knowing I delivered her into the hands of evil."

Mark's body relaxed as he placed his hands on the chair before him, mirroring her. He lowered his head and said, "Fine. I don't like it at all, but you're right. We can't leave her out there. And you're right—you do know this place better than me."

Jennifer's heart filled with relief, but she held down the desire to show any sign of victory. Instead, she quietly moved around the table and wrapped her arms around her husband once again. This time, he reciprocated and held her close. "Thank you, Mark. We are a team. Understand?"

"Yes," he said. "I was lost when you died, and I was never whole again—not until you found me again tonight. And I have Lara to thank for that."

They stood in each other's arms for a time, each thinking of how to proceed. Jennifer looked towards the living room and noticed someone was sitting in one of the large parlor chairs. It was a woman, quite old by the look of her, wearing a midnight blue dress, staring out the front window.

"Mark," whispered Jennifer. When he looked at her, she nodded towards the woman.

"Hello?" called Mark. "Who's there?"

"Why Officer Warren, I am surprised you don't remember me," said the woman as she turned to look at them. She was pretty for her age, almost striking, with a royal air about her, though with a warmth mixed in that made her seem approachable.

"Mrs. Bennett?" Mark said, surprised.

"Very good! You do remember, though you may call me Genevieve, dear," the woman said.

"Of course, I remember. It's only been a few hours since we spoke," said Mark.

"Has it? Oh dear, forgive me. Time passes oddly in odd places, and I have indeed traveled to some very peculiar places since we last spoke. I was here, but a few *hours* ago, you say?"

"Yes, at most—maybe less. I'm a little unsure of the time," Mark said.

"Ah, wait! You were going to do something if I'm not mistaken. Let me think; don't tell me. Ah yes! You were going to stop a ritual, correct? A gate-opening ritual! Find the gates and save the child? Or something like that?"

"Boy. Yes, that's right," Mark said, chuckling.

Genevieve smiled. "Judging by your demeanor, all went according to plan?"

"Yeah, I think so," he said. "We believe it worked."

"Wonderful! That is most excellent news. I did hope to be here sooner, as I may have been of some use, but I'm afraid my spirit was clinging rather loosely to this world. It wasn't until I felt a tugging that I was able to return, curious that I should feel it *after* all has been said and done." Genevieve then turned her attention to Jennifer. "And this must be the lovely wife I've heard so much about. Please bring her closer!"

Mark took Jennifer by the hand, led her around the table, and into the parlor where he presented her to the old woman with a mock flourish. "Here she is, the beautiful Mrs. Jennifer Warren!"

Genevieve extended her hands, and Jennifer took them into her own, kneeling before the stately woman, feeling suddenly shy. To Jennifer, this woman's gaze cut through her, into her very soul, reading her thoughts and learning everything she ever was.

"Hello, Mrs. Bennett, I'm happy to meet you finally," Jennifer said.

"Tut-tut—*Genevieve*. How I longed for this moment for years, watching you helplessly through the windows of this house as you were dragged to and fro by that awful daughter-in-law of mine. I so wished I could release you from her, but my powers ended at the threshold of this house, as yours do now."

"We have power?" Mark asked.

"Indeed you do," Genevieve said, patting Jennifer on the hand.

"You have power over anyone who enters this place, so long as you are here. But like me, your power fades once you step outside. Such is the privilege of owning this lovely home. I am very sorry I could do nothing to help you, dear."

Jennifer quickly wiped a tear from her face and said, "No, it's ok. Seeing you through these windows brought some hope to me."

"Then I'm glad. I cannot imagine what you went through, though I could guess it was something like hell."

"I thought I *was* in hell," Jennifer said.

Genevieve leaned in, holding Jennifer's hands tightly in her own, motioning for Mark to join them, and said, "Knowledge is our best weapon against the evil in this place, and make no mistake, there is much evil here. However, we are not in hell. This is another place entirely, and in it, you will find an evil as you've never seen before. But it is also true that, hidden in places where you might least expect it, there is good."

The Warrens nodded in understanding before Genevieve continued.

"Now, both of you, tell me your story. Everything. From the beginning."

3.

Lara Fanning soared through the sky like a missile, holding tight to the rotten arms of Griselda Bennett as they punched a hole through the low-hanging clouds. She deduced that flying was not a gift Griselda was blessed with, given how deeply the old lady was digging her fingernails into Lara's arm.

Though the cumulus was thick and dark gray, Lara had a rough estimation of her position. She was flying roughly parallel to the ground and had been for a few minutes. However, she had been losing velocity gradually and had no idea how to correct herself. If she didn't figure it out, she would soon crash back to earth. If that happened, she wanted to be as far away from Griselda as she could get. She pried at the old woman's bony fingers, but their grip was steel.

Griselda whispered into her ear, "Oh, you'll not be rid of me so easily, you dirty slut. You've ruined my perfect night, and for that, you will pay *dearly*. You don't belong here, little vampire, but here you will stay with me forever."

Reminded by her nemesis that she was, in fact, a vampire, Lara smiled. As the wind and cloud water vapors rushed across her face, she opened her mouth and felt four sharp canines slowly grow out from her gums, followed by a surprising amount of pain. She adjusted her grip on Griselda's arm and held it up before her face, like a decaying turkey leg. With one quick movement, she bit down on the arm, and immediately, the taste of death and rot filled her mouth causing her to gag, but she held her jaws tight, pushing her teeth into the old woman's flesh. In response, Griselda let out a piercing scream that rang sharply in Lara's ears and, for a moment, loosened her grip in a reflexive attempt to pull her arm away from the pain.

This was all Lara needed. She flung her head back and ripped a mouthful of skin and meat from Griselda's forearm then tore the other arm from around her neck, flipping around to face the hag. Smiling wickedly, Lara thrust out her hands, punched the woman's chest with a sickening crack, and with one swift movement, launched the old woman out into the night sky. She watched with relief as Griselda plunged into a bank of clouds and out of sight.

Lara reveled in the victory for only a moment as the relief of escape was quickly followed by a wave of exhaustion. She would have to land soon, though she had no idea how to accomplish the task. Looking toward the clouds below, Lara turned herself in that direction by willing herself to do so. Within seconds, she had broken through, finding herself flying over a vast forest stretching out in all directions below. She glided just above the treetops, most of which had few, if any, leaves. It was as if this world was in a constant state of autumn—the dark and dreary kind—the kind Lara liked least of all. She loved the colors of fall, bright and orange-red, but this place looked like a graveyard of trees.

Barreling to the earth, Lara tried to slow herself any way she could, first by willing it and then by turning herself, so she was flying belly first, and then by flailing wildly in the air—none of which worked. Eventually, she resigned herself to the inevitable and curled herself into a ball, trying to protect her body as much as possible from the violence of the impact.

First, she hit a large oak tree. Her momentum brought her into it with such force the trunk broke apart quickly into a thousand shards. She didn't feel it at all. However, the next tree, which she hit with a glancing blow on her side, broke her right hip and half her ribs, bouncing her straight into a three-ton boulder, which broke her other hip and all the ribs on that side, shattering her femur. After the stone, Lara went into a long series of somersaults and belly-flops across the uneven ground, breaking her neck and crushing her collarbone until she finally came to rest under a large dead elm tree at the side of a rippling creek, like a raggedy doll.

She lay there for a while, unable to move and unable to feel the various cuts, bruises, and compound fractures across her body. Lara almost felt lucky being spared the pain she would undoubtedly be feeling if she hadn't severed her spinal cord just below the base of her skull. However, as her vampire healing kicked in, all the nerves came slowly and painfully back to life.

Lara Fanning lay there under the elm tree, lost and broken, in excruciating pain. However, she did not scream or make a single sound. Instead, she channeled all her energy into praying Griselda didn't find her before she finished healing.

4.

Randy Wall held tight to Leo Lourogen's back as the Honda 750 roared down Eighteenth Street. A false morning light gradually faded into darkness. Randy's right arm was killing him. At first, he thought he must have injured it during his fight with Jimmy Vance, but then he remembered something else. The spot of pain in his forearm emanated from the very place where the devil Surgat had grabbed him earlier, digging his demon claws into Randy's skin. Randy let out a small groan.

"Don't worry, buddy. We'll get you home to rest," Leo called back to him over his massive shoulder.

"Why is it getting dark? I thought it was morning," Randy said.

"Nope, it's the middle of the night."

Randy felt a headache coming on. "Then what was that light?"

Leo grunted and shrugged. "Don't matter. It's gone now."

As they crossed Middle Road, they heard gunfire in the distance, sounding like several shotguns fired off in succession.

"Who's doing all that shooting?" Randy asked.

"Anybody with a gun," Leo said. "Brother Jones raised an army of undead, probably to distract people from what they were doing to Jack tonight. But don't you worry about that—you just rest."

Randy could hear the concern in his cousin's voice. Over the years, Leo had been called many things, but *sensitive* was not one of them. However, this newfound concern for human life was only one of the many revelations Randy had about his cousin tonight. It was all too much to think about right now. Sleep was what he needed and lots of it.

Soon, the motorcycle had pulled up to the front of Randy's house. Randy's parents, Tom and Maggie Wall, burst through the front door just as the Honda came to a stop in the driveway. Leo stood and pulled Randy into his arms with surprisingly little effort.

"Where the hell have you been? It's after three in the morning," Tom Wall cried as he approached them.

"You've had us worried sick. Don't you know what's been going on around town tonight? Wait—Randy, are you OK? Why are you carrying him, Leo?" Maggie Wall asked.

"Ah cripes. Is he drunk?" Tom asked.

"No, Dad! Jesus, I'm injured," said Randy.

"Yeah, he needs to rest, Aunt Maggie. Best we get him up to bed."

"What happened? Did he get attacked by those crazies out there?"

Leo shook his head. "No, Uncle Tom. He just got bit by a stray dog, a big one, but he'll be OK. Just needs some sleep, I think." Leo sounded like even he didn't entirely believe his own words. He never was a good liar. "Let me get him upstairs and into bed. He could do with some rest, I reckon."

"Oh, poor Randy," said Maggie. "What hurts?"

"Just my arm, Mom," Randy said.

Once they made it upstairs and Leo tucked him into bed, Randy's mom got an ice pack and some ibuprofen and brought them back up to him. Leo did his best to cover for Randy, but the Walls were just happy he was home safe. Leo said his goodbyes and assured Randy that he'd return when he could to check on him.

"Might bring someone with me to check you out," Leo added before he left Randy's room.

"Who? Since when do you know so many people, Leo?" Randy mumbled through a yawn.

Leo looked at his shoes for a few moments, rubbing his forehead and muttering to himself as he sometimes did, before answering. "I reckon I oughta tell you some things when I get back. A lot of things, I guess."

"Yeah, seems like it. No more mysteries, you understand?"

"Okie dokie," Leo said, somewhat sheepishly. "I gotta go out to the church and check on things there. Shaun and Joe were heading out there to get away from Brother Jones's undead. I need to make sure they made it OK."

"What the hell? How did *they* get caught up in all of this?" Randy asked.

"Oh, buddy, I think everyone's caught up in this now. The boys were at Whitey's having ice cream when the undead attacked. I got them out of there, but I had to find you and Jack, so I dropped 'em off by a cornfield and told them where to go. Hopefully, they got to the church—they'd be safe there. Safe as anyplace else, at least."

"Shit," Randy said, as his eyes started to close. He had a million more questions, but he could not keep his eyes open another moment.

"I'll be back as soon as I can," Leo whispered, and he slipped out of the room just as Randy drifted off into a deep sleep.

It would not be a restful sleep. Dreams were waiting for Randy, dark dreams filled with a mysterious figure—and a demon's fingers digging into Randy's arm.

5.

"Careful, Jack," Anne Davies said, as she helped him down the last few steps onto the expansive lawn behind the Bennett mansion. "You're weaker than you think."

"Yeah, I think you're right—pretty sure I'm gonna crash as soon as I get home." Jack Davies rubbed his forehead and glanced back at Ava, seeing lines of worry burrowing into her forehead. "Don't worry; I'm fine. I just need like a day of sleep. We survived—it's over. Right?"

Ava replied, "We survived. I can't say it's *over*—far from it, I think. We still have a lot to do, Jack."

"You're right," Jack admitted. "I was just hoping everything could go back to normal, I guess."

Ava laughed. "*Normal* might need a new definition. Gather your friends and explore the town, Jack. Find out what's happened but be on your guard. Many of the devils' followers escaped last night, and though diminished, they could still be dangerous, even in a small way. And, of course, Brother Jones and his minions are still around. Be careful around that church."

Jack stared at her sideways for a moment. "Hey, what do you mean 'We need to gather?' You sound like you're leaving."

"I am," Ava said.

"Seriously? Right when we need you most?"

"I won't be gone long, only a few days at most. I have friends who may be able to help us. I need to speak with them."

Bettie Stone interrupted them, staring up at the sky. "Hey, guys.

Why is it getting darker? I thought it was morning. Did we just skip the whole day?"

Jack looked up and saw that, yes, it was getting darker again as if night had fallen in the middle of a cloudy morning. He pulled out his phone and saw the time said five after three in the morning. "Hey, it's still night time. Bettie's right."

Ava said, "I bet it was the remnants of the power Surgat used to open the gates. I bet it illuminated the entire town."

"What do we do until you get back? What happens if Brother Jones and these cultists come looking for me? What are we supposed to do about that army of undead?" Though he tried not to sound hurt, Jack was unable to mask his disappointment. A shadow passed over his mind, and he wondered when he would see her again.

Ava took his hands, and with a nod of her head indicating for Bettie and Anne to give them privacy, she moved closer until she stood face to face with him, staring into his eyes. Once again, Jack felt the blood rush to his face as she kissed him softly.

"You don't need me following you around. Last night, you survived a much greater enemy than I have seen on this earth in many years. The preacher and those cultists are powerful to have summoned those devils—and it wasn't only due to Betty. But without Surgat and his brothers, their strength is greatly diminished. I imagine they're more afraid of you than you are of them. After all, they probably think Opus and Maximus are still here with us. Of course, they'll figure it out soon enough. But for now, I think they'll lick their wounds and regroup." Ava lifted herself on her tiptoes and gave Jack a long kiss.

"But why do you have to go?" he asked, pulling away reluctantly.

"Do you remember what I told you the first night we met when you asked me if I'd be back?"

Jack thought for a moment and then said, "You said you doubted you could stay away from me, even if you wanted to."

"And that's still true. But there is much danger here, and even more is on its way, so we must do what we can. I'll let Bettie stay in my house. She'll be safe there—I'll make sure of it—but check in on her if you can. And keep Anne close—we don't know why or how she became flesh. Best to keep her a secret until we figure that out, as well. I will return."

With that, she kissed him on the lips for a breathless moment, turned, and was gone before Jack could open his eyes.

3

FIGURES IN THE FOG

Lara opened her eyes as a glorious rush of pain-free tingling danced across her skin. The torture of her body repairing itself had been almost too much to bear, but in the aftermath came a cool calming sensation that pushed the earlier agony almost entirely out of her mind. She lay there several minutes, staring up at the cloudy sky and basking in the sensations.

Sitting up and taking stock of herself, Lara seemed to feel as good as new, which was odd, given just how broken her body had been only minutes ago. She was still dressed in her Halloween costume—Sally from Nightmare Before Christmas—but her shoes had slipped off her feet as she flew into the clouds. Her black and orange painted toes looked back at her, bringing a welcome smile to her face.

She was in the middle of a forest, though most of it appeared to be dead or dying. There were leaves on some of the trees, but mostly, there was nothing but crooked branches overhead. She had no idea how far she had flown into the forest—it could have been several miles or more.

A slow-moving fog billowed along the ground between the trees. Everything was silent, almost oppressively so. Only the whoosh of a cold breeze and the soft scraping of a dozen leaves tumbling across the ground broke through. No sounds of living things, dead things, or undead interrupted the silence.

"What's wrong?" she whispered into the trees. "You've never had a teenage vampire drop out of the sky before?" She chuckled to herself, and a sudden pang of loneliness ached in her stomach. Lara was, after all, only seventeen years old, and though she was mature beyond her years, she had never been entirely on her own before. Definitely not like this, lost in some strange wood of an alternate reality.

Lara had always been an independent child from the earliest age. When her dad left their small family without so much as a goodbye note, Lara had handled it with more strength than anyone would have expected from an eight-year-old. There was a brazen individuality about her that intimidated some people. Now, she wanted nothing more than to be lounging on the living room sofa, watching whatever dumb show her mom liked. Sadly, Lara feared those days were gone forever.

Where am I? She asked herself, shaking the thoughts of loneliness out of her mind for a moment.

It was a question she couldn't answer. Lara didn't even know *how* she had come to this world in the first place. Officer Warren's wife, Jennifer, had brought her here, but how she had accomplished it was a mystery. Lara had no idea how to get back if she *could* get back. So many changes.

Out of nowhere, a piercing scream cut through the quiet, sending a wave of panic through Lara's chest. The trees seemed to turn their attention away from the odd vampire girl and toward the source. It came from no more than one or two hundred yards away, deep in the forest to Lara's right.

Griselda.

Lara crept into the trees with as much stealth as she could

manage, a monumental challenge with all the dead leaves covering the ground. It seemed as if each step she took echoed through the forest as if broadcast on a loudspeaker. Another scream pierced the night, this time somewhat closer than before. A great loathing overcame Lara at that moment, and it was all she could do to keep from heading in the direction of the screaming to offer herself to the hag. Instead, she forced herself away and behind an old tree.

I must be silent, she said to herself in an oddly commanding tone, and to her surprise, the next step she made was silent—not a sound. She looked down, and her eyes widened with wonder and an acute anxiety as she realized her bare feet were no longer touching the ground. She was hovering above it, only a few inches but high enough to keep from moving a single leaf.

Now, how do I move?

As soon as the thought of the word "move" entered her mind, Lara lurched forward, slowly gliding across the forest floor, just inches above the thick carpet of withered leaves. Keeping her balance was difficult, at first, which reminded her a little of the first and only time she had tried surfing years ago on a family trip to California. However, the young vampire managed to keep herself afloat well enough to move a full twenty feet into the woods before she finally dropped back down to the earth. She stood there for a minute, quite pleased with herself.

However, before she could revel in the newly discovered talent, she heard a sound to her left—footsteps. Lara peered through the trees and spotted a small road only a few dozen yards away. It was little more than a wide path winding through the dead trees and bushes. It occurred to her that her senses were much sharper now—whether due to the effect of this strange world or her new vampire abilities or both, Lara did not know. Her skin tingled now with a pulsing alarm, tickling her senses just enough to set her concentration on full alert. With danger ahead and danger behind, Lara crept behind a nearby grove of trees just before the edge of the road and waited.

As she chanced a look around a tree, she saw a figure of a

woman standing next to the road with her hands held up in the air as if to block an attack. Lara ducked back behind the tree, hoping she had not been seen. She leaned against the trunk and listened for any sound of movement. Slowly, she stole another look around the trunk. The woman still stood there in exactly the same position, as if frozen. Her hands remained raised above face as if shielding herself from an attack that would never come

Then Lara noticed several other figures, similarly frozen in place on either side of the path. There were men and woman, children and old people. Some distance away, Lara saw what looked like a pack of wolves, or coyotes, their backs arched as if cowering from some unseen menace. There were other creatures too, ones Lara didn't recognize as anything she had ever seen before. None of them moved an inch, and it occurred to her just what she was seeing. They were statues—dozens of them, all facing in different directions.

So, who made the footsteps?

No further sounds came, though the cold wind continued to blow and seemed to pick up speed as the moments passed. Lara began to wonder if the sound had been her imagination, but as she peered again at the road, she saw the dark figure of a man standing some yards away in the middle of the path. He wore no clothing, but his lean body was firm and muscular, though lanky. His long hair hung down in greasy strands and through it shined two gleaming orange eyes, the only discernible features on his face. He made no movements nor spoke a word, but what emanated from his presence was pure hatred, worse even than Griselda.

Suddenly, the man blinked out of sight, disappearing entirely. Lara frantically searched the road to see where he had gone. At first, she saw no sign of him, but then to her horror, she found him standing on the road again, now several yards closer to her than before, as if he had magically teleported forward ten yards. Again, he blinked out of sight and then, seconds later, appeared once again several yards closer than before.

As he slowly drew nearer, Lara felt his hate. Her heart raced and her hands trembled. A tight knot slowly formed in the pit of her stomach. Paralyzed by an acute fear, Lara leaned against the tree trunk and gasped for air. Debilitating anxiety threatened to overpower her equilibrium. Tears ran down her cheeks as. She struggled to control her emotions. She slumped to the ground between a pair of serpentine roots and bit down on her tongue to keep from crying out in despair. She desired nothing more than to end it all and cross over forever into nothingness. Words ran through her mind.

Give yourself to me. . .

Lara pulled herself up to her feet. As if in a trance, she stepped around the tree and was just about to offer herself to the creature, when she felt a cold hand slip around her face from behind, covering her mouth, and soft lips pressed against her ear. A girl's soft voice whispered to her in an unfamiliar and thick accent, and when she spoke, Lara could feel the girl's icy breath blow against her neck like a cold winter wind.

"Shh, young vampire, not so fast. Where do you think you're going? Off to end your sweet young life so soon, yes? No, no, no, calm yourself and hear my voice. Concentrate." As the girl spoke, the tension in Lara's body relaxed, and though part of her still longed to join the man on the road, the desire inched itself away from her thoughts, little by little. "Is a *good* vampire, yes? Do not follow the call of Dreadman—his touch will break your heart and leave you as a shell. Then you will join the others, lifeless and lost forever like these others you see."

"Dreadman?" Lara's own voice sounded far away.

"Yes, Dreadman's touch will make you go away, and only your body will remain for Meurt to mourn."

Lara's eyes widened as the realization hit her. The figures at the sides of the road were not statues at all. They were people and other creatures, frozen in terror and lost in time, touched by the hand of this thing.

"Stay with me, vampire girl. Stay with Meurt and live, yes?"

Lara concentrated, focusing her thoughts on the soothing sound of the girl's voice, and soon, her thoughts turned away from the darkness of the man on the road. In moments, she felt like herself again. She turned to the girl and nodded as if letting her know she was back in control of herself.

This Meurt was small and pixie-like, with pointed ears and an elvish face. She appeared to be Lara's age with bright white-blue eyes and long snow-white hair that flowed past her waist, cut into even bangs in the front. Her skin was shimmering and pale, almost translucent, and her voice, light and melodic, sounded like a dozen icy wind chimes ringing through a dry breeze. She too was barefoot and wore a simple tweed waistcoat and pants that somehow seemed to blend into the shadows whenever Meurt peered around the trees to look at the Dreadman.

"Not a sound," Meurt whispered, glancing back to the road.

The Dreadman blinked out again and moments later reappeared, standing directly in front of them, only ten or so yards away. This time, he was turned to face them as if he knew they were watching him. Lara held her breath as the dark man turned his head in their direction, his sparkling orange eyes scanning the area, looking at them briefly, then back in the direction from which he had come. He stood there for a few more moments, then blinked out and was gone.

"Quickly," Meurt said. "Follow me now, before he returns!"

Meurt pulled Lara by the hand, and without hesitation, the two girls were tearing through the woods so fast they would have looked like nothing but a blur to anyone nearby. As quickly as she had pulled her, Meurt stopped and brought Lara behind a tree, raising one finger to her lips and peeking around the trunk. "Look there, vampire girl. You are lucky Meurt found you," the pixie whispered.

Lara looked in the direction from which they had come and saw the Dreadman, fifty or sixty yards away, standing in the exact spot where they had been hiding only moments before. He was looking all around, searching for them, sniffing the air.

"When Dreadman disappears again, we will run to the hill behind us. You keep running until Meurt says stop. Yes? You must keep up and step where Meurt steps, hop when Meurt hops, and leap when Meurt says leap."

Lara agreed, and they waited until the Dreadman once again disappeared. When he did, Meurt grabbed Lara by the hand and sprang off through the trees with the grace of an antelope, yelling, "Keep up, vampire girl!"

The branches and brambles cut through Lara's costume like razors, but her skin was barely grazed. The exhilaration of overwhelming speed raced through as she followed Meurt away from the Dreadman. Within seconds, they had covered hundreds of yards, and by the time Meurt finally directed Lara to stop, they had run almost a mile.

"You are fast, yes? Almost as quick as Meurt—and that is very fast, indeed!"

"Thank you. Who are you? How did you find me?" Lara asked after she had taken a moment to gather her thoughts.

"I am Meurt. I did say this before, yes?"

"Yeah you did, but I don't understand."

"You will. And what is your name?" Meurt asked.

"Lara. But who *are* you? What are you? Who was that–Dreadman? Where am I?" Lara felt like all the questions in her brain were about to come spilling forth.

"In time, Lara, the vampire girl. We have lost him for now, but he will not be lost for long. We must go to a safe place, yes," Meurt said.

"By all means, take me someplace safe." Lara had no idea who this Meurt was, but she did know she was running out of choices. She would have to trust this person until she could find a way back to the Warren's *if* they were still alive.

"Meurt's home is some miles from here in a small valley, near a quiet river that is haunted by a pair of Indian lovers. Master is waiting for Meurt to come home. You will be safe with Master and Meurt until you must go, yes."

"But I must find my friends. Your house is, like, in the totally opposite direction," Lara said.

"You may go where you wish, vampire girl. Meurt only *offers* you safety; she cannot make you accept it, yes? But if you want to see your friends again, you should not go that way—not yet. Dreadman will follow you, and he will find you, oh yes he will. We must lose him first and quickly."

Lara knew there was no arguing—she had no choice but to accept Meurt's offer. And as for the Warrens—she wouldn't do them any good by leading this Dreadman right to them, nor would it benefit anyone if she was dead.

"OK, fine. Lead the way."

It was all she could do to keep up with Meurt. The pixie seemed to have a gear that Lara couldn't come close to matching. In fact, she sensed Meurt was holding back to keep from pulling too far ahead. For hours, they ran over hills and across valleys, through streams and over ponds, sometimes following through a river or diving into a lake. Meurt doubled back a few times, and Lara wondered if the girl was trying to cover their path to confuse any pursuit. At one point, Meurt stopped dead in her tracks at the top of a small hill and seemed to be listening for something. She then whispered some inaudible words into a thicket, grabbed Lara by the hand, and pulled her along behind.

Finally, after more zigging and zagging, they came upon a small river, and at its edge was a little wooden cottage. A thin line of gray smoke snaked its way out of a stone chimney. Its frosted windows glowed with a warm light in the perpetual darkness of this world. Meurt and Lara stood there for a time, staring at the sweet calm of house.

"This is Rivervale, my home," Meurt said.

"It's lovely," Lara said. "What river is that behind us?"

"It has many names, young vampire. But I believe you would know it as the Wapsipinicon, yes?"

"The Wapsi?" Lara asked, surprised to hear the name. "But how can that be? I feel like we ran a hundred miles. The Wapsi is not that far away."

"There will be time for questions later. But now, you must meet my master, the lord of all these lands."

The door to the cottage opened and through it walked a man

unlike any Lara had ever seen. She tried to speak, but no words would come forth for many minutes, so overwhelmed was she by his presence. Meurt giggled and danced across the river's edge to kiss the man's cheek. He smiled when she did so but did not take his golden eyes from Lara's. He stood there with his hands on his hips looking down at her with a melancholy smile and the smallest hint of sadness in his eyes.

Meurt's voice seemed to float on a soft breeze between them. "Master, this is our new friend, a young vampire girl I found hiding in the middle of the woods. She is called Lara. Lara, this is my master."

4

A SORT OF HOMECOMING

Bettie followed Ava up the front walk to a stone cottage style house on River Drive, just east of the Bettendorf-Davenport city line, with a close view of the Mississippi River. They had walked all the way across town to Jen Graver's house, where Ava had left her car at the party earlier. Coroners and detectives from half the counties were still there, working together to clean up the bloody mess created by the vampires, Stephanie Caine and Emily Scott. With the authorities immersed in the horror of the scene, the girls snuck into Ava's car and drove off without being seen.

Ava's house sat downtown on River Drive, just east of the border between Bettendorf and Davenport. A waist-high stone wall buttressed the property where the yard met the front sidewalk. Two large oaks dominated the front yard—half of their bright orange and red leaves still hanging on in the mid-autumn breeze. Bettie had seen the house numerous times when her family had driven this way to Davenport, and she always thought it was the most delightful house in town. It had been featured multiple times in local papers and real estate publications, so whenever her family would pass it, her mother would invariably say, "My, what a lovely home."

To which her father would mechanically reply, "Oh, yes indeedie."

Bettie shook away the memory of her parents and asked, "Have you always lived here?"

"No, I bought it a year ago, when I moved to Bettendorf," Ava said as she stopped short of the front steps.

Bettie gasped. *"You* bought it—"

Before she could finish the question, Ava shushed her with a quick wave of the hand, staring at the front door. Bettie looked around but saw nothing but falling leaves and heard nothing but the quiet sounds of the night. She watched Ava, who craned her neck and tilted her head like an animal, sniffing the air.

"What's wrong?" Bettie asked.

Ava whispered, "Someone's inside."

Bettie looked at the front windows but saw nothing. "How can you tell?"

"I sense it. I need you to come and stand at my side, *quietly.*"

"OK," Bettie said.

"Put your arms around my neck. I'm going to pick you up and run around the side of the house to my car. I'll be moving quite fast but don't worry. I won't let go of you. I promise. OK?"

Bettie clasped her hands around Ava's neck and readied herself. Ava bent down, picked her up and, in an instant, sprinted around the side of the house with such speed Bettie saw nothing but a blur of dark colors. In fact, only a second or two passed before they were standing outside the passenger door of a black, mint condition, 1967 Ford Mustang. Bettie opened the door and got in. A moment later, the driver door was open, and Ava was turning the key. The low rumble of the engine sounded loud in the dead of night.

Suddenly, an enormous crash, like shattered wood, came the front of the house, and Ava threw the car into reverse onto Sixth Street, trailing a billow of white smoke before them. With one quick motion, she thrust the stick into first gear and peeled off down the street.

As they tore past the front of the house and squealed onto State Street, Bettie saw a tall man with bright white skin and a bald head covered in burns and scars standing outside the shattered ruins of what had been Ava's front door. He stood there, watching them drive away into the pre-dawn morning. He made no move to follow, but Bettie had a suspicion they had better keep going and put him out of sight.

Ava was apparently thinking the same thing, because she kept her right foot on the gas as they pulled onto the I-74 bridge, heading across the Mississippi to Illinois at a speed that brought Bettie's stomach into her chest.

"Who was that man?" Bettie asked.

"It wasn't a *man*," Ava said.

"OK. What was it?"

"I'm not entirely certain what it was. It's taken the form of a man, obviously. I guess we can say for sure something got through tonight."

"A demon?"

Ava shrugged as she dialed a number on her phone. Moments later, a man's voice came on the other line, barely audible over the rumble of the car engine. Ava spoke to him in a language unlike any she'd ever heard—it sounded to her almost like a combination of French, Russian, and Japanese. They communicated only briefly before Ava hung up, tossing the phone on the dashboard.

Bettie watched Ava as she drove. She was still in her Halloween costume, an old-school Harley Quinn outfit that managed to be sexy while avoiding the usual hot-Halloween-costume stereotypes. Though the woman was disheveled and covered with spatters of blood, mostly her own, Ava somehow managed to look beautiful. However, as impressive as she was, Bettie was struck more by the confidence the woman exuded. Physically, she appeared little older than Jack and Randy, but Ava held herself in a way that betrayed an age much older.

"Why are you staring at me?" Ava asked with a smirk.

"Where are we going?" Bettie asked.

"Chicago."

"Why?"

"I know a man there—someone who can help us, I hope. We'll get a room on Michigan Avenue and get some sleep. Then tomorrow night—or *tonight*, I guess—we'll head to his house and find out some things. I'll do my best to get you to school by Monday, but I can't promise anything," Ava said.

Bettie laughed. "Oh, school is the last thing on my mind, right now. And I'm pretty sure I'll need to switch schools, anyway. I doubt the headmaster will take kindly to one of his students spoiling the big night."

Ava laughed as Bettie lay her head on the headrest. When she awoke, they were rolling into downtown Chicago as the first rays of sunlight glowed into the sky-blue-pink horizon over Lake Michigan.

5

ATTACK AT FOREST GROVE ROAD

Joe and Shaun stumbled through the seemingly endless rows of corn, still following what they assumed to be the North Star. Shaun had seemed oddly distracted, a condition that was only intensifying the further they walked. He kept looking back over his shoulder, and twice he stopped, cocking his head as if he heard something.

"Dude, what the hell are you looking at?" Joe finally asked. "You're freaking me out. Do you see something?"

Shaun didn't answer him right away, his attention fixed someplace behind them. Finally, Shaun muttered, "It's nothing. Don't worry about it."

Joe groaned. Whenever Shaun Porter said *don't worry about it*, Joe knew there was something to worry about—probably a *lot* to worry about.

Unfortunately, Joe was not accustomed to walking long

distances. The fact that he was six foot four and weighed around two hundred seventy pounds made it especially difficult to be stealthy trudging through muddy fields of dead corn. However, he would gladly walk the whole night if it would keep them away from the brain-eaters at Whitey's.

Directly ahead, Joe saw that the cornrows curved sharply to the right, running east-west. He had spent enough summers detasseling corn to recognize the shift in direction meant they were coming to the end of the field. Both of their phone batteries had died, so Joe couldn't be sure what time it was, but he guessed they had been walking for about an hour. They had to be close to their destination. As expected, when they finally broke through the end rows, they came upon a ditch above which sat an old gravel road. Joe scrambled onto the road as quickly as his tired legs would take him. "This has to be Forest Grove Road but no church," he said, taking a moment to catch his breath. "We must have missed our mark."

"Yeah," Shaun said, still in the ditch. He stood there, staring back into the corn.

Looking further down the road, Joe barely made out a thin steeple poking above the fields, lit by a small floodlight. They had indeed missed their mark but not by much. If they jogged, they could be at the church in a few minutes, though Joe doubted he had the energy for it. He looked into the ditch and said, "Hey dude, I see the church up there about a quarter of a mile away. Let's get going."

"Too late," Shaun said flatly. He was still staring into the field.

Following his line of sight, Joe saw nothing but corn stalks and shadows. "What do you mean?" Joe asked.

Not turning his head, Shaun said, "You should go."

"Me? Us. *We* should go, Shaun. We should go right now. What the hell is wrong with you?" Joe stumbled down into the ditch.

"It's too late. They're here." Shaun backed slowly away from the corn stalks.

Joe put his hand on his friend's shoulder, drawing him away from the field then grabbed hold of his upper arm, pulling him up the bank and onto the gravel. Then he heard them. Footsteps crunched through the dead corn leaves, getting closer with each step. The tops of the corn stalks rattled back and forth, nearer and nearer, until three people emerged from the field and stepped into the ditch. It was the girl from Whitey's, followed by two men, who were also apparently undead.

"Shit," Joe muttered. "Dude, we gotta run now."

"You go," Shaun said.

"Bullshit. I'm not going anywhere without you."

Joe tightened the grip of his massive hand on Shaun's arm and took off running down the old road. At first, Joe was dragging his friend down the gravel, but Shaun seemed to snap out of whatever spell he had been under and was soon running on his own.

The undead were somewhere off to their right, still in the cornfields. Joe could see the tops of the stalks rattling in his periphery. Though these undead were strong—superhuman, at least—they were not any faster than the boys or at least not faster than Shaun. Joe, on the other hand, was lagging and began to fear he wouldn't make it to the church before the creatures overtook him.

As if sensing the same thing, Shaun called back to him, "Follow me!" as he darted off the road to his left and onto the front yard of a farmhouse.

Joe dug deep and sprinted across the yellowing grass all the way to an old red barn situated just behind the house. Looking back, Joe could see no signs of pursuit. He stopped outside the barn door to catch his breath as Shaun wrestled with the giant wooden door. "Dude, what are we gonna do?" Joe asked.

"We gotta hide. Maybe find something inside the barn to defend ourselves," Shaun said.

"They don't seem that fast. Maybe we could keep moving through the field and cut around over to the church. I think we lost them."

"No, we didn't. And they weren't running as fast as they could—they were herding us."

"What? Why?" Joe said, standing up and putting his hands on his head as he continued to catch his breath.

"They want me."

"What are you talking about?"

Finally yanking the barn door open far enough for them to pass inside, Shaun said, "Doesn't matter. There's no time. Just remember, she wants me not you. If we get cornered, you run. I'm not kidding, either. Run away and don't look back, you hear? They're not after you."

"What the hell are you talking about? Dude—"

"Just do it," Shaun said, cutting him off. "Keep quiet—they're coming."

The boys pulled the door closed behind them and found a two-by-four to bar it closed. They quickly searched for anything resembling a weapon. Unfortunately, the farmer had recently completed a brand-new aluminum barn on the other side of the property, and this one was being readied for demolition. All they found in the whole place was an old pitchfork and a discarded Phillips screwdriver.

"Well, if these three are zombies, just stick the screwdriver into their skulls. Should do the trick. It works on TV, anyway," Joe said, as they found a hiding place in an old corner horse stall behind a few bales of hay.

"The guys are *kind of* like zombies, you might say. I think the girl is something different. But yeah, a screwdriver through the skull is enough to take care of pretty much anyone, zombie or not. You keep the pitchfork, and when you get a chance, run as fast as you can out of here. Right to the church, you hear?"

"Dude, you're crazy."

Shaun grabbed him by the shirt and pulled his face right in front of his own. "I'm serious, Joe. You hear me? Just run to the church. Don't worry about me."

"OK, OK, I'll run if it comes to that. But we should hide and hit them first, you know? They're too strong for us, but if we surprise them, we might have a chance."

Shaun sat there for a moment and seemed to be analyzing Joe's

impromptu plan. "You're right. I'll hide in that horse stall across
the way, and you hide in this one. When the guys come down the
center, we can spring out and hit them with everything we've got.
The girl won't be with them."

"How do you know that?"

"Just trust me," Shaun said, and he ran across the barn to the
horse stall opposite him, crouched down, and waited.

Joe almost whispered something to Shaun, but before could
say another word, he heard movement outside the old barn. A
pair of shadows moved back and forth between the wood slats,
growing larger until they stopped just outside large doors. Joe's
heart raced as he glanced across the hay-strewn dirt floor. Shaun
lifted one finger to his lips and peered over the half-wall of his
stall.

Rotting fingers slithered in through the opening, and the barn
doors began to shake until finally the two by four holding them
in place was split in half. The doors blew open, clanging loudly
against the walls to either side. The males stepped inside first,
remaining on either side of the doorway, then the female slowly
stepped into the opening, her arms and legs spread wide as if
to catch any escaping teenage boys. She still wore her Catholic
school uniform with black converse high-tops. Her legs were
gray, dirty, and covered in cuts and bruises. Her face was hidden
in shadow, but Joe could see her yellow eyes shining out from
between strands of greasy hair. She nodded her head forward,
and the two males moved ahead, searching the stalls, one by one.

Joe leaned against the half-wall, holding his pitchfork
diagonally across his side, the tip of the fork at eye level. He didn't
need to see the undead men—he could hear their footsteps as
they shuffled through the barn until, at last, the one closest to him
came around the wall and into view. Joe leaped out of his stall and
immediately rammed the pitch fork straight into the man's skull
until the prongs were jutting out the other side.

Across the way, Shaun wrestled with the other male, trying
unsuccessfully to jam the screwdriver into the guy's forehead.
Joe attempted to get back on his feet, but before he could get

his weight under him, a powerful force knocked him backward, slamming him back again into the barn wall. Wood splinters and paint chips rained down upon his head as the entire backside of the barn vibrated from the violence of his impact. He heard another cracking sound in his shoulder, and intense pain shot through his body as he crashed back again onto the dirt floor.

As Joe lay there, eyes closed and wincing, he heard Shaun's voice. "Hello. You're Lucy, right? I remember you from grade school."

The girl moaned something in response, and Joe, still lying on his back, turned to look. The girl was sauntering toward Shaun. He couldn't tell whether the girl was going to ask Shaun to dance, or crack him in the skull and spoon out his brains. Her head tiled back and forth, like a dog attempting to decipher an unfamiliar sound.

"Shaun, you gotta run, dude. Save yourself," Joe managed to croak out through the waves of pain rippling through his shoulder.

"It's OK. I think it's going to be OK." Shaun's voice sounded like it came from the other side of the cornfield.

The girl continued toward Shaun until she stood directly in front of him, her face inches from his. Then, to Joe's horror, just when he thought she was going to take a bite out of his friend's face, she reached out, grabbed him by the back of the head, and kissed him, long and deep—and worse, Shaun was kissing her back. This creature with rotting arms and legs, with sores and bruises covering her body, this girl with blue lips and white-blue eyes was making out with Joe's best friend.

Shit! She's got a spell on him. I know it. In a few seconds, those French kisses will turn into feasting—on Shaun's tongue! "Dude! That's effing gross!"

Slowly and with effort, Joe stood and quietly reclaimed the pitchfork, which lay only a few feet away. He took several deep breaths and then, with all the strength he had left in him, ran straight into the back of the girl, jamming the pitchfork into her back until the four prongs jutted out through her chest. The girl gasped and coughed then let out a high-pitched shriek.

"Out of the way, Shaun!" Joe yelled as he continued forward until he had rammed the pitchfork, along with the girl, deep into the soft pine wall of the horse stall.

"Joe, what did you do?" Shaun asked. He sounded pained.

"I saved your life; that's what I did! Come on. Let's get out of here before she pries herself loose," Joe said, noticing the girl was indeed attempting to do just that.

Grabbing Shaun's hand and ignoring his pain, Joe led them out the barn door, though the farmyard, and eventually across Forest Grove Road. Once, he had to stop and kick Shaun in the side to get him to stand up and run, but when they had gotten far enough away, like before, Shaun snapped out of his trance and ran along with Joe with what little energy remained in him.

The boys flew around the back corner of the church so quickly they missed seeing two small shrubs planted just outside the main church doors. Joe's foot struck the nearest one, sending him tumbling onto the front sidewalk, with Shaun collapsing on top of him. Before they could get their bearings, the church doors were flung open, and a half-dozen men in hunting fatigues sprang out at them, their rifles trained directly on the boys.

"Oh, shit," Joe muttered, holding his hands up in the air.

Then a large, well-built man in a red and black flannel shirt stepped behind the gunmen, letting out a bellow of relieved laughter. "Oh, keep yer guns down, fellas. These here boys are alive, yes indeedie. These must be the boys Leo told us about. Welcome to Forest Grove Church. You're as safe here as anyplace else in this town, I reckon."

Joe, exhausted and in pain, let his head fall back onto the sidewalk. Feeling safety for the first time in hours after fearing for their lives the whole night almost made him want to cry. But when he looked at Shaun, he saw something different—an emotion that seemed out of place, given what had just happened to them. Though he could not be sure, it looked like disappointment.

6

THE VOICE IN THE CAVE

Randy stands on the burning shore of a lake of molten rock. The heat singes his hair down to the root, leaving nothing but bare skin the color of ripe tomatoes. But he feels little pain, only a pulsing ache in his left arm—dull, like a distant memory he cannot shake. However, something other than pain is coursing through his body as if his veins were flowing with the same lava that was now roiling and bubbling before him. Though it does not hurt, the sensation makes him nauseous, and he leans down with his hands upon his knees for a moment, expecting to belch a stream of white-hot vomit onto the fiery lake.

Randy rights himself, turns and steps away from the lake, seeing a dead forest before him, spreading out for miles. With some effort, he moves his legs one after the other and stumbles toward the burned wood. As he approaches, the dead trees seem to part before him.

The ache in his arm is still throbbing just enough to make him aware of it, like a kitten tapping his forearm with its paw. As he moves deeper into the forest, the landscape does not seem to change at all. There is nothing—no other living creatures anywhere to be seen. Still, Randy cannot shake the sensation that he is not alone. Something is aware of him.

"Hello?" he calls out. "I know someone is out there. I mean you no harm. Shit, I'm only dreaming, anyway."

He hears a sound that is so unexpected, at first, he cannot place it. As he listens closer, he recognizes what he hears–laughter. And as he looks in front of him, he sees that he is suddenly standing at the mouth of a cave, though he cannot remember how he came to be there.

More chuckling rolls out of the cave, echoing throughout the forest.

"Who are you?" Randy asks.

Another round of laughter, this time louder.

"You must be *thinking* funny shit, cuz I haven't cracked a joke yet. Doesn't matter, I guess. I'll be awake pretty soon, and then *I'll* have a good laugh."

"This is not a dream," says a voice, one that is familiar to Randy, though he cannot place it.

"Who's there?" Randy asks.

Another laugh.

"Is that all you can do? Just laugh?"

The laughing stops, and the voice says, "Oh, no, young one. Laughing is not *all* I can do. No, indeed it is not, though I am happy to have something to laugh about."

"Yeah, you're a real barrel of laughs. What did you mean, I'm not dreaming?"

"You are not. You have traveled here," says the voice.

Randy scratches the back of his head and looks around as if seeing the dead landscape will somehow make sense of what he just heard. "Traveled? Yeah right. I didn't go anywhere. I'm lying in my bed right now, sleeping like a blond baby."

"Is that so?"

"Yep."

"Well, then, try waking yourself."

"Huh?"

The voice chuckles again and says, "If you are, as you say, sleeping like an infant in your bed, then why don't you wake yourself? Now. Go on, try."

"OK, I will. I'll wake myself right up, M-Effer." Randy blinks vigorously and jumps around, stomping his feet as hard as he can on the dry dirt. He slaps his face to the point of pain then clamps his eyes shut and pinches himself in both nipples at the same time, even twisting them until they slip out of his grip, but when he opens his eyes again, he is still standing in the molten world, staring at the black cave entrance.

"It appears you are not in your bedroom—or you're sleeping so soundly you cannot wake—perhaps you'll never wake."

"Oh, I'm in my bed. I'm sure of it. Maybe I *am* too tired to wake up. I had a long weird night, after all," Randy says.

"Randy Wall, you are not in your bedroom. In fact, I'm certain that, if your poor parents come in to check on you, they will undoubtedly find an empty bed and wonder if you snuck out the window. You have peregrinated or something nearly like it. You're in the middle of an old memory."

"I've never been to a place like this in all my life, not until now, anyway. How can I remember something that never happened?"

"I didn't say it was *your* memory."

Suddenly, an unfamiliar voice screams in Randy's mind, startling him and causing the world around him to falter for a moment.

You must leave, Randy! Get out! Now!

"Come to me, and I will explain everything, young one," the voice in the cave says.

Randy, still shaken by the screaming in his mind, asks, "Who are you?"

"Do you not know?" the voice in the cave asks.

Out, Randy! Do not listen to him!

"No, I don't."

"You do. You know who I am."

Now, Randy. You must turn and run.

"Come to me, Randy. Enter my cave," says the voice in the cave.
Run to the tree by the lake of fire.

"Come into my cave, and all will be revealed."

Run to the tree and lay your hand upon its trunk. Now or you will die!

"I'm sorry, weird cave creeper, but I gotta go." With that, Randy turns and sprints straight for the gnarled dead tree at the shore of the lake of molten rock. Just before he lays his palm upon its cracked trunk, he hears a faint sound coming from behind him.

Delirious laughter.

7

JACK'S NEW NORMAL

Sunday morning. Everything has changed.

Jack pulled on some sweats and crossed the hall to the guest room where Anne had slept. After knocking several times, he creaked the door open, whispering, "Anne?" Peering into the room, he noticed the bed was made and the room was empty. A rush of anxiety rose through his chest.

Where did she go?

For reasons he couldn't place, Jack found the idea of Anne wandering the house and speaking to his—*their*—parents terrifying. How long had she been up? How long had he been sleeping? It had been difficult task, explaining to his mom and dad just why Anne needed to spend the night with them. Their first reaction was that she must be a secret girlfriend—the girl was beautiful, after all. However, Anne had made up a lie about having an abusive dad and a drunk mom, which played right into the Davies' highly developed sense of empathy. Jack wasn't sure how long the subterfuge would last, but for now it was the best he had.

Anne suggested they tell their parents that her name was Sarah to avoid any odd-coincidence feelings, which Jack agreed was a good idea. Truth be told, it was odd how easy it was for her to come up with the lie. He'd never seen her do such a thing before—didn't think she was capable of speaking anything but the truth. In fact, Jack had assumed that *he* would be the one who'd do all the talking, but Anne handled it like a pro, cool and calm.

But where was she now?

Jack ran down the stairs, through the hall, and into the dining room to find everyone at the dining table, empty plates pushed to the middle and coffee cups half-full. His mom was telling a story about Jack. She was laughing so hard the words were almost unintelligible, but from the few he could understand, it was evident his mom was telling the infamous story about how Jack somehow fell off a dock at Lake of the Ozark's during one of their numerous camping trips.

"Oh, my goodness," Anne said, giggling. "How old was he? Weren't you scared for him?"

"Oh, no, he was a Freshman. It was just a little over a year ago! HA!"

Diane Davies, a sucker for any physical humor, loved it when one of her kids—usually Jack—did anything clumsy. And when one of her sons managed to trip over something or run into a wall, no one would laugh louder than their mother.

"Oh, Jack! I was just telling Sarah all your best stories," Diane said between laughs.

"Yeah, really funny," Jack said as he sat down.

Anne wiped a couple of tears away and said, "I'm getting to know a whole lot more about you than I ever knew. Pretty interesting."

"Oh, Jack is good at many things, but coordination is not one of them. That's ok. He's smart and good-looking, and I don't care if I'm biased. Would you like some pancakes, Jack?"

Jack nodded as his mom and dad exited to the kitchen. Once he was sure they were out of ear-shot, he whispered, "So, what are we going to do? Where will you go today? You're not gonna be able to stay here forever. They'll get suspicious soon enough, or they'll call child services or something like that."

"Don't worry, Jack. I've got it handled," Anne said, taking a sip of orange juice.

"What do you mean?"

"She likes me—they both do. I think they're going to suggest I stay with them for as long as I need to," Anne said, sitting back in her chair.

"What makes you think that?"

"Just wait. You'll see."

Jack watched her for a moment. There was something different about her, aside from not being a ghost. She seemed to be more *confident*.

"I need to take a cue from you. You're like all, *'whatever.'* I'm freaking out," Jack said. "I mean, you don't have an ID—no social security, no birth certificate. Shit, I don't know what we're supposed to do. Sorry, I'm just stressed out."

Anne leaned in, reached across the table, took his hand and said, "It's to be expected. Jack, what you went through last night was more than any person has experienced in many years. You just worry about yourself and keep yourself safe. You've got school tomorrow, and you're going to have to get your life back to normal as much as you can."

"Normal? How the hell can I go back to high school now? Everything has changed. Everything! Hell, I wouldn't even know what normal feels like."

"Quiet," Anne whispered. She looked over Jack's shoulder into the kitchen.

"I'm sorry," whispered Jack. "But there's no way I'm going back to school. You know how many people were in that cult last night? How do we know who to trust? They all know who I am, but I don't know who they are."

"That's true. But you must go back to your life now, Jack. You won last night. I don't think they'll bother you for a while."

It occurred to Jack that Anne was unusually cavalier about the whole situation, but before he could decide what that meant, their mother returned to the dining room with a stack of pancakes. She sat down and continued telling stories about Jack's childhood, some embarrassing and some silly. He knew, any minute, the photo album would make its way out of the living room cabinet, and the two of them would sit on the couch for hours looking at pictures of Jack and his brothers at every awkward stage in their lives.

Through all of this, Jack sat at the dining room table, forcing himself to finish the stack of flapjacks slowly as his mind raced from one thought to the next. Anne was right; he knew it. He could not just hide away from the world in his room or run off to California. Whatever evil had infiltrated Bettendorf would find him, no matter where he was. Ava was right too—Jack could not wait for help to come. He had to find a way to handle these problems himself. Now was the time to find out just who was involved in the cult and what they were planning to do going forward.

There were a few people he already knew were involved—Brother Jones, Stephanie Caine, and that nasty Jimmy Vance. What was their connection to the others, the ones in the robes? None of it made sense. Jack could see no way that any of those people would know each other, let alone conspire to kidnap him and open a gate to hell. The cult was obviously wide-spread and dangerous.

So, what does all this mean? He asked himself. *I wish Ava was here.*

If he was honest, he wished Ava were there for more reasons than one. He desperately wanted to touch her again—to get to know her and find out her likes, her dreams, her favorite movie or book. He wanted to go out on a date and kiss her again. Jack had kissed girls in the past, but they were nothing like Ava. She was confident, intelligent, and exotically beautiful, more beautiful than anyone Jack had ever met. And she wanted him.

How on earth had that happened? That was as much of a mystery as anything else, but now she was gone, and Jack was alone.

No, not alone. I've got Anne and Randy. And, anyway, Ava said she would only be gone a few days. I can manage that long. I must.

Pushing up from the table, Jack took his empty plate into the kitchen and trudged back up to his room as Anne and his mom continued talking like two lost friends. He picked up his phone, which he'd managed to charge during the night, and found that Randy had texted him.

Randy: Hey. Call me when you wake up.

When Jack called him back, Randy answered the phone with a voice that sounded like someone in a lot of pain.

"Hello?" Randy grunted. Static crackled through the connection.

"Hello? Where are you? It sounds like you're out in a cornfield," Jack said.

"No, I'm home. I don't know. The connection has been like this all morning—in and out of service. It's like we're in the middle of a cornfield. Hey, have you heard from Joe or Shaun?"

"No, yours was the only message on my voicemail. Why?"

"I don't know. I've called them both, and I texted them like a hundred times. They haven't answered. I'm a little worried."

"I just woke up. Maybe they're in bed."

"No, when Leo took me home, he told me he had dropped them off out past Whitey's near a farm. He said there were all these zombies running around killing people out there at Whitey's, and he was gonna go back and find the guys. He hasn't come back."

"On Middle and Devils Glen?"

"Yeah," Randy said. "And he dropped them off out on Crow Creek Road and told them to hide so he could come back and help us. Maybe something happened to them."

"What should we do?"

"I don't know. Shit, I'm no good right now. My arm is killing me. That effing Surgat really dug his nails—" Suddenly, Randy's voice broke off, and Jack could hear him groaning through the static in the connection.

"Randy?" Jack called into the phone. "You there?"

After a few moments, Randy finally responded, "Yeah, I'm here. Jesus, I think we should get together and look for them."

"You don't sound so great. Maybe you should rest."

"And let you have all the fun? Screw you—I'll hop on my bike and meet you at Sunnycrest, OK? We can ride up towards Whitey's and see what's going on. By the way, I'll be happy when one of us gets our license."

"OK, fine. But if you keel over on me, it's on you."

"Got it. I'll see you there," Randy said and abruptly hung up.

"Where are you going?" said a voice from behind, startling Jack from his thoughts.

"What?" Jack asked, turning to see Anne standing in the hall outside his door.

Anne laughed. "Didn't mean to startle you. But you said you were going someplace. Where?"

"Oh, Randy and I are gonna ride up Middle Road and see if we can find our friends, Joe and Shaun."

Anne's eyes narrowed. "Are they missing?"

"Yeah, looks like it. I don't know." Jack explained as much as he could about how Leo had left his friends by the side of the road and the undead army that came out of nowhere.

"OK, well I'm coming with you," Anne said.

"Oh, no you're not."

"Oh, yes I am."

"You don't have a bike. You'd just slow us down."

"Mom has one, right? I can use hers. You're not going to leave me here, not when you're out doing something dangerous. I've been left in this house far too long, as you know. I'm coming with you."

Ten minutes later, Jack and Anne were pedaling their bikes down Mississippi Avenue under a gray and cloudy sky with the chilly November wind pushing them along.

8

REVELATION AT CROW CREEK

When they arrived at Sunnycrest Park, Randy was already there sitting on a bench next to the kiddie swings, his bike lying on the grass next to him. He was hunched over with his head between his knees, holding his left arm tightly against his stomach, his head swallowed up by a gray University of Iowa hoodie.

As Jack and Anne pulled closer, he looked up and grunted, "About time."

Jack pulled back the hood of his Chicago Cubs sweatshirt and said, "You don't look so good."

"I'm OK."

"I mean it—you should be home in bed. We can handle this without you, I think."

"I said I'm OK. I'm coming with you. Who's this?" Randy asked, looking at Anne. Jack realized that Randy did not know about Anne's resurrection, as it were.

"Randy, this is Anne."

Randy's jaw hung open as his eyes shifted back and forth

between them. Finally, he said, "What are you talking about? Anne? Your sister—who's *dead*?"

"Yeah."

"Hello, Randy," Anne said, extending her hand. "I feel like I already know you."

Randy took her hand and said, "Pleasure's mine. So you gonna explain this to me or what?"

Jack shrugged. "Honestly, I don't think I would know where to begin. It seems like something happened last night when the cult was trying to open the gates. Must have brought her back to life. That's about as far as we've gotten."

"Huh," Randy grunted. "What's one more un-friggin-believable thing, right?"

With that, Randy stood and gingerly swung himself onto his bike. Soon, the three of them were cruising down Middle Road. News of an attack by some "crazed lunatics" had already swept across Bettendorf, so the streets were almost empty, even at eleven o'clock on a Sunday morning. Only a few cars and trucks passed by them on their way past Palmer Hills golf course. As the threesome made their way through the intersection at Middle and Devils Glen, Jack saw the telltale signs of a battle.

A burned-out police cruiser and a totaled SUV still sat where they were left the night before. Trash still littered the streets. Whitey's parking lot was covered in dark dried blood, and the building, usually pristine white, was splattered red.

As he surveyed the carnage, a frightening thought occurred to Jack. "Hey guys, let's keep our heads on a swivel. If the cops haven't come back to clean this place up, there might be a reason."

"I agree," Anne said. "Whoever did all this might still be around."

Randy scoffed. "Shit, who cares? We've got the key here. Didn't you cause an earthquake in the high school cafeteria? Why should we be afraid?"

"You know I can't control that, Randy. I don't even know how I did it in the first place. If I did, I could have avoided a lot of pain last night; that's for sure."

At the mention of the previous evening's events, Randy doubled over in pain, grabbing at his left arm.

"Jesus, Randy. What the hell is wrong with you?"

"I don't know, dude. My arm is killing me—I swear to god. It feels like a hot brand is being pressed up against it every time I think about last night." Randy once again winced in pain.

"Is that the arm that Surgat grabbed?"

Randy screamed out and fell off his bike, landing hard on the cement. "For God's sake, don't say that name!"

"I'm sorry," Jack said as he and Anne laid down their bikes and knelt next to Randy. "Why would that name make the pain worse?"

"It's a demonic wound," Anne said, quietly.

Jack and Randy fell silent for a moment and looked at her. "What?" Jack asked.

"A demonic wound. When a demon or, in this case a devil, hurts a mortal, it sometimes leaves a part of itself behind in the wound. That's why it hurts so much whenever you say the name or when you think about it. The wound remembers."

Randy stared at Anne silently for several moments before finally asking, "What can I do about it? How do I heal it?"

"You can't."

"What do you mean? I'll have this wound forever?"

"Of course not."

"Thank God. So, it'll eventually go away on its own?"

"No, I meant you're mortal; you won't live forever. The wound will possess you, or you'll die," Anne said, emotionlessly. Then she looked across the parking lot and said, "I'm gonna go over to Whitey's and look around. I might be able to figure out where these creatures went."

Jack watched her walk away. He felt a tickle in the back of his mind, like a small warning. Looking around, he could see nothing and no reason to worry. So why did he feel so wrong?

"Dude, your sister has a great bedside manner," Randy said as if mirroring Jack's thoughts.

"Yeah, sorry about that," Jack said. "She was never like this before. She seems kinda cold."

"Resurrection will do that to ya, I guess. But shit, what do I do with this new information? I'm gonna die or become possessed by an ancient evil? Eff that! There's gotta be some way we can cure this. Maybe Ava knows something about it. I mean, she's got to have some friends someplace who are like her, doesn't she? Let's call her."

"She took off last night to find help—told me she'd be back in a few days. We can ask her when she gets back."

"Demonic wound. How does Anne even know about demonic wounds if she's been a ghost stuck in your house all these years?"

"She probably learned it in the land of the half-forgotten," Jack said, almost to himself.

"The *what?*"

"Never mind. Here, let's get you up and back on your bike."

As Randy stood up and carefully pulled himself back onto the leather seat of his bike, he watched Anne, who was looking around Whitey's parking lot and mumbling to herself. "Hey, Jack."

"Yeah?"

"Anne. Now that you mention it, she seems to be adjusting well to life. I mean, twenty-four hours ago, she was just a ghost who never left your house, and now, she's riding bikes and seems unfazed by much of anything she's seeing."

Jack turned to look at Anne. "I'm not sure she's adjusting all that well," he said.

"What do you mean?" Randy asked.

"Well, she's been—*different* since she came back. It's weird."

"How?"

"She just seems *odd*—not herself, I guess. It's like her emotions are stunted. It's weird. But I imagine that's to be expected if she's trying to figure out her place in all of this. Getting used to being a living, breathing human wouldn't be easy, I guess—not to mention, she's never actually been outside our home before last night."

"Yeah. By the way, how does she know how to ride a bike?" Randy asked.

Jack sat there for a moment with no reasonable answer. "I hadn't thought of that. Weird. What do you think?"

"Hell if I know. But we should keep an eye on her. Something's telling me this isn't right."

The boys watched as Anne walked past them and across Middle Road, looking north. She stood there for a minute or two then continued down the sidewalk twenty or thirty yards before jogging back. She hopped on her bike and asked, "What intersection is this?"

"Middle and Devils Glen," Jack said.

"OK, I see body parts strung out along Devils Glen Road, going that direction," Anne said, pointing north. "What's down there?"

Randy said, "Just neighborhoods—houses and condos. A mile or so down is Crow Creek Park."

"I think they went that way. The body parts lead in that direction. There were a whole bunch of undead here last night, killing people and eating them, it looks like. I think the bones and half-eaten limbs seem to indicate these creatures had discarded them on the sidewalk as they made their way down the road."

"You mean they were snacking on people?" Randy asked, looking like he wanted to vomit all over his handlebars.

"I think so. Who knows how many people were killed here? We should see where they went."

The three of them raced down Devils Glen, while keeping a lookout for any sign of undead. Fortunately, their trip was uneventful, and within minutes, they were gliding down the slight incline of the entry into Crow Creek Park. As they coasted along the drive, Jack immediately saw what they were looking for. In the Northeast side of the park next to the kiddie playground equipment was a large patch of burned grass and melted plastic. The stench of charred flesh hit them as they drew closer to the playground.

"Holy shit," Randy gasped. "What the hell happened here?"

Jack shook his head. "No effing clue."

As they made their way off the drive and across the grass to the playground area, Jack got the feeling something horrible had happened during the night, probably while he was being tortured by Surgat. Judging by the numerous tire marks and footprints, the area had been cleaned up by the police only recently.

"Well, if Shaun and Joe were here, we won't know until the police sort it out," Randy said.

"I'm at a loss," Jack said.

Suddenly, Anne stood straight up, staring into the trees just beyond the playground equipment. Eyes wide with fear, she began to back away as if bracing for an attack. A low growl rumbled from deep within her chest, a sound Jack had never heard from her.

"Anne, what's wrong?" Jack asked, unable to see what she was looking at.

Anne shook her head, her chin quivering. "I don't believe it."

Randy glanced back and forth between Anne and the trees. "What are you looking at? Is something in there? You're freaking me out!"

Anne then glared at Jack and laughed maliciously. "You stupid boy." Anne's voice was different now, guttural and angry. But that was not all—she *looked* different, almost as if her skin was changing. It seemed to be shriveling and dying before their eyes. Pieces of it dropped and melted like hot mozzarella cheese.

"What, Anne? What's happening? Your skin!"

"How did you summon that—*thing*?" she asked Jack. Her eyes were bulging in their sockets, like something in her skull was trying to push them out from the inside.

"What are you talking about? What thing?" Jack asked, confused. "Anne, please tell me what's going on."

Anne slapped her hands at her temples and let out a piercing scream, then she glared at Jack and said, "You don't know what you've done, do you? You don't have control over it! You draw these things to you, and you change the world around you, but here you sit oblivious to your own doing. You're going to be so easy for *him*. You have no idea what's coming. Ha!"

Jack felt light-headed. He stumbled and fell to his knees as he felt his entire world begin to crumble. *Why does she sound like she's someone else?* Then, in the corner of his eye, Jack saw a figure emerge from the trees.

It was a girl dressed only in some burned up rags and her undergarments. She was tall and thin with long, lean legs, and her milk-white skin was covered in dirt and ash. Her hair was jet black, and even from a distance, it was possible to see she was of East Asian descent. She was a student at their high school, but she had not been there long.

Randy said, "Hey, it's that foreign exchange girl. Tatsu!"

The girl shot a look at Randy. Her eyes were red as flame, and waves of heat seemed to be emanating from her skin, rising into the air above her. It then struck Jack precisely who this girl was. They were in Algebra together; she sat a few rows in front of him. She was a foreign exchange student from Japan or Korea—he could not remember which. Jack recalled that Tatsu had seemed almost unapproachable, though he quickly found out she was quite friendly, and her English was better than most American kids he knew.

"Tatsu?" Jack called to her. "It's me, Jack Davies."

She stared at him for a moment as if she was trying to remember something important, but then Anne spoke, breaking her thoughts.

"What are you doing here?" Anne asked.

Tatsu spat, "I could ask the same of you. What are you?"

Jack looked at Anne, and to his horror, he saw that her appearance had changed further. It was as if her face had melted, like a photograph left on a radiator. The bottom lid of her left eye drooped half an inch, and her lips contorted into a twisted snarl. Jack's eyes filled with tears as he watched Anne transform into something else entirely.

"Jack, what's happening to your sister?" Randy asked.

Tatsu spat, "Sister? There is no way this is your sister—she's not human. Don't you see? Can't you see what she is? Oh God, what is happening? She's a demon!" Tatsu's skin began to glow yellow and red. She crouched down to steady herself, her eyes rolling back in her head.

"Anne?" Jack pleaded from his knees.

"Ha!" The creature laughed as the disguise disintegrated further. "I'm afraid this girl is correct. I had so enjoyed our time together these hours, dear Jack, but it's nicer still to break your heart. I had hoped to keep the charade up for a bit longer, but alas it was not to be. The magic fades and I must return to my master. Goodye, Jack. You will find us in your nightmares!"

"What do you mean? You're Anne! You came to life after the rite last night. We're going to live together like a real brother and sister. Fight it, Anne! Fight whatever's inside you!"

"Your sister is gone, dear Jack. She is gone from this world forever. She was taken by my master and never will you see her again."

The rest of the skin fell to the ground, revealing slimy blue-black skin and large yellow eyes. However, this form did not remain but continued to change until it finally morphed into a small floating ball of flesh and bone. It continued to evolve until Jack could see wings and feathers, and it became something like a hummingbird with wings flapping a thousand times a second. The bird hovered here for a moment and then darted into the sky and out of sight with a burst of energy like the pop of a bottle rocket.

Jack, stayed there on his knees in schock. Waves of nausea swept over him as the whole world spun around him. Tatsu looked at him, her eyes filled with pity. It seemed for a moment like she might come and wrap her arms around him, but instead, she looked down at herself, covered her body as best she could with her hands and arms, and sprinted back into the woods.

Randy knelt and put his arm around Jack. "I'm so sorry, Jack! You hear me? I'm so sorry."

Jack stared up at the clouds, feeling lost and alone under the gray November sky.

9

AN EMPTY SPACE

1.

"Jack," Randy called from behind him. "What the hell just happened?"

Unfable to form words, Jack only shook his head. His hands and arms trembled as he gasped for air.

Randy knelt in front of him, placing his hands on shoulders, and looked into his eyes. Randy's face was a distorted mix of worry through the tears. "Jack. Hey, Jack snap out of it. Stay with me, buddy. We'll figure this out. I promise you."

"What happened?" Jack finally asked. "I don't understand. Why did that Tatsu girl say? What the fuck did she say to Anne?"

"That wasn't Anne. I don't know *what* it was, but it wasn't Anne. Whatever it was turned into a bird and flew away. You saw it, just as well as I did. We gotta figure this out, man. Your sister. We have to find her."

"Yeah," Jack mumbled. "We gotta find her." With that, Jack fell onto his back. The moment he hit the ground, a dark curtain dropped over him, cutting him off from the physical world. His vision went black and Jack drifted away from consciousness as his physical body disappeared before Randy's.

A fraction of a moment later, Jack found himself in a different world in the dead of night—a dark gray place surrounded by a thick forest of dying autumn trees.

He had peregrinated.

2.

Randy stood there staring at the space on the ground where Jack had been lying only moments before. He had disappeared without a trace. Randy looked back at Tatsu, who seemed just as startled by the development as he was. He yelled, "What happened? He was just here! Where did he go?"

The girl shook her head and opened her mouth to speak, but before she could answer, a sharp stabbing pain sliced into Randy's arm, and the scabbed-over tooth marks where Surgat had bitten him the previous night began to swell and pulse agonizingly. Blood and yellow pus seeped out of the wounds. Unlike past episodes, the pain didn't stop but continued to throb with increasing intensity, until Randy doubled over and began convulsing in dry heaves that produced nothing but thick lines of spit.

"You have a demon inside," Tatsu called to him from the trees.

"What do you know about it?" Randy cried. "Who the hell are you?"

"I know nothing of you. But I see it as clearly as I see the bile dripping from your lips."

Randy grunted. "Getting a good view of the show?"

"What happened to your friend?"

The pain continued, and Randy finally fell on his side, wrapping his arms around his knees and screaming in agony. From the ground, he could see Tatsu standing at the edge of the woods. Her skin had stopped glowing, but she looked just as wild as before. She glanced back and forth across the park then ran across the playground and knelt next to him. "What's wrong with you?" she asked, touching his head with the back of her hand. Her skin was burning hot.

"I'm in pain, goddammit! Are you blind?" Randy looked up at her and saw that her eyes, which moments before had been fire red, were now a dark chocolate brown–her hair singed, and her body covered with dirt and ashes. She still wore what was left of her blouse, but it barely passed for clothing. Her white bra and underwear were dirty but had survived whatever fire had consumed the rest. Oddly, her skin appeared to be unhurt—no scars or burns at all, only dirty and ash.

"Try to relax and think of nice things—fun things! And breathe." Tatsu caressed Randy's forehead. Her touch soothed him, and as she continued to whisper in his ear, he slowly felt the pain receding. Within a few minutes, it was nothing more than a small annoyance.

"What did you do?" Randy asked, feeling like himself again.

"Nothing. You relaxed; that's all."

"Bullshit. You did something. Your hand was warm."

"I have warm hands. Is something wrong with warm hands in Iowa?"

"Yes. Iowans are very suspicious of warm hands," Randy said sarcastically as he slowly sat up. "I'm feeling better."

"Good. Now, could you do me a favor and bring me some clothes? And find Allison Murphy. She's probably looking for me. Tell her I need clothes."

Now that the drama of the situation had subsided, Tatsu was suddenly self-conscious about the state of her attire. Randy, realizing he was now staring, averted his eyes and said, "Sure, no problem. Give me a minute to gather myself, and I'll hop on my bike and—"

He was cut off by the sound of an old school bus roaring down the road. It bounced along, slowing gradually until it finally pulled off to the side of the road on the other end of the park. It was an ancient purple monstrosity and looked like it hadn't seen much action, or paint, over the past twenty years. Randy drew Tatsu aside, pulling her behind a charred piece of children's playground equipment that, at one time, looked like a pirate ship.

A man wearing a St. Louis Cardinals baseball cap and thick glasses stepped out of the bus. He stood outside the bus door surveying the park until his eyes focused on the burned patch of grass only feet away from where Randy and Tatsu lay hidden. Another figure stepped off the bus, and Randy ducked back behind the equipment. "Shit," he whispered.

"What?" Tatsu asked. "Who's there?"

"Just this idiot kid, named Jimmy Vance, except he isn't a kid anymore. He's—and don't call me crazy for saying it, not after all you've seen today—but he's a *vampire*." Randy shook his head as if he could hardly believe he was saying it.

"Vampire?" she asked. "What is a vampire?"

"You know, they suck your *blood*? Like Dracula?"

"Ah! Kyuketsuki?"

"Uh, if that means monsters-who-will-suck-your-blood-dry, then yes, kyuket—whatever you said."

"But they aren't real," Tatsu said. It was almost a question.

"Again, with all you've seen today?"

"I don't understand—the sun is out. If he is a vampire, why is he outside in daytime?"

"I have no idea. All I know is he will kill us if he sees us. You understand *that* shit? By the way, they keep pointing in this direction. I think they're gonna come over here. We need to leave, like now." He glanced to his left and saw that his and Jack's bikes were both several yards away in the open. "Shit, we're gonna have to leave the bikes behind. Let's make for the trees back there, OK? We can cut through the woods to the quarry and head south from there. Once we're away from this place, we'll find a place for you to hide out while I get you some clothes, OK?"

Tatsu nodded, and the two of them tore across the playground and dove into the trees.

3.

"You see that?" Jimmy Vance asked.

"Uh huh," Carl said, staring at the trees where, moments before, Randy and Tatsu had run off.

"It was that Wall kid with some half-naked chick."

"Yep."

"Should I go after them?" Jimmy asked.

"Nope."

"Why not? He deserves to get taught a lesson, and I want to be the one who teaches him. Hell, we owe him for what happened last night!"

"You're a half-vamp," Carl said.

"So what?" Jimmy said.

"Well, It means you've got limits. You can walk in the sun, which is a nice bonus, but you got no power 'til nightfall. In daylight, that kid could kill you easy as anybody else. Hell, even at night, you're not as powerful as a full-vamp. That kid about ended you last night as it was—face it, fighting ain't why you were made. Now, grab that shovel over there and carry that bag."

"Randy Wall? He couldn't do shit to me. I could kill him, vamp powers or no vamp powers, with my damn two hands!"

"It's not what we're here for. The Wall boy don't matter, not now anyway. Something out there fried almost a quarter of our army last night, right over there in that black patch of grass. Far as we know, there ain't nothing can do something like that. We need to figure out what new rival we're dealing with. If you haven't noticed, things have changed around here, and not all of it is for the better. Got it?"

"Yeah, I get it. But that little turd hit me with a baseball bat! I will *not* forgive that shit. Believe me."

Carl handed him an empty bag and started across the Crow Creek Park toward the burned patch of grass carrying two shovels. "Yes, I believe you. And maybe you'll get your chance to pay him back someday. But not today."

As they walked, Jimmy asked, "Why ain't I a full vamp?"

"Because Brother Jones don't want you to be a full vamp, not yet, anyway. You're more useful to us this way."

"Gee, that's great. So, that slut Stephanie gets to boss me around all night, rub it in my face, and I gotta take it?"

"Yep."

"That's bullshit."

Carl smirked, but as they approached the burn, a strange expression crossed his face. He immediately dropped the bags of equipment and got down on his hands and knees, sniffing the blackened earth. He moved to the burned up pirate ship and sniffed where Randy and Tatsu had been hiding. After several moments, his head shot up, and he looked back at the trees. "Looks like you get your wish. You better go follow those two, after all."

"They did this?" Jimmy asked.

"One of them did it. And this wasn't done by nothing normal; that's a fact."

"That Wall kid doesn't have any power. He's just a doofus."

"Didn't say it was him."

"You think the girl did it?"

"The Wall kid was with us last night—gotta be the girl. That's why you need to follow them, but don't get seen. Just keep a watch and see where the girl goes. Find out where she lives," Carl said, still looking at the burned spot on the ground. "I'll find out what I can about this place. You get movin' before they get away."

"What about the Wall kid?"

"Leave him be, for now—and that's an order. He doesn't matter to us right now. But don't you worry, Jimmy—Brother Jones will be dealing with him soon enough. Believe me, that boy and all the others will pay for what they did to us."

10

BEGINNER'S LUCK

Anxiety threatened to overwhelm Jack's senses as he stared at the strange world around him. One moment, he had been lying on the grass of Crow Creek Park in the middle of a bright but cloudy day, the next he had traveled to—*here. But where is here?* Jack asked himself. The trees above him creaked and groaned as a cold wind drove through them, sprinkling the ground with what remained of their dying leaves. However, the trees were not the only sounds he heard. A subtle crunching of leaves sounded from the woods.

"Hello?" Jack called into the shadows as he pulled himself to a sitting position.

"Hello?" a soft voice echoed.

"Who's out there?"

"Who's out *there?*" the voice asked with a laugh.

Sudden dizziness came over him, and Jack struggled to stand as he scanned the forest but slumped back down onto his behind. His eyes had not yet adjusted to the darkness, leaving him temporarily blind to the surroundings, but he sensed a presence amongst the trees. Still reeling from the loss of his sister, Jack was in no mood to play games—a dangerously odd mixture of rage and ambivalence rose within him. He knew it would not take much for the blood red rage to overwhelm him again. His elbows on his knees, he bowed his head into his hands and rubbed his temples with his thumbs.

"Show yourself, or go away," he called in a stronger voice than he had intended, as another wave of nausea washed over him. Sweat beads dotted his forehead, and his vision became a light shade of crimson.

"Not so fast, *peregrinator*. I do not succumb easily to words of command, and I think you do not yet know what you're doing. You're lucky I happened to be in this area—very lucky indeed. But don't worry. You've got the traveling sickness, I think. It'll go away in a moment," said the voice.

Jack couldn't tell whether it was a man or a woman, a boy or a girl, but seemed to him that it was perhaps a little of each. "How do you know I traveled?" he asked.

"Didn't you?"

"Answer *my* question first," Jack said.

"Oh, I don't know. Perhaps I was staring at that piece of ground upon which you sit, hunting a particularly juicy field mouse, when poof! My savory dish ran off into the shrubs, and there's a boy in its place looking confused and, frankly, rather stupid. Handsome, though, yes he is."

"Who are you?" Jack asked.

"I am me. And you?"

Jack struggled to stand but could only stumble a few steps before he had to step over to a tree and lean against its trunk to steady himself. Again, he scanned the trees, noticing that his sight had already adjusted to the darkness. "I am me," Jack answered.

"Good answer," said the voice, chuckling. "Best not give away too much too soon, I always say. But your identity is not hard to guess. Your coming to this land was foretold and expected and perhaps even arranged if truth be told."

"Arranged?" Jack asked. "I came here through my own power—I'm pretty sure."

"Oh, I don't doubt it one bit. But that does not mean you had everything to do with why you came to be here. Why *did* you travel here, peregrinator? Do you even know?"

"To find someone," Jack said. He was not entirely confident with that answer, but he thought it best not to show this person any weakness. *Let her or him feel I had every intention of coming here.*

"Ha! Good for you!"

"Why do you say that?"

The voice laughed again. "You told the truth right off the bat! I thought there would be much more digging and dodging, but here you go and tell the truth straight away. Such a relief!"

"How do you know I'm telling the truth?" Jack asked.

"Now, there you go, just when you were doing so well! Tedium is not an attractive quality, no matter which world you're in. Go back to being bold and handsome, young man."

"You are the tedious one," Jack said.

A low growl rumbled from the shadows. "Oh, you will do well to watch your tongue. Of the two of us, *I'm* the one who knows where you are."

"Are you saying you can help me?" Jack asked.

"Of course, I *can* help you, and there is no doubt in my mind you need my help. However, I haven't yet decided whether I *will* help you. I have many things to do, and time runs queer in the Woodland of Weird. I imagine your coming will make it even worse, so truthfully, I'm disinclined to offer my support."

In the shadows, Jack found hints of light, places where his eyes, now rapidly adjusting to the conditions here, could make out details of the forest. Within the gnarled arms of the myriad branches, he picked out a form, not human but animalistic like a wolf, though smaller. It moved stealthily between the trunks and seemed to make no sound as it padded here and there. Occasionally, its head would peer back at him with two glowing eyes reflecting what little light there was in this place. The entire world was partly illuminated by some source besides the moon, currently hidden behind a thick veil of glowing clouds. Some other light was here, faint but present, like the ghost of daylight from some long-dead sun buried in the cold vastness of whatever space surrounded this dimension.

"If you refuse to help me, I guess I'll find my way," Jack said. "It's better I don't trust you, anyway."

The voice laughed. "Oh ho ho! Don't play the trickster with me! Tell me who it is you seek, and I will decide whether to help you or not."

"Why would I say anything about myself if you won't even show yourself to me?" he asked as he squinted into the forest and stepped forward.

The shadow slipped between a pair of trees and drew closer. "I see your eyes upon me, so you know perfectly well I have revealed myself to you. Why do you choose to lie about obvious things?"

"But you're in shadow."

"And? So are you."

She was correct—he was indeed standing in the shadows of the surrounding trees. From her viewpoint, he probably looked the same to her as she did to him, a silhouette. "OK, I'll step into the light," he said and stepped over to a small patch of open space several paces away until he felt the brightness of the strange illumination on his face.

The creature paused for a moment in the trees, staring at him. Slowly, a dog-looking shadow crept toward him, and as it did, the animal seemed to transform into something else. At first, it became a misshaped mass of black, like a malleable ball of black clay, but soon, the edges of its ambiguous shape reached out on all sides until it finally twisted into a human form. Finally, the creature stepped into the light and stared at Jack.

The canine creature had become a girl—naked and petite—just over five-foot-tall with long, gray and tan hair that flowed down her shoulders, past her small breasts, all the way to her hips. From her face, she looked to be about the same age as Jack. She was thin but healthy, with narrow hips and lean muscular legs. As she stepped closer to Jack, staring up at him defiantly, he saw her eyes were bright yellow. Her skin seemed to glow in the ghostly light. There was a feral look about her, and her wild face appeared to convey a mixture of emotions, from exhilaration to fury to amusement, all in succession, and sometimes all at once. Her lips parted with a wicked grin, and a red serpentine tongue curled up out of her mouth, the tip running slowly along the contours of her front four teeth like a predator holding a field mouse under its paw.

Jack's heart raced.

She said, "And now that you have seen, what do you make of me?"

For the one-millionth time in the past two weeks, Jack was speechless. She placed her hands on her hips and watched him as his eyes awkwardly scanned her entire body. She was beautiful and wild, like a wolf or coyote, and appeared to be equally dangerous. However, there was something about her that immediately struck Jack as being out of place. Here was a person who looked in every way like a girl, except for one small part hanging lightly from below her pelvis between the tops of her thighs.

Jack cleared his throat and asked, "I don't mean to offend you, but I have to ask—are you a boy or a girl?"

She smiled at him for a moment, tilting her head. "I am both. And I am neither. I am what I wish to be at any time of any day I choose to walk in these woods. If you are examining me and noticing something that looks like one thing, while other parts look like another, well, all I can tell you is this—I am both, and I am neither."

"I get that, but there's more to you than just being a boy or a girl or neither. A minute ago, you were a wolf—"

"—a coyote."

"And then you turned into a girl, sort of. What are you?"

"There are many names for what I am, though I find none of them satisfying, so I prefer not to use any. I am more than what they call me, as are you. Take me as I am or not, but let's leave the names to those with tiny brains."

"How did you know I can peregrinate?"

"Because you were not here before, but here you are now. I was padding through this wood, looking for a bite to eat, and there came a flash of white light and a sharp sound, like the piercing of tight skin followed by the smell of charred air. And there you were. Though it has been some time since I encountered one who travels, I do know the signs."

"I'm Jack. What's your name?"

"Faelith," she said, leaning closer to sniff him. She squinted her nose slightly and laughed.

"Nice to meet you, Faelith. But I'm afraid I have to find out where the hell I am and how I got here. Unless you plan to help me, I should probably say my goodbyes."

Faelith studied him, smiling. "I have not yet decided whether to help you. Perhaps I will accompany you for a time until I am sure which is the best course for me."

Jack sighed. "OK, that's fine. But could you cover yourself?"

"Ha! What? With clothes?"

"Yeah, that would work if you have any."

"Do you see any clothes here? No? Sorry, but there's not much I can do when I spend most of my time in animal form. Alas, you must get past your shame."

"I'm not ashamed of anything," Jack said. "If you want to walk through the woods buck naked, knock yourself out."

"Ha! Such a boy. Now that we have that sorted, why don't you tell me how you got here, and I'll tell you if there's anything I can do to help you."

"I'm looking for my sister," he said finally. "She was stolen from my world, or so I was told. How I got here, I don't know." Jack explained to her the incident at Crow Creek Park and how the creature disguised as his sister had revealed itself. "After that, I fell to the ground feeling defeated, and the next thing I knew, I was here in these woods. And then you came along."

Faelith raised an eyebrow and stared into his eyes then sniffed the air between them. "This creature told you that your sister was taken from your world?"

"Yes."

"And you know she was taken to this world? Is that why you peregrinated here?"

Jack rubbed his forehead. "That I don't know. I didn't control any of it—I just wound up here. I mean, if it happens that I just magically traveled to the same world where a demon took my sister, then I guess it's dumb luck."

"You haven't been trained in traveling?" Faelith asked.

"No, I don't know anything about traveling, *peregrinating*, or whatever it's called. People in my world don't do that kind of shit. Hell, I never even knew *I* could do it until a few days ago. I don't know a thing about my abilities. Zero."

Faelith stared at him with a mixture of pity and something else. Was it excitement? Curiosity? Or was she thinking of ways to exploit his weaknesses? A rush of nausea passed through Jack's guts as he realized how much of his vulnerability he had just revealed to her.

Stupid me! Have I given away too much?

"Hm," she mumbled. "This is a sad story, indeed. If you don't know how you came to be here or how to use the powers you have, how can you ever help your sister? How will young Jack find his way home?"

"I don't know. Honestly, I've been flying by the seat of my pants. I have no idea what I'm doing. I want someone to tell me what the hell I'm supposed to do!"

"I must think on this for a time." She motioned for him to follow. "Your story sounds earnest, which makes it all the more confusing. How could you have come here without being trained to peregrinate? I admit it's not something I'm too familiar with. I've only known two peregrinators in all my life, but I have an inkling you didn't come here by accident, and my inklings never lie. Honest, they are, my inklings. If you came to this place, there had to be a reason. And so it stands to reason that, if your sister was kidnapped and taken from your world, you came here to find her."

Jack grabbed her by the shoulders and turned her to face him. "Can you teach me? Can you show me how to find my powers?"

She slowly removed his hands and calmly set them back at his sides. "Never touch me again, young man. Do you hear?"

"I'm sorry," Jack said, his face turning red.

Faelith laughed at him, and Jack's embarrassment grew. "You're an odd one. I don't like being touched unless I've given an invitation, which I have not—at least not yet." She gave him a sly wink and continued into the forest as Jack followed.

"Where are we going?" he asked.

"It's best not to stay in the open too long, especially you. Your entry was clumsy, and if I were made aware of your presence, others would have been too. You're fortunate I happened upon you when I did, most fortunate indeed. In fact, you might almost call it fate. There are some in these woods who would have taken advantage of your situation and eaten you for dinner or worse."

Jack laughed, hoping Faelith was joking, but the girl gave no indication one way or the other. "So, are we going to your home?" he asked.

"Home? Ha! I have no home. I go as I please, and I stay where I want to stay for as long as I wish to stay there. However, I do have many dens. In fact, I have one not far away—a place for me to rest and feed. We will go there, and I will decide what to do next. I admit you do present a puzzle for me, and I must have time to think."

"How am I a puzzle for you?"

"Because I so happen to be on a quest of my own—one that has taken me many miles from my usual hunting grounds to this god-forsaken land of dead things."

Jack stopped. "Well, I have to find my sister! I can't sit around while you decide whether you want to help me or not. Who knows what's happening to her!"

Faelith turned and snapped, "Then go right ahead. Go! Find her yourself if you think you can. Perhaps you'll happen upon her captor's hideaway by accident. You'll blunder into it like you seem to blunder into everything else. Silly boy! You have no idea where you are, and as far as I can see, I'm the only chance you've got to turn your fortunes around. That is *if* I think you're worth it!"

Jack struggled to maintain his anger, but his frustration mixed with fear and confusion began to boil inside him. His teeth chattered, and his hands clenched at his jeans until he thought he might rip ten holes in them. All the frustrations of the past twenty-four hours boiled up through his body, threatening to spill out of every orifice.

Suddenly, his vision turned red, and everything changed.

Jack became aware of everything—every molecule of every dead tree, every fallen leaf, and every cell in Faelith's body. The girl's face, which had up to this point held little more than snarky contempt, was now filled with surprise—surprise and then fear—not fear of Jack but of something else. Her head darted all around, a thousand times in a second, and Jack suddenly realized the ground was shaking beneath them, just like that day in the cafeteria. The trees swayed right and left before him, and for a moment, he thought he could hear them whispering to each other as they stared down at him with disgust. He tasted their hatred for him—it permeated the air all around.

Faelith leaped in front of Jack and grabbed him by the shoulders, yelling, "Stop! You idiot, stop this right now! You'll kill us both!" When it became apparent that Jack was in a trance, she said, "You fool of a boy." Then she rose to her tip-toes, looked into his vacant eyes as a tree branch fell behind her, and kissed him full on the lips.

Quickly, the anger subsided as a new sensation nudged its way into Jack's mind. Faelith's lips tasted like something sweet, like candy and pumpkin pie and chocolate cake. Electricity, nearly as intense as the one he had experienced with Ava, began to course back and forth between them both, and almost involuntarily, Jack slid his hands around her small waist, pulling her body closer. In response, she slid her hands behind his back and laced her fingers through his hair, turning her head to the side and closing her eyes.

They stood like this for what seemed like hours. Jack was fully aware he was standing in the middle of a forest in some strange alternate world, kissing a naked coyote girl—who was not quite a girl—and though he knew with every ounce of his being they were in danger, he found it impossible to stop kissing her, even after the ground had stopped shaking. His mind was not his own. Finally, he heard her speak through their kisses.

"Fool, stop kissing me. We. . .must. . .leave."

"You. . .stop. . .I. . .can't," Jack said.

"You truly are a teenager," Faelith growled. Then she reached back with a clenched fist then punched him hard in the chest directly above his heart.

It felt like his entire chest might cave inward, smashing his heart and lungs. He staggered back and bent over with his hands on his knees, panting. Faelith knelt on the ground and gasped for air as well.

"Bloody hell," she said. "Do you kiss like that all the time?"

"I don't have a whole lot of experience. I'm pretty sure it must have been you."

"Ha! I've never kissed anyone in all my years of existence, young man! I'm quite sure *that* wasn't me!"

Jack looked at her and laughed. "Maybe it's beginner's luck for both—"

Faelith's head shot up, and she sprang into a crouched position, letting out a low growl into the woods. Quickly, Jack saw them too, dozens of them—people, hooded and robed in gray—silently hovering above the ground twenty or thirty yards away in the forest, watching them. With the fog, it was hard to see much. How they had appeared so quickly, he couldn't tell, though Jack wondered if they had been watching them the whole time. He could not see their faces through the misty air, but he sensed hostility and instinctively backed away, whispering to Faelith, "I don't like the looks of them."

"Nor should you," Faelith whispered back. "Your show of power brought them upon us. Others will follow, I'm sure, but I doubt any could be worse. I'm afraid we may have met our end, young Jack. Beginner's luck, indeed."

"Who are they?" Jack asked.

"They're called the Visitors by some," Faelith said, sniffing the air. "But my kind call them the Host."

"What are they?"

"You don't want to know. You only want to run. As fast as you can."

"OK, I will try. But I don't think I'm very fast, probably nowhere near as fast as you."

"You don't think you can make the ground rumble again, maybe?" she asked, keeping her eyes on the visitors.

"I don't think so. I've lost it again. I'm sorry, but your kiss took it out of me."

Faelith sighed then grabbed him by the arm and, in one smooth motion, swung his entire body onto her back, laughing as she cried, "Hang on!" And in a flash, she had him in her arms, sprinting through the dense dead foliage of the Woodland of Weird.

Though she was dodging rocks and leaping over fallen trees, Faelith never lost her footing nor her balance, and as she ran, her laugh rang through the trees like a fresh morning rain. Like a thoroughbred at full gallop, her gait was smooth and steady. Her footfalls never faltered, and she covered the ground making hardly a sound.

Jack looked behind and saw nothing.

"Hey, I don't think they're following us," he said.

"Oh, they're with us, and they're gaining fast. I don't know if we'll make it to my den."

Jack looked back again. "I'm telling you, Faelith. They're not behind us."

"Look up," she said.

Jack lifted his head and there, high above the trees, he saw them. The Host, dozens of them, glided silently, their long gray cloaks flowing freely in the night sky like a horde of flying wraiths. Now, with their hoods thrown back, Jack could see their faces. Each was beautiful and terrifying—human-like, with high arching brows above piercing eyes that seemed to glow in the darkness. There were men and women, all with long blond, almost white hair flowing out behind their billowing robes. In the dark and cloudy sky, it was impossible to see much else. They made no sound or none that Jack could hear, as they followed along, seemingly content to remain at a discreet distance.

"Jack," Faelith cried. "You've got to reach out for whatever power you have and try to find it. Get angry if you need to. Fight! Think about your sister. What are they doing to her, whoever took her? Where do they have her? What have they used her for?"

Jack concentrated, though it was hard to do, riding on Faelith's back. However, remembering what the creature in the park had said about Anne helped him focus. The anger he felt as he lost what he thought would be a new life with his beloved sister intensified, and soon, his vision went red. The anger snowballed, fueled by the fear of what was above him, but also by the knowledge that, if these creatures took them, he might never see Anne again. And if he didn't save her, who would?

The blood rose within him, and his vision again turned crimson. A great upheaval in the earth burst the ground below them, sending the nearby trees toppling over and showering everything within twenty yards in an avalanche of dirt and rocks. Jack looked up and saw the Host weaving and dodging the debris with ease. This made him angrier, and another upheaval, more massive than the last, sent piles of earth and trees sailing into the air, knocking a handful of the Host out of the sky.

Unfortunately, Faelith could not navigate the breaking ground. She stumbled to her right and lost her footing in the wreckage of a broken tree. As she fell forward, Jack lost his grip on her back, and the two were sent tumbling in opposite directions, somersaulting over the ground. When he finally came to a stop, Jack ignored the pain now pulsing across his back and looked up to find three attackers shooting right for him, like missiles. He reached out for his power and, with his right hand, leaped to Faelith and grabbed her by the arm. Clenching his teeth, Jack concentrated until suddenly everything went black.

And just like that, Jack and Faelith were gone.

As the outstretched hand of one of the Host—a tall, thin female with hair as bright and golden as the morning sun—reached out to grasp nothing but thin air.

11

HEAD IN THE WOODS

Randy stumbled through the small grove of oak trees, his head pounding and his stomach rumbling with what little breakfast he had eaten that morning. Tatsu helped him along as best she could, propping him on her shoulder. She had long ago lost any shyness about the state of her clothing. The throbbing in Randy's head kept his mind only on one step at a time.

"Where we going?" Tatsu asked.

Randy stopped for a moment to catch his breath. His home was the easy answer, but there was no way he could bring her there in her current condition. "Well, I was planning to take you to my house or Allison's house if you knew the way, which it seems you don't."

"I think she lives on Tattlefeet Lane."

"You mean *Tanglefoot?*" Randy asked.

"Yes, that's it," Tatsu said.

"Ok, that's to the west over there," Randy said, pointing to their right. "I don't know what to do about your clothes, though."

"Do you have a phone?" Tatsu asked. "Mine melted in the fire."

"Yeah, but I don't know Allison's number. I don't suppose you memorized it, did you?"

"No."

"Well, then I guess I'll have to walk over there, get your clothes, and meet you back—" Before he could finish his sentence, Randy heard a sound behind them—little more than the crackling of leaves.

"What is it?" Tatsu asked.

Randy whispered, "I think we're being followed."

"You hear something?"

"Yes."

"That boy from the park?"

"Maybe. Sounds like one person. I gave Jimmy quite a beating last night, and he's not used to that. He's probably pissed as hell."

"You fought him? Why?" Tatsu asked.

"Eh, it's a long story, a really long one. We better get moving and figure out what happened to Jack. He needs our help; I'm pretty sure—"

"Oh, boo hoo," called a familiar male voice from somewhere in the copse of trees behind them. "Too bad about your poor friend. But it doesn't matter—he's gonna be dead soon anyway, and so are you, Randy Wall."

Randy closed his eyes and rubbed his forehead as a new sensation began to grow within him, and a cold voice spoke in his mind. Though the words dripped with menace and hate, Randy could not help but be mesmerized by the sound of it. *Kill him. Kill him*, the voice said.

"Shut up!" Randy called out.

Jimmy laughed. "Why don't you come here and make me, you little shithead. Your friends aren't here to help you this time, and I don't think this naked girl is going to be much of a challenge. Maybe I'll show her a good time, Vance-style, once I'm done with you, that is."

You can do it. Kill him.

"*Vance* style? What the hell would that be—drink a fifth of whiskey and slap her around before you pass out on the couch?"

Jimmy glared at him. "Keep talking, little bitch, and you'll see what Vance style is all about."

Jimmy stalked around a tree and stood in front of Randy, a dirty grin spread wide across his face as if he had not a care in the world that his prey held any power at all. For a moment, Randy almost felt sorry for the boy, as he felt a strange power growing within him—one he knew was far superior to anything the Vance kid possessed.

Now's your chance, fool. Kill the little bastard.

"I don't want to," said Randy.

Yes, you do. You want to kill him. You've always wanted to kill him.

"Oh, you don't?" Jimmy said. "Well, then I guess you can stand there while I rip your throat out, like the little pussy you are. Maybe I'll leave you with just enough life in you to watch me take this little Jap girl on the ground here, right next to you. Show you how a real man does it."

"Boy. You should be careful," Tatsu said.

"And why is that?" Jimmy mocked.

"You are weak," she said.

"Ha!" laughed Jimmy as he shifted on his feet. "The fuck you know about me?"

"I know enough to know you're making a mistake right now."

A new fury burned in Jimmy's eyes. "Oh, you think so, do you? Well, just you wait. I'll show you, you little Jap bitch."

"You know it's true," she said. "I see how weak you are—everyone sees."

Jimmy stood there watching Tatsu with his mouth hanging open. His eyes shifted back and forth between Randy and Tatsu, and then he said, "You gonna let the chink talk for you, pussy? You gonna let her fight your battle? Is that it? Ha! I always figured you for a pussy, Wall, but letting a slut like this fight for you is a whole other level."

Randy felt weak, not physically but mentally, almost as if someone had seized control of his body, like a car passenger sliding over and sitting on his lap to take the wheel. His vision turned red and yellow. Words came from Randy's mouth, but he wasn't the one speaking them.

Dak bat caelvyrn, ack bant-Vampyr! The voice cried out in his mind, and Randy repeated them aloud. "Dat bat caelvyn, ack bant-Vampyr!"

"What the hell did you say?" Jimmy asked, his eyes wide.

"Crawl back to your hole, half-vampire—you are a slave, nothing more. It is all you ever will be. This one is mine, and so he shall stay."

Randy struggled against the power within him, realizing too late he was possessed by it. The entity was malevolent and ancient; he could feel its dark energy surging through him, but he also knew this demon was not yet in full control. Randy struggled with the power, pushing it back into the recesses of his mind. A claustrophobic panic set in, as if he was being held down by a massive weight.

No, you fool. Let me have him, the demon growled.

"This is *my* body," Randy said aloud. "I will do what I want. You're not in charge!"

"Who the hell are you talking to, freak?" Jimmy asked. His signature sneer remained glued to his face but now accompanied by a rising fear.

Tatsu watched Randy as he continued to struggle. Finally, she gathered herself and turned back to Jimmy. "You should run, Jimmy. Run fast. Now!"

Though Jimmy Vance was never known for being the wisest kid at Bettendorf High School, he possessed enough smarts to recognize danger when he saw it. A slight sliver of fear flashed across his face.

At the same time, a new desire grew in Randy, like a wolf spotting an injured doe, and the dark red haze filled his eyes. For the first time in his life, Randy began to have dark thoughts—genuinely violent thoughts—ideas no sane person could ever have.

Good! Yes, he must not live. Kill him.

"I can't. He looks like he's ready to run," Randy said.

"Who's gonna run? I sure as hell ain't gonna run, not from you, anyway," Jimmy said. Though his words were all bravado, his voice gave away the anxiety filling his chest.

He will kill you when he gets the chance, and you know it's true. He will kill you or one of your friends. Perhaps this girl? Or your friend, Jack. Jack Davies? If you let the Vance boy get away, someone you love will die, and it will be your fault. Kill him.

Randy doubled over and screamed. He called out into his mind—to the thing within it, *Shut up! Shut up! I am in control, not you! It's my body!*

Yes, yes, that is true, young Randy. You are in control, so you must do this thing. You must do it now, or let your friends die. It matters not to me.

Randy stood, and his vision still filled red as a fire burned just under his skin. How long had it been there? Did it start only moments ago, or had that fire burned within him his whole life? At that moment, Randy was one with the fire. He let it bathe over him, and instead of pain, Randy felt a soothing calm. Then he noticed that Jimmy was no longer there.

"It's OK," Tatsu said. "He ran away."

Though he knew he should be relieved at her words, Randy spat and glared into the trees with hatred filling his heart. Without a word, he charged after Jimmy with a newfound speed he had never possessed. It was not superhuman speed, like Lara or Ava, but faster than he had ever run, as if he had suddenly harnessed all the human potential of his own body. Soon, Randy was tearing through the woods like a cat, leaping over fallen trees and ducking under low branches until, at last, he spotted his quarry.

Jimmy had slowed down, probably due to his stubborn cockiness—a weakness that would soon be his undoing. In fact, it seemed that he had hesitated for a moment, perhaps considering whether he should go back and kill the Wall boy, just to teach Tatsu a lesson.

Within moments, Randy was on Jimmy's back, driving him

to the ground, and with one graceful motion, flipped the boy around and turned him so that Jimmy was on his back looking up at him from the forest floor. Desperation lit the boy's face, his usual expression of vile contempt nowhere to be found.

"What the fuck! Get off me, you homo!" Jimmy cried.

Randy said not a word, but with methodical efficiency placed his hands on both sides of the boy's head and began twisting it right and left. Randy Wall was filled with power, giving him more than enough strength to subdue the Vance kid but not enough to rip his head off with one clean motion. Instead, Randy continued to twist back and forth until he could feel the boy's vertebrae cracking between his hands.

"Stop! Randy, stop!" cried a voice behind him, but he did not stop. Finally, with one last thrust of his hands and one final upward ripping motion, Randy separated Jimmy's head from his shoulders. He held the head in front of him, staring at the boy's death mask as the sound of Jimmy's final piercing scream echoed through the trees.

12

THE LAGOON

When Jack opened his eyes, he found himself in a small meadow, softly illuminated by some strange light that seemed to come from nowhere and everywhere at once. Next to him lay Faelith, blinking her eyes as if she had just awoken from a dream. Exhausted, Jack sat up slowly and scanned the area to his right. He was aware of the soft sound of a small stream coming from not far away. Behind him, he heard crickets and frogs and other sounds of another watery area. It was all familiar to him, somehow, like he had been here before.

That's impossible. I don't have any memory of this place.

"How did you do that?" Faelith asked.

"Do what?" Jack asked.

"How did we get here?"

Shrugging, Jack said, "I peregrinated."

"No. How did you take me with you?"

"I don't know. I was scared, so I got us out of there, I guess."

"You peregrinated both of us away from that place, right at the moment of our greatest need. You *must* know how to do it," Faelith said. She stared at him with that same mysterious half-smile she had given him before, holding it for some time until Jack began to feel uncomfortable.

"Not really," Jack said. "Seems like I can only do this stuff when I'm mad or scared maybe."

"Hm. Yes, I see that—probably a defense. I think you must have hidden your skills deep in your mind. Perhaps you can only use your powers when you truly need them."

"Maybe. If I hid them from myself, that would be the dumbest thing I could have done. I could've avoided a lot of shit if I'd known what the hell I was doing, especially the past week or two. Hell, I could have been a star on the varsity football team. But whatever I did, I don't remember doing it at all. I'm obviously an idiot."

"It was smart. You had no one to teach you—no one to show you how to control your abilities. Power like yours, young Jack, is not easy to control. Most who have it, die young."

"How?"

"Simple. They wind up traveling to places they shouldn't, or they never figure out how to get back. Many use the power too often, until it consumes them or drives them mad. You must have hidden the power away—forgotten it—to protect yourself."

"The hymn of forgetting," Jack said, remembering Anne's song.

"The *what?*" Faelith asked.

"A song Anne sang to me when I was a kid to help me forget bad memories."

Faelith smiled. "You're something else, Jack Davies."

Jack snickered. "Yeah, I'm one in a million."

"Yes. Just like the rest of us."

"Yeah, you certainly *are* one in a million. Part boy, part girl. Part human, part coyote. One in a *gazillion*, more like it."

"Yes." Faelith glanced down at her feet. "That is true."

"Are there others like you?" Jack asked. He hoped he had not said the wrong thing.

"Of course, there are others like me! I didn't just spring out of a cave in the earth. I had a mother and a father like all living creatures. And I had brothers and sisters too."

"Where are they now?" Jack asked.

Faelith looked up at the sky for several moments then back at Jack and smiled half-heartedly. Then she waved his question away and said, "Come, we don't have time for stories now. Let's look around and see if I can recognize where we are."

Jack did not pursue the subject but followed her segue. "This place looks familiar to me, but I can't put my finger on why. I hear running water beyond those trees, and it sounds like there's a lake or a marsh behind us."

Sure enough, as they searched the area, they came upon a peaceful lake, partially concealed by a slow-moving mist. It appeared that the lake was at least a few square miles, oblong-shaped with still water like glass. At its center was an island with oak and elm trees flourishing upon it, the only vegetation Jack had so far seen that looked like it might be alive. The trees were covered with healthy red, orange, and yellow leaves.

Faelith let out a small laugh. "Your 'accidental' travelings are fortuitous, Jacky-boy."

"What do you mean?"

"This place of all places. I won't believe we happened upon it by accident. No, I will not. In fact, if I'd had more time to think before the Host appeared, it would have been the first place I would have thought to bring you."

"What lake is this?" Jack asked.

"Its exact name I don't know, but I have heard it called The Lagoon."

"Yes!" Jack clapped his hands and laughed. "That's it! The Lagoon!"

"What?"

"This place is just like the lagoon in Bettendorf, the town I'm from back in my world. It's just bigger, a *lot* bigger. I mean, the Bettendorf lagoon is not much more than a pond with ducks and a few geese and some sunfish and a tiny island in the middle—this is more like a lake. Aside from the size, it's the same, right down to the island in the middle. Which means that water back there behind us must be this world's version of Duck Creek, and that hill over there on the other side of the lake should lead right up to Middle Park. Oh, my god! It's just like Bettendorf, but it's not. The same, but different. I mean, there are no houses, and the scale of everything is a lot different, but it's like an alternate version of my town. Holy crap!"

Faelith arched an eyebrow at him and shook her head. "I have no idea what you're talking about, but *this* lagoon is quite an interesting place. Again, your ability to aimlessly pop yourself exactly where you need to be is remarkable."

Jack gradually became aware of music in the air—a hymn being sung, quietly, almost like the whisper of a song. It was unmistakably a woman's voice, soft and sweet as a gentle breeze blowing through a cavern—haunting in its melody.

"Do you hear that?" Jack asked.

"The singing? Yes, of course. Did you not hear it the moment we arrived?"

"I don't know. I was confused. It's strange—I'm not sure I heard it before now, but it feels like it's been playing ever since I came into this world, even back where we were before we peregrinated."

"*You* peregrinated. I rode along," Faelith said, laughing.

Jack ignored her. "I think I was drawn here. Not just today, but my whole life."

"OK," Faelith said, taking his right hand into both of hers. "Don't get all dramatic on me. I'm sure there is a reason you came to this place. I've heard there is a lady who lives on that island, and she is most strange. As you might guess, she is called the Lady of the Lagoon. She never leaves her house, which sits on top of a small hill at the center of the island—or so the story goes."

"Do you know this story? Can you tell it to me?"

"I only know bits and pieces. I never thought much about it until now, to be honest. I always figured it was little more than a fairy tale told to children at night. But legend has it the Lady of the Lagoon was a powerful witch, who was sent here long ago to fight off three equally powerful demons, who had crossed over from some forgotten hell. A great battle was fought, and she eventually defeated them and cast them out of this world forever. As the story goes, she became ever more dominant after the war with the demons, so she was eventually imprisoned on this island by whoever ruled these lands at that time. This place is supposed to be guarded by a great army of ghostly wraiths, who hover all over the waters of the lagoon. I don't see them anywhere, so that part of the tale may not be real."

"Ha! You're not much of a storyteller, are you? You left out all the exciting details."

"Shush! What does it matter? You're *here*, my dear Jack, and if there is any place you might find someone to help you, it would be on that island. That is, *if* the stories are true and *if* the lady doesn't turn you into a toad."

"How do we get over there? If it was the lagoon in Bettendorf, we could just wade over. The water only goes up to your waist, even at its deepest point, but this lake seems deeper."

"Can't you swim?" Faelith asked as she walked toward the lagoon, pulling him along behind her.

"Yeah, I guess, but I don't think I've ever swum that far before."

"Well, you're in luck. I can adapt," she said, and she ran to the shore of the lake where she leaped head-first into the waters.

Jack followed her, startled by her impromptu night swim. When he got to the shore, he found only the widening circles of water marking Faelith's entry through the surface, but the girl was nowhere to be found.

"Faelith!" he called, but no answer came. He stood there for several minutes, scanning the lake from end to end and all around, until finally, a tail fin broke up out of the calm water, sending a shower down upon his head. Then Faelith surfaced, showing her top half as her usual human-like self and her lower half as a fish.

"Hello, Jack," she said with a giggle. "Do you like?"

"Ha! You're a mermaid!" he exclaimed with glee.

"Ha! I'm no more mermaid than I am coyote, or girl, or boy," she said. "You were right; this lake is quite deep. So, take off your clothes and climb on. I'll get us across in a jiff."

"A jiff?" Jack laughed.

"Yes, a jiff!"

"Take off my clothes?"

Faelith smiled devilishly and swam closer to the shore. "What's wrong? Are you shy?"

"Well, no—I mean, yes!"

"OK, you can certainly jump in here wearing your clothes, if you wish, but you'll be stuck walking around the island all wet and cold. Or you can leave them here, and I'll come back for them after I've dropped you off on the other side. They'll be perfectly dry and warm."

He sighed and looked up at the dark sky then back at Faelith. "OK, fine. But you can't look."

"Oh, please. You don't have anything I haven't seen before, or rather, you don't have anything that I don't *have*," she said and broke into another round of giggles.

Jack thought about it for a moment, and realizing that dry, warm clothes in this weather were far better than wet clothes or no clothes, he slunk behind a small family of shrubs and stripped off his clothing down to his boxers. When he was done, he gingerly tiptoed through the sharp twigs and crusty fallen leaves to the edge of the lake where Faelith was wading patiently, again smiling her wicked grin, eyes wide in mock anticipation. Jack exhaled once, placed the clothes at the edge of the lake, and leaped into the cold waters of the lagoon, letting out a shivered groan at the shock of the water's temperature.

"Oh, my god," he said through chattering teeth as he grabbed hold of Faelith's shoulders and slid himself upon her back. "This water is frigging freezing."

"Yes, it is," Faelith said as she flipped her tail and began the swim to the island. "It's deep, *very* deep, and legend says there is a great beast at the bottom sleeping there for over a thousand years. Some say it may never wake again, or so we hope, for the chill of these waters is made colder by the muffled snores of the beast."

"What kind of beast is it?" Jack asked.

"Who knows? At any rate, I don't wish to go down there and wake it to find out."

As if on cue, several enormous bubbles of air burst through the surface not ten yards away from them, hurling a half-dozen good sized waves that crashed straight into Jack and Faelith, pushing them several feet off their course. The surprising force of the waves caused Jack to lose his grip on Faelith's shoulders momentarily.

"What the hell was that?" he asked.

"I'd rather not venture to guess. You'd best wrap your arms around my waist—I think we should get to the island and quickly. Hold on tight and take a deep breath!"

Jack inhaled and wrapped his arms around her as she told him, holding on as tightly as he could, as Faelith thrust her tail with two powerful flaps, leaping into the air and clearing the lake by at least three feet. Then kicking her backside up and ducking her head, she plunged them back into the water. Jack's grip slipped slightly, but Faelith sensed it immediately and grabbed his forearms, holding them close to her stomach with a vice-like grip. Soon, they were cutting through the water faster than any speedboat Jack had ever been on, cruising swiftly across the remainder of the distance until with one great thrust of her tail, Faelith launched them back out of the lake and into the air. In the split second before they crashed back to earth, she somehow changed back to human form, so when they hit the ground, she had her legs again, landing gracefully on the island's picturesque shore.

"Ha! We did it!" Faelith cried.

"That. . .was. . .amazing," Jack said, struggling to get back his air.

"Sorry about the landing, but I do have a flair for the dramatic. Anyway, back I go to get your clothes. Stay right here; I won't be a minute." With that, the girl ran back to the lake, the silhouette of her a perfect darkness against the ghostly light glistening from the rippling water. As Faelith soared once more into the air, her legs quickly morphed together, changing back into a fishtail, before she popped down into the water and was gone, leaving hardly a ripple to mark her entry.

Jack became aware that the song he had heard earlier was somewhat louder now that he was on the island. Whoever sang it was still a little ways off, somewhere deeper within the island's small forest. Though he could not make out the words, Jack got a feeling that the song had shifted. It was a similar melody, but the cadence had changed. There was a darkness to it now, like a requiem sung by a woman.

Jack waited for several minutes, seeing no sign of Faelith anywhere. The far shore was covered in a mist, and at this distance, he was unable to see much of anything. Still, given how fast she could swim, she should have made it back by now with his clothes.

Maybe she's left me here to face the lady by myself, he thought with a twinge of sadness. Though he had only just met her, Faelith had already made an impression on him, and he hoped to know more about her.

His worries were soon allayed as he saw a wake cutting across the glassy surface of the lake at great speed. A moment later, Faelith sprang once again from the water, her tail flashing off a rain of water and changing back into two legs before she landed perfectly on her pale feet. Her hands were empty.

"Where are my clothes?" he asked.

"That's a good question." She shook her head with a broken laugh.

"Oh, come on. No games, give me my clothes."

Faelith shot a quick look at him. "Does it look like I have your clothes on me? I'm not playing games—they weren't *there*."

"What are you talking about? I left them right on the edge of the lake, like three minutes ago. How could they be gone?"

"How should I know? When I got to the other side, they weren't where you left them."

"Maybe you missed them. Maybe you went to the wrong place."

"I never go to the wrong place. But just to be sure, I swam all up and down the shore, then I went on land as a coyote to have a sniff. That's when I came upon something interesting. Someone had been there—probably just after us."

Jack stared through the mist to the further shore and the trees beyond. "What the hell was it? Who was it? The Host?"

Faelith sighed. "I don't think so. The Host have a unique scent, unmistakable. This was different. It smelled like—like death."

"And it took my clothes?" Jack asked.

"That would be a safe assumption, but that's not the important thing. Whoever or whatever was over there wasn't just looking for clothes to steal. I think it was following us."

"Huh, well, I guess it's curious maybe, wanted to play a trick on us."

"No, that's not what I mean. The scent—I think I caught it when we first met, just after you appeared in the woods, and again while we walked together before the Host came."

Jack froze. "When I first appeared? And again here? That would mean—"

"That means it can peregrinate."

13

AN INCONVENIENT GROUNDING

"What the hell!" Randy said. "What. . .the. . .hell!"

"Oh my god, what did you do?" Tatsu asked.

"What does it look like I did? I just ripped Jimmy's goddamn head off! And look! His mouth is still moving! He's looking right at me!"

It was true. The last bits of electrical impulses still firing off in the former head of Jimmy Vance made it seem like the boy was still in there, perhaps cursing Randy Wall forever. Its eyes blinked, its jaw open and closed repeatedly, and its nose even wrinkled like it smelled something awful. The voice in Randy's head laughed hysterically.

"Stop staring at me, motherfucker!" Randy yelled at the head, then he grasped it by the hair and promptly chucked it into the woods, where it bounced around among the tree trunks and roots with a half-hollow sound like a coconut.

"Why on Earth did you do *that*?" Tatsu asked.

"He was going to kill me. What else should I have done?"

"I get that. But why did you throw that head? We need to bury it someplace or dump it in the lake!" Tatsu ran into the trees. Moments later, she returned grasping Jimmy Vance's by the hair and holding in front of her at arm's length. "You're an idiot."

"Yeah, yeah, tell me something I don't already know. What the hell are we gonna do with his body? I don't have a shovel with me, and *obviously*, you don't either."

"I need clothes."

"Yeah. You have to be freezing to death—it's like fifty degrees out," Randy said.

"No, I'm fine. I feel warm actually, but I'm tired of being half-naked. Do you know where you can get clothes?" Tatsu asked.

"My sister has a crap ton of clothes in her closet, but she's not your size; you're a lot taller than her. But she left some sweats, and I have some t-shirts you could wear, and I bet one of her hoodies will fit you—she likes them big."

They turned back to Crow Creek Park so Randy could get his bike, now that Jimmy was no longer a danger. When they arrived, they found Carl hauling what looked like four large sacks of dirt up the hill and tossing them into the old church bus. When he had finished packing up his things, Carl stood in the doorway of the bus staring out across the park.

"What's he looking at?" Randy whispered.

"Your bike, maybe?" Tatsu said.

"Ah, crap. Don't take my bike; just leave it be," Randy said. At first, he was speaking mostly to himself, but then he heard the voice in his mind talking almost like a spell. *You have better things to do, old man—work that must be done. Go back to your master and leave that bike alone. You don't have time for that stupid Wall kid, anyway. Jimmy will handle it.*

Carl then checked his watch, shrugged, and climbed onto the bus closing the door behind him with a high-pitched squeal. Once he had turned the old bus around and was driving back down Devils Glen Road, Randy turned to Tatsu and said, "OK, just wait here. I'll bring you the clothes as fast as I can but don't leave these woods no matter what. OK?"

"Yes, but hurry! Please!"

Randy sped his bike as fast as he could all the way down Crow Creek Road and cut through some yards once he hit eighteenth Street. Though he knew he should be exhausted, an unusual energy was flowing through him. He was fully alert, and though he should still be in bed resting after the horrendous events of the previous night, Randy's mind was focused.

Funny isn't it? How killing makes us feel alive.

"Shut up, asshole!" Randy said out loud.

You still think that's all I am?

Randy pushed the voice away and stood on his pedals, pumping his feet with all the force he could muster. He flew down Tanglefoot Lane, the crisp November air rushing past him as he pushed himself harder and harder, praying his parents were still out running errands. He had no desire to have a conversation with them about staying in bed.

Unfortunately, his parents were home, sitting in the formal living room, reading—never a good sign. The only times he found them sitting in that forbidden place was when company was visiting from out of town, or when they were mad at him about something and wanted to have a talk. Any other time, that room was empty and off-limits.

"Ah crap," he muttered as he stood in the entryway. "What did I do?"

"Do?" Maggie Wall said. "It's not what you did. It's what you're not doing right now—sleeping! Where were you?"

"I wanted to go for a ride on my bike; that's all."

"After what happened last night?"

"Yeah, come on, you dope," his dad said. "Why are ya running around all day when you were out half the night and got bit by a damn dog? Jesus Christ, you need to rest, Randy. And what the hell are doing outside by yourself, anyway? Didn't you hear about all the nuts out there attacking people?"

"That's right! It's all over the news. Why, the Scofield's down the street? Their boy Todd, the one that works at Whitey's? He was killed," his mom said.

"Got his goddamn head ripped off."

"Tom!"

"Well, it's true."

"You don't have to be so—anyway, Randy, I hate to do this to you, but you're grounded until all this—*craziness*—clears up."

"What?" Randy said. "No, you can't ground me! I have to go and help this girl—"

"Ah, sorry buddy," Tom said. "No girls, no friends, and no leaving this house until we get a coast-is-clear from the police."

"Don't think it's just you, Randy. The whole town is under curfew until further notice. No one can go out after sundown until the mayor says it's OK. Even your sister was planning to come home from Iowa City today, but we told her to stay up there and come back next weekend. So, there isn't much choice. Just hang tight, and we can watch movies or play board games. Think of it as an early snow day!" Randy's mom seemed a little too excited about the idea of being cooped up together every night.

Randy shook his head slowly. "No, seriously guys. I *can't* stay here. I have to leave, like right now!"

"Bah! Quit your belly-aching," Tom said. "It won't be so bad. We'll sit tight here for the day and, hopefully, everything will be back to normal tomorrow. It's just one day, after all."

Dejected, Randy shuffled over to the stairs and said, "OK, I'm gonna go lay down."

"That's a good idea, honey! Try to rest and let me know if you need me to put anything on that wound!" his mom called after him as he started up the stairs.

"Oh, and one more thing," his dad said, stopping him as he was halfway up the stairs. "Where's Jack?"

"Huh?" Randy grunted, and a rush of anxiety swept over him. "I. . .uh. . ."

"His mom called looking for him. She said he told her he was gonna meet up with you. Did he?"

"Uh, no, I just went for a ride by myself. I don't know where Jack is," Randy said, and he continued to his room in defeat.

14

THE SONG OF THE AUTUMN KING

Lara sat at the dining room table, her head filled with music she had never heard before in her life, if made by instruments never heard on earth. Their sounds had a profound effect on Lara—she could not think, listen, or focus on anything but the music. She sat in an oversized wooden chair next to a thick oak table, transfixed by the sound that seemed to be coming from nowhere and everywhere all at once. Her eyes played tricks on her. Flames from a fireplace in the next room danced along the ceiling, over the walls, and across Lara's face, tickling her skin as she laughed until tears ran down her porcelain face.

"What is that music?" she managed to whisper after some time.

Meurt appeared by her side and answered, "We are moving the house, young vampire. Fear not; you are in the Autumn King's home—the home of my master—the first home in the valley of the river of sorrowful songs. It is my master's song. It is beautiful, yes?"

Lara tried to answer the question, but a crescendo of the music rose around her and within her, and she forgot what she wanted to say. The exhilaration thrilled her and threatened to overwhelm her new vampire senses. She breathed deeply and became aware of a whole new set of sensory experiences. The fresh aroma of sumptuous food—subtle herbs, a potpourri of flowers, burning wood, and the glorious flesh and blood of her hosts conspired to send Lara into a heightened ecstasy from which she begged never to be released.

"Where are we going?" she asked when she finally learned to cope with the sounds and the smells.

"Where we need to be, young one," Meurt said. "Master knows the way, and he will take us where we must go, though you may be surprised at what you see when at last you leave this house."

Fighting through a wave of joy, Lara whispered, "But I don't want to leave this house. I want to stay here forever."

"I do not doubt it, dear one. I do not doubt it at all. And perhaps, one day, you will stay here if you like, even forever. I do not see your path, but you will do as you will do, yes."

"Sometimes your words make no sense," Lara said.

Meurt let loose a peal of laughter that sounded like the ringing of church bells and sent forth a string of sparkling lights that danced in the air above Lara's head. "That is the song, vampire—the song of my master, the song of the Lord of the River, the Autumn King, the King of the Wood. Even I, after all these years, find words difficult while he plays it."

"Why do you call him your master? Are you his slave?" Lara asked.

"I'm not his slave, though I am not free."

"I don't understand."

Meurt laughed. "I would not expect you to understand any more than I would expect to understand your world if I were to go there, yes?"

If hours passed or days, Lara could not have said. And so consumed was she by the music and the atmosphere, Lara could not discern the time of day or even how long she had been in that house. Whenever she finally left this house—a thought which immediately pained her—would all her friends be old or dead? But most of all, Lara felt an overriding sense of peace, unlike any relaxation she had ever known. She dozed off now and then. For hours or days, she could not say.

Soon, the music descended in volume and intensity ever so slightly, and Lara got the sense that perhaps the song had begun a long decline toward an ending. At the thought, sadness swept over her, and she whispered into the room, "Please, don't let it stop. Keep playing."

"Oh, young one, all things must end, yes? Have you never heard this saying before?" Meurt's voice, filled with delight, tickled her ears.

"Yes, I have heard that saying. I'm not a fan."

Again, Meurt laughed, and immediately Lara's sadness lifted to joy. "I do understand, young one. My master's song brings joy and peace and every glory of the sky. But even his song must end if only to pause, for the time is pressing, and your friends are in need."

At the mention of her friends, a flicker of memory flashed through Lara's mind, and she felt herself awaken as if from a dream. Not realizing her eyes had been shut for some time, Lara opened them and lifted her head from the back of her chair. The house was just as it had been before the song had begun, but with a little less sparkling dust in the air.

"Yes," Lara finally whispered. "My friends need me, though how can I help them? Maybe I should stay here."

"You are welcome to remain here if you wish, so said my master while you slept. But I think you'll find it difficult to abandon them once you return to yourself. You have traveled far for them and changed quite a lot. I think you may find your efforts have not been in vain, but danger still lurks in the shadows of the world. I believe you must soon make a hard choice between contentment and struggle."

"How do you know so much?" Lara asked.

Meurt put her hand on Lara's shoulder and said, "Do you not remember telling your tale? Perhaps you do not. The song affects some people like that, and even vampires are not immune to its charms, so it seems. You told us your tale, and Master listened while he played his song and smoked his pipe by the fire, staring at the flames and thinking. You are a unique creature, young Lara, unlike any to have entered this home in many years, yes."

"How am I unique?" Lara asked.

Nothing about Lara had ever stuck out in any way. Her grades were average—not horrible, not great—and she had never been the most athletic kid in class. When PE class went for a run, Lara was invariably smack dab in the middle of the pack of runners. She never got the big awards, the gold stars, or the honor roll bumper stickers. However, she did not get into serious trouble, either. In fact, she doubted any school administrator ever had any cause to know her name.

"You are a vampire in our home, yes? This is something that has never happened in all the long years of this place. My master would never allow such a thing, and yet here you are sitting at our table. That alone should tell you all you need to know."

"But why me? You and your master know nothing about me."

"It is true. I don't know anything about you, other than you don't belong in this world. But my master, that is a different matter. He knows more than you would believe. His eyes see through the walls of words, and his mind comprehends much on sight alone. And of course, you told us much during the song. I could answer every question, but it would take much time, and *that* you do not have."

The Autumn King entered the room, his deep green eyes solemn and mournful. He stood before the table and looked down at Lara. A long beard grew down from his face with mustaches that seemed to be living entities all their own, curling out slightly at the ends, moving independently. The color of both his hair and his beard could only be described as purely and simply autumn. It was as if the colors of all the trees of October—bright reds, brilliant yellows, dark browns, and warm oranges—had sprouted from his skin and come to life on his face. This king's countenance gave the impression of a man at the height of his powers, but his eyes belied a thoughtfulness and generosity of spirit, combined with the weight of some inevitability. He wore heavy tweed pants tucked into large brown boots, secured by an elaborate pair of laces winding all the way up to his knees, and a long coat of shifting colors with a large hood he had thrown back as soon as he entered the house.

A fresh breeze swept in with him, and on it floated a scent of pine cones, burning leaves, chestnuts, and the morning fog. When the king spoke, his voice held within it the crackling of campfire flames and the rustling of leaves. There was almost a melody to his words, and his manner of speaking felt to Lara at times like hearing a song.

"The house is set, the way is clear, no sign of Dreadman lingers, far or near. A nasty creature is he, but no match is he for the Autumn King. You must have care, young one, while traveling in the wood; there are few now living within it who are good. As Meurthanasa said, you may stay if you wish for as long as you wish. You will be safe in our wonderful home by the river—in our noble house by the river."

Lara smiled and said, "You'd let me live here with you and Meurtha. . ."

"Meurthanasa," he corrected.

"She may call me Meurt," Meurt said.

The Autumn King laughed—a deep rumbling sound—shaking his head. "A name too brief for one so beautiful and strange, for one so lovely and strange. Our home is open to you, young Lara of the Vampyr, sweet Lara the young Vampyr. But alas, my heart readies a song of sad parting, and with it will come many tears—and from it will come many tears."

Lara nodded and forced herself to look away from the overwhelming majesty of the king. "I know you're right, but I'm scared. I know my friends need me, but I don't know what I'm supposed to do for them. Maybe I'm meant to be in my own world, helping Jack Davies. I want to go home, but I don't know how to get there." Suddenly, a thought occurred to her. "Can you send me back? Can you send me back to where I'm from?"

"I do not have such power. I am not a peregrinator, though even if I were, your world was closed to me and my kind many long ages ago, before the pull of Lunis cast out the Fae and the world was split in two—before the world was broken in two. Your story is bound with those of your kind, and if ever you will return to your world, your song will be sung by them." The Autumn King stepped next to her and lay a large warm hand on her shoulder, sending waves of serenity flowing across her skin.

"I know," Lara said. "I won't leave my friends to fight alone. And, honestly, I think if I am ever gonna return to my world, I'll need Jennifer's help to do it, anyway. I guess I don't have a choice but to leave this house."

"Do not say you have no choice, for it demeans the glory of sacrifice. There are many choices and many paths, young vampyr, and though the correct one often feels like the only one, you could always find another. I do believe your road will lead away from our home but do not despair—the road away must also lead back. You may sit if you wish for as long as you wish, and I will tell you many tales ere you go; I will show you such things ere you go."

Lara stared back into the king's eyes and again lost all sense of time. When she finally found her voice again, she said, "I don't want to keep my friends waiting."

"Fear not. Though in this house much time will pass, less than a day will have gone by in the world outside our door. Rest your head, drink of my ale, and listen as I tell you my tale; be still as I tell you the tale."

For what seemed to be days, Lara listened as the Autumn King told her countless stories of his travels in this world, including some that involved Jack Davies and his sister, oddly enough. In fact, Jack's sister came up in his stories time after time, Lara realized. Though she felt as if she was drifting through another sleepless dream, she was remotely aware of periodically drinking something amber and tangy-sweet. It filled her and refreshed her more deeply than any food or drink she had ever consumed in her life.

Meurt was with her through most of the story, though sometimes, she would stand and dance near the fireplace, and it seemed to Lara that fireflies hovered in the air all around her. When the Autumn King finally finished his tales, he stood up from his massive chair and strode directly to her.

"Lara of the vampyr, there is one last thing I must tell you before I open the door for your parting. Your friend, Jack Davies, needs your help. His sister is here, somewhere in the wood."

"Anne? Jack's dead sister? The ghost I met at his house that night?" Lara asked.

"Your words are as a mystery to me. But here the girl is quite alive and imprisoned in a house in the woods. I believe your path leads to her. Do not leave this world nor return to this house before you have done what you must do. If you heed not my warning, much suffering will come of it."

"Can you help me?" Lara asked. "Can you come with me and help me find her?"

"This is your story, not mine, and I shall never leave these miles near this house again. And now, I must speak words only you can hear, young vampyr—words you must never repeat."

Meurt skipped across the room and out the door into the night. A silence came over the place right then, and Lara could no longer hear the crackling of the fire, nor the creaking of the old wooden house. The only sounds remaining were the Autumn King's clothes shifting together and the squeaking of the leather on his boots. When he finally spoke, his voice was solemn and sad.

"Meurt is my servant and my love. I hold her dearer than any living thing I have known in all my days. Though she does not remember it, fate has cast a melancholy end to our tale, for though she will be my love to end all loves, so too is it foretold that she will be my bane. When the time comes, she will find a branch from deep within the wood, one golden and alive, and she will bring it to me and strike me down, ending my long years at last. Then will she take her final reward and live out her days as a queen, until at last spring comes to break her own heart. As for you, Lara, there are three riddles you must know ere you depart."

"Riddles," Lara said, dreamily. "Tell me."

"First, the boy cannot win until he is whole. Second, only the dragon can slay the demon. And last, the secret is hidden in the cellar."

With that, the Autumn King patted Lara once more on the shoulder and strode out of the house, leaving the door open behind him as the cold fall air rushed into the room, waking Lara from her reverie. Then a sad but hopeful song filled the air, and Lara's eyes ran blood red with her first vampire tears.

15

THE BURNING ARROW

Mark Warren, still wearing his standard issue policeman's uniform, led Jennifer by the hand out the front door of the guest house. They turned and said their goodbyes to Genevieve Bennett, who cautioned them to remain vigilant. "You never know who or what you'll come across in the woods. You must be careful with each step you take."

"We will," Mark said, squeezing his wife's hand. "Will you be here when we come back?"

Genevieve thought about it for a while and said, "I can't say if I will or I won't. My spirit clings loosely to this world, but I have no doubt I will be back from time to time if I'm not. Oh how, I envy you. It's the best part of making a journey—never knowing if it will turn into an adventure." Blowing a kiss to each of them, the old matriarch closed the door and drifted away down the hall.

"Mrs. Bennett was right. We have to be careful, Mark," Jennifer said as they made their way down the stairs onto the front pathway. Before them, an immense forest loomed against the dark gray sky. "These woods are strange. Griselda had a name for this area—she called it the Woodland of Weird, a play of words on the poem by Poe, I guess."

"The Raven?" Mark asked. He was never all that versed in literature—such things were Jennifer's domain, though she had made some impact on his culture. Whenever she could, she would coax him on a trip to Chicago to see a play or an opera.

"No, it was Ullalume."

"Don't remember that one," Mark said.

"Yes, you do. 'It was down by the dank tarn of Auber, in the ghoul-haunted woodland of Weir.' Remember?"

"Oh yeah! You used to read that to me every Halloween."

"Yes, I did," she said. "Glad to see my efforts to give you some culture weren't for nothing. Well, anyway, this forest runs for miles and miles. I'm not even sure there's an end to it. Of course, I didn't get to travel much." Jennifer's voice drifted off, and her eyes betrayed the intrusion of unwelcome memories.

Mark turned her to face him. "All of that is done now, you hear? We're together now, and nothing will separate us ever again."

She smiled. "I thought this day would never come. I hoped I would somehow be able to get away from Griselda, and I almost did once or twice, but I never thought we'd be together here. It's probably not right for me to be happy you're stuck in this place, instead of someplace better, but I can't help it. I am glad you're with me."

"Buddy, I wouldn't want to be anyplace else," Mark said, kissing her once, and turned back to the woods. "You sure you want to do this? I mean, if we run into Griselda, I don't know what we could do to defend ourselves."

Jennifer shivered and said, "Yes, I think we have to try. Lara doesn't know the area at all. If she somehow found a way to get away from that woman, she would still be lost out here."

"And if Griselda does have her? What can we do about it?" Mark said.

Jennifer thought for a moment and said, "I don't know, Mark.

But I think there must be something we can do. If we're here, in this strange world, there must be a reason. I believe we have a part to play here."

Mark agreed. "We do have a part to play, or at least we can't let Lara fend for herself."

The Warrens stepped off the porch and walked down the front pathway that sloped down a small but steep hill and into the Woodland of Weird. A cold breeze blew through the empty branches, and the only sounds in the forest were those of blowing leaves and creaking tree trunks.

Mark felt a chill, and not from the crisp air. He glanced over his right shoulder and saw the Bennett Mansion on the hill behind them, staring down like a great sleeping giant. In this world, the house looked almost like a living being. Its windows were rectangular eyes, devoid of emotion, but imposing nonetheless. In one of the upstairs windows, a small candle still burned—the only light emanating from the otherwise dark house.

"Do you know who lives there now?" Mark asked, nodding to the mansion.

"I don't. Griselda never went there—I don't think she was able, or *allowed*," Jennifer said.

"That candle up there. Know why it's always lit?"

"No, but she used to stare at it, sometimes for an hour. She'd just stand there on the lawn below and look up at that window. I don't know if she was sad or angry, but I think it bothered her somehow. She never said a word to me about it—she never spoke a word to me about anything that wasn't cruel—but still, I got the feeling it touched something inside her."

"Really? Could that hag be affected by something? Hard to believe."

"The whole forest is dead now," Jennifer said, shaking away the memories again. "But it wasn't always like this. When I first got here, there was some life in these woods. The leaves you see on the ground, they were still on these trees, though most were changing colors. It was all green and red and orange, but I guess that was like a mirage. Everything was dying."

The Warrens continued down the hill and did not speak again until they came upon a path barely wide enough for the two of them to walk side by side. Jennifer told Mark that this was what passed for a road in this world. She figured it ran about where Mississippi Ave had run in the living world.

"So, why are the mansion and the guest house the only buildings in this world? I mean, this place looks like our world. It's like Bettendorf exactly, without the houses and streets. Yet, the Bennett estate is exactly like it is in the real world. Why is that?" Mark asked.

"There are other houses here. Some are hidden in different parts of the woods. But you're right; aside from the estate, it's mostly forest, and I don't know why."

The breeze picked up strength as they moved further into the forest until Mark found it difficult to find a path to follow with all the blowing leaves and rolling mist moving across the ground. Fortunately for both of them, Jennifer seemed to know exactly where they were headed and even cautioned him along the way to look out for hidden holes in the ground or hard-to-notice tree roots. After they had walked the better part of a mile, they came upon a more distinct path that Jennifer referred to as a road, though it barely constituted a walking trail. They followed it for a mile before Jennifer veered off into the woods.

"From here, we should stay out of sight and make as little sound as possible," she whispered.

"Are we in danger?" Mark asked.

"We're coming to a weird place. I would take us far around it, but I don't think I'd know my way back to the road, and I'd hate for us to get lost. When I last saw her, Lara seemed to be flying roughly in the direction of this road, so I think we better keep to it as much as possible. Still, even the hag avoided drawing attention in this place. She talked about creatures who lived here, but one in particular worried even *her*. She called him The Dread."

"Creepy name. Who is he?"

"I don't know," she said. "I only saw him once from a distance, but that was more than enough for me. Oddly, it was the one time I felt relieved to have the hag with me. Whatever evils lived inside *her*, I knew this creature held a thousand times more and a thousand times worse. It was like fear emanated from him—the worst fear I'd ever felt in my life. It paralyzed me. Even *she* seemed affected by it. It was all she could do to drag me away through the forest to escape."

"What did he look like?"

"I only got a glimpse of him, but that image will remain in my mind forever. He seemed like a shadow, a moving shadow, with bright eyes and long ragged hair."

Suddenly, a thought occurred to Mark. "Wait. Is this the same path she took you on? Couldn't she be on it, too?"

Just then, behind them, came the sound the crunching leaves. The skin on Mark's neck tingled. He looked back and saw an old woman in a black dress only twenty yards away. Her face was shrouded, but the veil was transparent enough to see two black holes for eyes and a mouth open wide. Two skeletal arms stretched down to her waist, the pale bones glimmering in the shadows. When the woman took a step toward them, her joints clicked together.

Jennifer gasped, and Mark grabbed her by the shoulder with one hand, covering her mouth with the other. They stood there, frozen, praying the woman had not heard them. Through the veil, Mark could hear the woman sniffing the air, and soon, a grotesque laugh shook her body. When Griselda finally spoke, Mark felt Jennifer convulse as she sobbed silently in his arms.

"Little crickets, little crickets, where are you hiding? Little crickets, little crickets, where are you hiding? Do not worry, old Griselda will find you, by and by. And when she does, the things she does will make you want to die."

Griselda sniffed the air. Her black empty eye sockets turned toward them, and she paused for a moment before a hideous smile grew across her old face, and a trail of saliva dripped down her chin.

"No, do not worry. Old Griselda will find you, by and by. And when she does, the things she does will make you want to die. Oh, Jennifer, my dirty whore. You must pay for what your friend did to me, Jennifer. Look what her bite did to my lovely flesh," Griselda cried out, holding her arms of bone above her head.

Suddenly, Griselda's head jerked forward. Mark didn't know if she could see through the empty sockets of her eyes, but she seemed to be facing them directly. Jennifer's convulsions became violent as she lost all control of her weeping. The hag had found them.

"Yes, when she does, the things she does will make you. . . want to. . .DIE!"

Just as the terror of the hag drained all hope from his soul, Mark caught a glimpse of some movement. Someone, or something, was standing behind Griselda in the middle of a small crop of trees. Looking closer, he could see the figure of a man in a hood, holding something in front of him. It looked like he was pointing straight at them. Then a small ball of fire sprang up in front of the figure and before Mark could register what he was seeing, the fireball shot forth, streaking through the trees like a missile headed straight for Griselda. When it hit her, Griselda froze, then all at once she burst into a pillar of flames that quickly towered above her into the trees, illuminating the area in a golden-orange light. The old woman let out a scream that stung Mark's ears and echoed throughout the forest. Griselda turned away from the Warrens and ran off in the direction of the Bennett Estate, flames flowing behind her like wings of hell.

Mouths hanging open, Mark and Jennifer watched the flames cut through the woods until Griselda was nothing more than a faint light fading into the darkness. Mark shot a look at the hooded stranger in the trees and saw a giant bow in his hands. The figure watched them for a few moments, shifting on his feet as if making a decision, then silently jogged over to them and held out one hand, speaking in a thick accent that sounded vaguely European. "Come with me. We must leave now."

"Is she dead? Is she finally dead?" Jennifer asked, tears running down her face.

"No. It would take more than flames to destroy that one, but she is injured—twice in the same day. She will not come back just yet," the man said.

"Who are you?" Mark asked.

"A friend."

"We don't have friends here," Jennifer said.

"Did I just now save the both of you?" the man asked.

"But we don't know you," Jennifer said, quickly.

"You're cautious; that's good. But you must trust me, I'm afraid, for no other choice do you have. It's follow me or remain and die. Danger approaches. Other things, worse things, will have been alerted to our presence, and I may not save you a second time. And as you might know, Lady Warren, being noticed in this place is less than desirable."

"You know our names?" Mark asked.

"Not yours, no. But I do know much about her."

"We're searching for our friend," Jennifer said.

"You will not find her if you are enslaved again or killed, which I assure you will happen if you do not come with me at once." Though they could not see his face, the man's voice seemed sincere. His bright eyes darted here and there behind them.

"I think we better go with him, Jen."

Jennifer stood there for a moment, still shaken by seeing Griselda, then she asked, "What's your name?"

The stranger stepped into the moonlight, and Mark saw that he was strikingly handsome. His face was dark brown a thick black beard, speckled lightly with gray, and his eyes were sky blue, almost white. He wore black leather pants and a dark shirt under a long gray cloak. "I am called Alexis. Now come with me at once, or you will never see me again."

Mark grimaced. If Griselda returned, she would finish what she started, and it would be foolish to hope for a second miracle. He took Jennifer by the hand and, together, they followed the stranger deeper into the Woodland of Weird.

16

THE WOODLAND OF WEIRD

"This is as far as I will take you," Meurt said as they approached the remains of a once high stone wall, now covered in thick moss and dead vines. A few feet away stood an archway that Lara supposed, at one time, had been attached to the wall. On the keystone of the arch was a relief depicting a young prince and princess, both with crowns upon their heads. Time and weather had stripped most of the other decorations, but the two faces were untouched.

"Can't you come with me? I could use all the help I can get," Lara said.

"No, young vampire. My master never leaves the boundaries of his property—such is the price of his sacrifice. As for me, I would join you, but he has forbidden it, and so I must remain, yes."

"But you were away from him when you found me. You can leave, can't you?"

"Yes, I can go for a little while, but Meurt will fade if she leaves too often or stays too long. I'm sorry, Lara of the Vampyr, but your road takes you away from the path of Meurt and her master, which I can assure you does pain me to say. But do not despair. I think your road will not be lonely for long. If my feelings do not deceive me, you will find help when you least expect to find it, though danger is all around. Good luck, my young vampire friend," Meurt said as she gave Lara a long hug.

"Good luck to you, Meurt," Lara said, her chin resting on Meurt's shoulder. "I hope to meet you again someday. I'd like to hear another song and sit by your fire."

"If you wish it, so it will be. Go straight through the arch, and a mile or so through the woods, you will come to a small road. You may take that path back to where I found you, though I suggest you be careful. The Dreadman may still be on it, and worse things, too. But fear not—if my feelings do not deceive me, you will find help when you need it most, yes."

"I hope so. And I hope you and the king share many wonderful years together."

Meurt blinked at her for a moment then turned back in the direction of her home. She opened her mouth as if to say something but, instead, closed it and smiled softly. "That is my wish as well," she whispered into the night air.

And with that, Meurt did not hesitate any longer but kissed Lara on each cheek and once lightly on the lips then turned and, without another word, sprang off into the night like a flash, the branches and undergrowth moving only slightly at her passing.

Lara stared into the space Meurt had vacated for several moments, allowing the feeling of loss to wash through her before returning her eyes to the stone archway. "Well," she said aloud, "I guess I'm alone now in a world I know nothing about."

If she had allowed herself, she would have wept right then and there, but instead, Lara wiped her eyes and made her way through the archway and into the woods. Everywhere she stepped was covered in dead leaves and shrouded by random patches of light fog. The trees were as thick together as the hair on top of her head, and she could find no natural pathway through them. If anything resembling a road had ever been here, it was long ago consumed by the ravages of life.

The Autumn King's words played in her mind as she slowly made her way through the thorny undergrowth. Even the memory of his voice mesmerized her. *First, the boy cannot win until he is whole. Second, only the dragon will slay the demon. And last, the secret is hidden in the cellar.*

More than once, she failed at navigating the treacherous brambles, wounding herself with a hundred tiny cuts in the process. She checked the sides of her arms and thought it looked like she had been whipped. Though her vampire speed would have come in handy on open ground, no clear path through the thorns made using it somewhat dangerous. When she glanced once again at her arms, she saw they were already healed.

I guess vampire skills come in handy, she thought.

Suddenly, an intense desire came over her. In the past twenty-four hours, or however long it had been since she was turned into a vampire, she had not eaten a single thing. The hunger pangs struck her hard and threatened to overwhelm her senses. Immediately, the only thing Lara could think of was blood.

Geez, I'm freaking disgusting.

Unfortunately, there seemed to be little life in this forest, or perhaps everything was aware of her presence and doing its best to hide. Deciding it would be best for her to slow down and try to hunt before she lost what little energy remained in her, Lara crouched down and quietly stalked into the woods. In less than an hour, she found two squirrels and a large opossum, which altogether provided her with enough blood to feel rejuvenated. Lara had wondered many times just what blood might taste like, and though it took her some time to get used to the *idea* of drinking blood, the taste was only marginally satisfying. What she desired was human blood.

I have become a monster.

As she continued through the forest, she felt the uneasy sensation that eyes were upon her. Each tree and every shrub seemed to be staring at her. At first, she dismissed this thought as nothing more than paranoia, but as she progressed deeper into the woods, she could not help but notice the feeling only grew stronger with each step. Everywhere she looked there were giant oak trees, old and withered, standing like ancient guardians, their tall, crooked branches reaching out above her head. Then, at the corner of her right eye, Lara saw a dark shape moving like the wave of a long thin arm, but when she snapped her head to look, all she saw were branches swaying lightly in the cool breeze. As she looked ahead once again, it appeared that the trees were different now as if they had huddled closer together.

Lara gasped. Her heart, which had been still since she changed into a vampire the night before, picked this moment to lurch into one heavy beat, causing Lara to jump a full three feet into the air. The trees swayed toward her. All of them seemed to have heard the beat too and began closing in on her as if hunting a prey. An icy wind cut through the branches, whistling past the dry wood and leaves, creating a haunting song of woe like the voices of a thousand ghosts crying out as one.

"Stop it!" Lara finally yelled out into the night, feeling overwhelmed by the ghostly symphony. The sound stopped, though the wind continued to blow, and it seemed that the trees took heed of her command. They swayed back and forth before her as if they were trying to puzzle out whatever mystery Lara presented. "I am done with creepy shit for tonight! Quit blocking my path and let me through. I mean you no harm—I love trees for Chrissake! And I plan to get the hell out of this world as soon as I can, so give me a goddamn break."

The trees again looked to one another, still swaying in unison. A low murmur rumbled just at the edge of audibility. Finally, the trees slowly formed into two groups, lumbering over the ground on large roots, moving to either side of Lara, creating a kind of thoroughfare. The young vampire girl stepped forward, glancing up at the trees to her right and left. She thought she could discern large brown eyes shining through the shadows, peeking out from the thick rugged bark–watching her. In fact, as she finally passed the final oaks, it seemed to Lara as if the expressions in their eyes were not of anger, as she had thought, but of worry.

Why would they be worried about me? Lara thought with a slight shudder. *Or are they concerned for me?*

As she continued into the woods, the wind picked up again, and with it, the trees returned to their song, but this time, it sounded more like a warning. Floating above the whistling sound, Lara could barely make out words faintly sung by the chorus of ancients.

Tuuuuurrrrrnn Baaaaaaaaaaaaaaack!

17

DREADMAN'S TURNCOAT

"What were the two of you doing out here alone in the wood?" Alexis asked as he led Mark and Jennifer through a maze of drowsy trees.

Mark, still uncertain whether to trust the stranger, paused for a moment and glanced at Jennifer, who nodded. He said, "We're searching for a friend. She was lost out here, and we want to find her—to help her get back home."

Alexis stopped for a moment and glanced back at them. "This friend, what does she look like?"

Jennifer described Lara's appearance as best she could. "Dark hair, white skin—um, she's pretty, though right now I'd imagine she's kind of dirty. Her eyes—I can't remember what color her eyes are."

"Brown maybe?" Mark said. "Hell, I don't remember either."

"Hm," Alexis said.

"Have you seen her?" Jennifer asked.

"I believe I saw someone matching that description. Earlier, I was hunting in the wood not far from where I met you when I happened upon a dark creature known here by some as Dreadman. Usually, he is hunting the roads and forests of this land, searching for the lost. This night, he seemed to be waiting for something. I hid behind a pair of trees and watched as three of his henchmen brought forth a young woman, perhaps less than twenty, tied to a large beast of burden. Dreadman led them away. I followed and watched as they brought the girl to a small house on a lonely hill not far from here. They took her inside, and that is the last I have seen of them. I did not get a good look at her, but I think she may fit the description you gave."

"Oh, no. I wonder if that's her. I suppose it has to be, doesn't it?" Jennifer asked.

"I would think it too much of a coincidence, you being here seeking a girl and, at the same time, a strange girl captured by Dreadman. He is not known for keeping prisoners," Alexis said as he fingered the end of his bow.

"That could be Lara. Please, I beg you to take us there now," Jennifer said.

Alexis shook his head and continued down the path. "That is not possible. The Dreadman is strong, and he has many henchmen—angry cruel things who live only to do his bidding. No, we cannot go there just the three of us. We will need help. I will take you to my home, where my family will be waiting. From there, we will decide what to do."

Mark followed the winding path behind the tall hooded gentleman. Jennifer did her best to keep up with them. Her exhaustion from the previous twenty-four hour caused her to stumble across the dark, uneven ground.

Mark took her by the hand and slowed his pace. "It's OK, buddy. We'll get to wherever he's taking us, and then you can sleep."

"Hopefully," Jennifer said.

As they walked, it seemed to Mark that their path was shifting, winding through the trees almost randomly, until he finally lost all sense of their direction. A slight twinge of anxiety struck him. Jennifer had said there were worse things in these woods than Griselda. Mark narrowed his eyes and watched Alexis as the stranger cut around a large elm, glancing back at them. Mark left his worries unspoken—no sense in troubling Jennifer. She seemed to trust him. She trusted him enough to tell the man about Lara. In fact, she had told him enough to betray their entire cause if it turned out he was not a kind Samaritan.

Mark became aware of sounds coming from deeper in the forest. At first, he assumed it was nothing more than animals stomping through the dry leaves, perhaps deer or coyotes, but soon he realized it was something else.

Jennifer tugged on his hand and whispered, "Mark, look."

At first, Mark saw nothing more than a thick fog, rolling through the woods, but as he looked closer, he noticed them—tall figures, dozens of them, moving in the trees on either side of the path, barely visible in contrast with the fog all around. They appeared as apparitions, like gray ghosts rolling through the brume, moving parallel with the Warrens, hooded in long nebulous cloaks.

"What are they?" Mark asked.

"I don't know. I've never seen these beings before," Jennifer said. "The hag must have avoided them, or they avoided her.

"They look like ghosts."

"They are not," Alexis said. "They are the Mists."

"Mists?" Mark asked. "How can fog take a human form?"

"I did not say they were fog."

"But they are made of mist?" Jennifer asked.

"From what they were made, I do not know. But they are known as Mists, or so they are called. What they name themselves is anyone's guess. They have resided in these woods for a great many years, long before the darkness fell. Their home is north some miles away, and they rarely leave it, so far as I know."

"Do they always follow you like this?" Jennifer asked.

Alexis glanced at Jennifer, his bright blue eyes seeming to glow from the darkness of his skin. "They are not following *me* at all, nor have they ever. I've never seen them traveling in the open, away from their land. They must be drawn to you, though I cannot guess why. Of course, I know little about the two of you, but you must be special indeed to draw the interest of the old woman."

"Griselda?" Mark asked. At the mention of that name, a low humming sound rose from the Mists. It slowly grew in volume until it hit a crescendo and then subsided after several moments.

"Best not to speak that name—it is tied to evil, and with it, evil does come. The Mists will not abide it, nor will I."

"You said 'before the darkness fell.' What does that mean?" Jennifer asked.

"This place was once a lush land of speaking trees, twinkling stars, and faeries who danced in the woods under the light of the moon. Wondrous things lived here then, but one day, the clouds rolled in. Darkness fell upon the land and changed it into a ghost of what had been here before. The magical creatures, or most of them, left long ago. Now, fell creatures like the old wight of the mansion are among the only things that remain. The Autumn King resides some miles from here, and his power allows life to hold on for a time. However, the Winter Queen will take his place, and on that day, sleep will come."

"Why are you still here?" Mark asked.

"I still believe." Alexis motioned for them to follow again and continued walking down a path that only he seemed to see.

"In what?" Jennifer asked.

"In hope. The coming of the Winter Queen will signal an inevitable end to this autumn, but nothing is forever, and Spring will have his day as Summer will have hers, and so it goes, and so it goes."

The three of them continued silently for some time, with the movement of the mists as the only audible sound, like a soft sheet of cotton pulled along the cold ground. Mark thought long about Alexis's words, and though a thousand questions flooded his mind, he did not voice a single one. A few times, he heard

Jennifer breath in and then sigh as if she too had decided to save her own thoughts for another time.

Finally, the threesome broke through the trees and into an open yard before a friendly looking wood house, its windows illuminated in a soft orange-yellow light. A slithering snake of smoke rose from a stone chimney at its roof, and the remnants of a once proud garden lay dead below its narrow porch. The home was large, almost like an old country manor, and looked to have several rooms under its steeply sloped roof.

The front door burst open, and a young woman with long white hair sprang out across the porch and down the front pathway barely touching the ground until she had wrapped her arms around Alexis's neck, who happily returned the embrace. "Oh, I'm so happy you're back, my love," the woman said. "I sense danger in the woods tonight, and I felt the presence of many strangers, ripping into this world only hours ago." Then the woman looked over his shoulder at Mark and Jennifer. Her eyes narrowed. "Who are these?" she asked, releasing her herself from Mark and stepping around him to get a better look.

"These are Mark and Jennifer Warren, my dear. They have traveled with me to our home and are in need of our aid," Alexis said, then he turned to the Warrens. "This is a wife, Laurel. The others are inside, I presume."

"A wife? You have other wives?" Mark asked.

"'I have?' We do not word it that way. We are together, all of us—wives and husband. None belongs to one but each to all."

"I see," Jennifer said.

Laurel turned back to Alexis. "Avenya returned this morning from the northern wood; she had been gone nearly a week with no word. Olga only just returned an hour ago. They're inside keeping watch over a strange creature Olga captured while scouting to the west. I think you will not be pleased with what she's done, but you must keep an open mind, husband."

"What *creature?*" Alexis asked, a furrow deepening on his forehead.

"As I said, love. Keep an open mind."

Alexis paused for a moment and sniffed the air in the direction of the house then grunted and glanced back at the Warren's with a frown. "Join us inside. I must see what evil these fools have brought to our home." He then raced into the house with such a surprising burst of speed, Mark could barely see but a blur in his wake.

"I said keep an *open* mind," Laurel called after him. Sighing, the snowy-haired woman motioned for the Warrens to follow her into the house, leading the way.

The inside of the house was rustic, yet stately, again what Mark imagined an English country estate to be like. The interior was dark but warm, with numerous candles illuminated by the same ethereal energy brightening the rest of the world. The entry opened into an expansive great room with a fireplace at the center of the far wall, enclosed by an elaborate hearth filled with carvings and stone relief sculptures depicting numerous incredible scenes of bizarre creatures. Several large chairs and two sofas were placed throughout the room. Laurel led them through the great room and down a darkened hallway to a room at the end, which led down an old set of stairs into a vast cellar containing several rooms.

In the middle of it sat an ugly gurgling creature in a long, dirty coat tied to a rickety wooden chair. It coughed and spat when Laurel entered the room but froze where it sat when it spotted Mark and Jennifer. Upon seeing the Warrens, its eyes twinkled in the torchlight with a curious expression. It raised an eyebrow and laughed once in spite of itself. In the shadows next to several large wine casks stood two impressive looking women—one was probably at least six feet tall and had jet black hair, wearing a long dark gown, while the other was bald and wore a leather coat, britches, and boots. Her eyes were completely black from lid to lid.

"What's *this*?" Alexis asked.

The dark-haired woman stepped closer. Mark saw that her eyes were a piercing light blue, almost snow white, much like

Alexis's. "Stay calm," the woman said. "There is much to tell and much to learn. Wouldn't you agree, Olga?"

"Yes, Avenya," the bald woman said. "Is much to learn from dis creature. 'E know more than 'e say, yes."

"Where did you find it?" Alexis asked.

"Near the road, not far from the house in the woods where they took the girl."

"This is—" Mark began.

Cutting him off, the bald woman said, "One of Dreadman's henchmen."

Alexis glared at them one by one, with an intensity that would be enough to terrify most people. However, these women returned proud defiant stares of their own, each of them an obvious match for Alexis. The tension hung thick in the air of the dark cellar, and Mark began to wonder if the room might suddenly break out in violence.

Laurel placed one calming hand upon Alexis's shoulder, and he seemed to relax almost immediately. "Husband," she said. "You must hear what he has to say. The girl—the one held captive by the Dreadman—she is not of this world. She was brought here."

Alexis turned to Jennifer and then glanced back at the creature. "Why?" he asked.

Surprising Mark, Jennifer pushed past him and asked, "What girl? Is her name Lara? Is she a vampire?"

At the mention of vampire, the others in the room shot Jennifer looks of astonishment, mouths open. But the creature only shook his head, vehemently. "*Vampyr*? Nach bant Vampyr! No, no, no. She no Vampyr! She just girl. The name is Davies. Yes, Anne Davies."

Mark looked at his wife, who stared back at him, obviously thinking the same thing. "Davies?" Mark asked the creature. "Her name is Davies? As in *Jack* Davies?"

"Yes, yes, yes! She his sister!"

Olga tilted her head in a way that seemed almost animal-like, then stepped toward Mark, sniffing the air between them, glaring at him with her pitch-black eyes. "You know dis girl?" she asked.

Mark's mouth hung open, unable to reply. Jennifer stepped in and said, "We don't know the girl, no. But we know her brother, Jack Davies. Or we know who he is, anyway."

"Why would this boy's sister be a prisoner of the Dreadman?" Alexis asked.

Mark, finding his voice, cleared his throat and said, "He's no ordinary boy. He's from our world, not this one. And he's a peregrinator."

Alexis and his wives looked to one another with various expressions of incredulity. Olga asked, "Dis girl? Dreadman's prisoner? She peregrinator too?"

Jennifer shrugged, "I don't know, but I don't think so."

Alexis looked at the creature tied to the chair and said, "You! What is your name?"

Spitting and coughing, the creature replied in a hoarse voice, "Krumuck! And I just lowly henchman. Me not know nothing."

"Which means you know *something*," Alexis said, laughing. "Is this true? Did you take this girl from her world and bring her to this one?"

Krumuck shivered violently then cried out, "Yes! He made us!"

Alexis shook his head. "Are you a peregrinator?"

"No!" Krumuck laughed then fell into a coughing fit.

"How you do it?" Olga asked.

"Gates were open dat night we took her. They open just a moment, then close, then open, then close. But long enough for Krumuck and friends to enter her world and take her back to Dread."

"Why did you bring the girl to this world?" Alexis asked.

"Because Dread tell us. We do as he say, or we die." Krumuck whimpered behind one scaly hand but peeked through his fingers to gauge their reactions.

Avenya stepped next to the creature and placed a hand on his slimy forehead and asked in a voice filled with kindness and warmth. "Master Krumuck, why did he want you to bring the girl here?"

At her touch, Krumuck's shivering slowed and his coughing

subsided. His eyes grew heavy and a wide smile spread across his face. "Ahhhh. So good. We bring girl here because Dreadman want her to be here with him. He have plan, yes, but he no tell henchmen. That all Krumuck know." With that, the creature fell into a deep sleep.

Alexis paced the room for a while, as Krumuck snored in his chair. The others separated throughout the room, each staring blankly at the stone cellar walls. Mark looked at Jennifer and put his arm around her, stroking her hair.

Finally, Alexis walked to the center of the room and motioned for everyone to gather. His white-blue eyes glowed brightly, a stark contrast to his dark brown skin. He said, "I think we have no choice, wives."

Olga tilted her head. "Agree, husband."

Avenya closed her eyes and touched her lips with her fingers. "Agree, husband."

Laurel said nothing, but stepped next to Alexis and kissed his cheek.

Alexis looked to the Warrens and nodded. "If Dreadman brought this Davies girl to our world, it can be for no good reason. And if her brother is a peregrinator, as you say, it answers many questions floating in my mind. I'm sorry, Jennifer and Mark. But I fear we must delay our search for your vampire friend. Rest tonight, all of you. Tomorrow we will search for the Dreadman's house in the woods."

18

THE VOICE OF
THE UNDEAD

Joe stood in the vestibule of Forest Grove Baptist Church, staring out a window next to the main doors. There wasn't much to see but a mostly empty parking lot. A giant cornfield stretched out beyond and on either side of the church for acres and acres. The church and the farmhouse across the road constituted a small oasis amid a golden ocean of corn stalks.

The man on the other side of the vestibule had just finished cleaning and loading his double-barrel shotgun and was now staring out at said cornfields. Other men, carrying similar guns, along with one or two with AR-14's strapped to their backs, were stationed near various windows throughout the single-story church. Two women and a teenage boy kept a lookout on the roof with a sniper rifle and a couple .22's. Leo Lourogen had returned some hours ago, appearing weary and injured, and was at the moment in an office meeting with a tall, gray-haired man, who seemed to be the church minister.

Shaun was still asleep in one of the offices down the hall of the east wing of the church. He had been awake most of the previous night, staring out the very window Joe was now looking through and had only recently fallen asleep.

Inside the sanctuary, almost two dozen people lay on cots, staring at a large screen television mounted next to the pulpit. They had long ago given up any notion that the news channels would be broadcasting anything about their situation. In fact, all radio and TV channels were oddly silent about the previous evening's events, only mentioning vague stories about *trouble in Bettendorf* and that the police had things *under control.*

Joe's cell phone had died hours ago, as had Shaun's. He had asked if he could call his mom and dad from the church's phone, but the lines were down, and no one could call in or out for the time being.

Leo finally emerged from the preacher's office, followed by a large man with an enormous stomach tucked into a pair of brown slacks, and a short, skinny woman, who was wearing a set of hunting fatigues in which she did not seem remotely comfortable. They were the church minister and his wife.

"Don't you worry, Leo," the minister said as they stepped out into the vestibule. "We are on the lookout. Those dead ones won't get within a foot of Forest Grove Church—that I can assure you. We're prepared for this, you know."

Leo nodded uncertainly, stepping up to the window next to Joe. "They're out there," Leo said, "about twenty or thirty of them, I think. More are coming."

"What do they want with us?" the minister asked. "Why did they come all the way out here?"

"Don't know."

"You think Jones sent them? Perhaps to kill off the competition, so to speak?"

"Maybe, maybe not. Maybe he don't know they're out here," Leo said, glancing back. "Don't know why he'd send these ones out here or why they ain't attacked yet."

"They've gone rogue, you think?" the small woman asked. Her voice was surprisingly loud for her size.

"Maybe."

Joe was taken aback—not by the information he was hearing but by the amount of respect the minister and his wife apparently had for Leo. These people, unlike just about everyone else in Bettendorf, actually took Leo's opinion seriously. When he spoke, the minister and his wife both nodded thoughtfully. The past twelve hours had held some incredible revelations, but for Joe, this was one of the biggest.

Joe interrupted, "Leo, can we get out of here? Shaun and I have school tomorrow."

"Nah. It's too dangerous, Joe. Them undead is out there waiting for us. They attacked me on the road, just outside the driveway. I barely made it here, and their numbers are growing. We're gonna have to bunker down for a while until we come up with a plan, or they decide to move off."

"You guys have guns, lots of guns. Why don't you go out and blast them away?" Joe asked.

The minister and the woman nodded as if it was an idea they had already discussed. But Leo shook his head, saying only, "Might have to come to that but not yet. They're fast and hidden in the field. Unless they come into the open, it'll be hard to hit them. We could lose a lot of people."

Joe understood. These people were not an army—they were friends and family, cousins and in-laws, congregants and neighbors. It was a simple country church, and though they had somehow been prepared for a day like this, they were not interested in sending out their people to die if waiting it out was a possibility.

The minister said, "I'm Brother Dale Adams. This is my wife, Sister Shirley. You're more than welcome to stay with us, Mr. Lambert. We've got enough provisions for months, if it comes to that, which it won't. We need to sit tight for a bit, and once the phone lines come back up, we can call for help."

"The police?" Joe asked.

"No probably not them," Dale said.

"Why not?"

"Well, it's a bit complicated to explain right now. But we're not sure who we can trust in city hall, you see?"

Joe was dumbfounded. "What? You think the cops released a bunch of zombies on the town? What the hell?"

"They ain't zombies," Leo said.

"Well, they sure as hell look like it."

The Dale cleared his throat and explained, "They're undead, which I understand might seem like the same thing, but they're quite different. Zombies are slow and dumb. These things aren't exactly geniuses, but they are excellent hunters and well-coordinated."

"How do you guys know so much?" Joe asked.

Dale and Shirley looked at each other again. Finally, Shirley said, "To you, I'm sure all of this seems brand-new and shocking. But people have been fighting this battle in Bettendorf for many years, long before you, or even we, were born. They are not the first to come here, and they won't be the last. I'm sure of that."

"Yeah," Dale agreed. "I'm afraid it's been happening for some time."

"But this is different," Leo said.

Dale nodded. "Yes, indeed it is. This is bigger and bolder than anything we've seen before, but we have been expecting it for some years now. You see, Mr. Lambert, dark forces have been fighting a war in this town for longer than any of us here can remember. Sometimes, they grow strong and have to be beaten down. Happens every couple decades or so, sometimes longer."

"That's what's happening now? They've become strong again?" Joe asked.

"Yes, I guess you could say that. Very strong," Shirley said.

"So, this has happened before?"

"Not like this," Leo said.

Dale interjected, "This time is a bit different like Leo says. They've been patient, gathering humans to do their work for them. They infiltrated the town government years ago along with some of the most influential people in the county. They're better organized this time too."

"And this time, they have the key," Leo said.

"Or at least they know where it is," Shirley added.

"What's the key?" Joe asked.

Dale looked at Leo, who answered, "Jack Davies is the key."

"Jack? Jack Davies? What the hell are you talking about?"

Dale put his arm around Joe, saying, "I know this will be hard to understand. Heck, you'll probably just walk back to your friend and shrug it off as nothing more than the ravings of some simple country folk who've had a bit too much devil-talk in their Sunday services. But my friend, it is the truth; I swear upon the holy bible. Your friend Jack? Well, he's got himself quite a skill. One that a lot of folks around here want to get their hands on."

Brother Dale proceeded to fill in Joe on every detail he knew, including the cult at Sunset Circle, the devils of the glen, and Jack Davies' place in all of it. Leo told him about the rite at the Bennett Mansion—about Opus and Maximus and how they saved Jack, and the world, from annihilation at the hands of demons from hell. Leo pointed out there were holes in the story, parts he didn't know and might never understand.

When he had finished, Joe stood there staring at Leo, unable to speak for several moments. When he finally found his voice he said, "This is just. . .friggin. . .I don't even *know* what. It's all crazy."

"I know it is, son," Dale said. "There's a lot of darkness out there in the world; that's a fact. But don't despair—there's a lot of good in it too. And we haven't been idle, no-siree-bob, we haven't. Our cellar's filled with enough food and water to last us a couple years if we ration it."

Joe shuffled back to the office where Shaun was sleeping, his head full of more questions than he thought it could hold. When he opened the office door, Shaun was sitting up on his cot, staring blankly at the wall in front of him. "Hey, you're up," Joe said. "Dude, you gotta hear what they told me. This is friggin nuts." Shaun continued staring at the wall with no response. "Hey, Shaun, snap out of it!"

Shaun glanced at him and said, "Huh? What did you say?"

"What's wrong with you? You look like a zombie."

"Sorry," Shaun said. "I'm just—tired. What did they tell you?"

"A bunch of crap that made no sense."

"Like what?"

"Like there is a massive conspiracy in town to open a gate to hell and that Jack Davies is somehow the key to this gate. It's frigging stupid."

"What did they say about the people who are chasing us?" Shaun asked.

"Not much. Apparently, they're *undead*, and they've got this place surrounded, but no one knows why they're here. Even Leo doesn't understand it—and by the way, he seems like he knows a hell of a lot more about all this stuff than anyone else. It's like he's a leader or something. Can you believe that shit? Frigging Leo *Lourogen*? But anyway, they don't know why the undead are here."

"I know why they're here," Shaun said. Through all of this, he still had not looked away from the wall. "They want me. *She* wants me."

"She? What *she*? Who are you talking about?"

"The girl from last night. She's out there in the field, waiting for me."

"Come on, man. I know the chicks dig old Shaun Porter and everything, but I don't think that undead girl wanted to bang you last night. She wanted to eat your effing brains and shit them out all over that barn."

"You're wrong. It's me they're after, Joe," Shaun said, with no hint of doubt. "She wants me."

"For what?" Joe asked.

"I just know," Shaun said, flatly.

"How?"

"She's calling out to me."

A chill skittered up Joe's spine. Shaun's statement was frightening not because it was so incredibly ludicrous, but because it made perfect sense. It made more sense than just about anything else that had happened in the past twenty-four hours. During the chase the night before, one thing stood out to Joe, and he had been avoiding the thought ever since. The undead, especially the girl, had paid no attention to Joe at all. They were focused exclusively on Shaun.

"She's calling you?" Joe asked.

"Yes."

"How?"

"With her mind."

"Her mind? And you can hear it?"

"Yes."

"How?"

"I don't know, but it doesn't matter. Everyone in this church is in danger because of me, and if I stay here, it's gonna be bad. They're all gonna die."

19

THE CALL OF THE UNDEAD

Shaun stared out the back window of Forest Grove Church as the sun's autumn orange and gold rays seemed to light the endless cornfields on fire. To anyone else, it might have looked like a typical, calm, Midwestern dusk—quiet and still. But Shaun's ears were ringing. Though he couldn't see her, he knew she was out there.

…waiting for him.

She had been calling his name for most of the day. At first, he had been surprised that no one else had heard it, so distinct was the sound to his ears. When he mentioned hearing something, Joe stared at him with a mixture of worry and confusion. Earlier, Shaun had heard Leo instructing Joe to keep an eye on him, which was understandable. He would have done the same thing.

So why am I not scared? Shaun asked himself. *Why does it feel like walking out into the corn would be the right thing to do? And why don't I want to tell the others about it?*

Joe Lambert's voice startled him out of his thoughts. "Hey, the preacher and a few of their guys went out to do a sweep of the cornfield. They haven't seen a sign of them for hours, so maybe we can go home soon."

"What? Who went out?" Shaun said.

"I just told you. Some guys from the church and the preacher. Why? What's wrong with you?"

"The undead aren't gone—they're still out there. These people here in this church are gonna get themselves killed, Joe."

For the tenth time that day, Joe looked at him like he was insane. "How do you know that? Have you seen them?"

"No. I just—it doesn't matter how I know. I just know. They're still out there, and they've got others with them now, like twenty or thirty."

Joe put his hand on Shaun's shoulder. "Dude, how could you possibly know that? You haven't stepped foot outside this church all day."

"I just know. You gotta get them to bring those people back to the church. They're walking into a trap!"

Joe paused and stared at him for several moments, considering what to do with Shaun's unusual request. "OK, fine," he said finally. "Let's find Leo. I think he's communicating with them on a walkie-talkie."

"He's not with them?" Shaun asked as they jogged down the east wing hallway toward the minister's office.

"No, the preacher refused him because he's been awake for almost two days now, so Leo agreed to stay back only if he could man the radio."

When they got to Leo, Shaun told him what he had said to Joe only moments before. The large man rubbed his buzzed hair with one large hand and stared back at Shaun. "How you know this?"

"It doesn't matter, Leo. I just do. You gotta bring those people back. They're walking into a trap. I know it."

"OK," Leo said after considering him for a few moments then held the walkie-talkie up to his mouth. "Brother Dale? Come in."

"Yeah, Leo, I'm here," Dale said, almost whispering.

"You better get back here on the double."

Silence for a few moments then, *"Why is that?"*

"We got some information here. Those fields ain't empty."

"Yeah, I think you're right." There was a pause followed by static on the receiver. *"We can hear them—they're all around us—though they seem to be keeping their distance for now. Haven't seen them yet."*

Shaun pulled the walkie-talkie away from Leo's mouth, covering it with his hand. "That's because they don't want them; they want me. Get them out of there. Now!"

"Dale, you better get back in here now," Leo said. "Turn tail."

A few crackling noises came through before Dale responded with, "Yeah, I think you may be ri—"

A scream rang out through the speaker, cutting him off mid-sentence, and a shotgun blast blared through the speaker before it turned to static. For the next few moments, the speaker cut in and out with pops of gunfire and screaming, then back to static, and finally silence. Joe held his breath.

"Dale! Dale! What's happening?" Leo cried into the mic.

"They're all over us! We're pulling back!" Dale's voice cried out, frightened.

"Shit! Get them back. She wants *me!*" Shaun yelled and, without another word, ran out of the room, down the hall, out the back door, continuing until he stood in the middle of the church parking lot, surrounded on three sides by a thick yellow forest of seven-foot-tall corn stalks. "I'm here! Leave those people alone! You want me! Lucy! I will come to you, but you must let those people go!"

The sounds of fighting stopped as Joe and Leo joined him on either shoulder and waited, both breathing heavily in anticipation. A few moments later, the church members came bursting out of the field. Most of them were crying, and a few were empty-handed, having dropped their weapons somewhere in the cornfield. Brother Dale was the last to emerge, limping and holding his shoulder, which he had crudely bandaged with a piece of his own shirt. Leo and Joe took hold of him under each arm and guided him back toward the church.

Then, just as Joe and Leo closed the church door behind them,

Lucy Doyle, still dressed in her Catholic school uniform, emerged from the corn stalks. Several of her followers lined up behind her, just inside the field. Lucy had blood, brain matter, and flesh smeared across her face and chest, soiling her formerly pristine white button-down top.

The undead girl's eyes found Shaun. An abnormal expression that might have passed for a smile grew on her lips as she held out one hand and waited patiently. Though Shaun could see no other undead, he sensed their presence in the fields surrounding him, a hundred or more. All of them waiting.

He became faintly aware of the church doors opening somewhere behind him, but though he knew Joe was standing there watching him, he did not turn to look. Shaun knew if he did, he would change his mind. Instead, he strode across the parking lot to the edge of the field and, taking the bloody outstretched hand of Lucy Doyle, disappeared into the golden forest of corn as the last rays of the setting sun colored the whole world in sky blue pink.

20

A DART IN THE DARK

Randy sat on his bed and ran down the list of oddities in his head.

Jack Davies—inter-dimensional time traveler or some such thing. Disappeared into thin air.

Leo Lourogen—sword-carrying, vampire-hunter.

Lara Fanning—a vampire.

Stephanie Caine—another vampire.

Jimmy Vance—again, vampire, and now headless.

Not to mention that Bettie girl, who lives up the street from Jack, who was now a witch or something.

And then there's Shaun and Joe, who somehow got themselves mixed up in all this stuff.

Last but not least, Ava, Jack's weird pseudo-girlfriend, who may or may not be some kind of witch or vampire—and who's probably like a thousand years old!

Jesus, what the hell is happening around here?

We *are happening here, Randy,* the dark voice whispered to him.

The day dragged on like this—one excruciating hour at a time. He had thought about sneaking out, but his dad had positioned himself in the kitchen with a shotgun and a clear view of both the front and back doors. Randy's bedroom window was too far above the ground to sneak out safely that way, not without breaking his leg in the process, which would do no one any good.

Finally, at ten o'clock, Randy found his dad asleep in the dining room chair. From the sounds of snoring coming from the living room, his mom had knocked out too, so he stealthily snuck into his sister's bedroom and grabbed whatever things he could find that might fit Tatsu. A black and gold pair of Iowa Hawkeyes sweats, and a Packers hoodie was all he could see, so he grabbed one of his dad's old REM t-shirts and some socks from his room. He wasn't sure what size shoe she wore, so he took a pair of flip-flops, a flashlight from his desk drawer, and a small gardening shovel from the garage, which he tied to the frame of his bike.

In no time, he was out the front door and riding down the street again. However, this time, he took all back streets in case the police were out looking for curfew-breakers. Sure enough, even on the side streets, he had to duck behind bushes and vehicles to evade patrol cars. There were very few cars on the road, so he didn't have to slow himself down too much, and within a half hour, he was rolling down the hill into Crow Creek Park.

When he reached the trees on the far side of the park, he called out for Tatsu in the best whisper-yell he could manage. The sound of wind blowing through bare branches whistled through the night, and the smell of burning leaves tickled Randy's nose, forcing him to hold back a sneeze. Laying his bike next to a tree, he crouched next to a tree and untied the shovel. Electricity danced along the underside of his arms like a silent alarm. Something felt wrong. Trees creaked and tumbling leaves crackled in the breeze, but no other sound emanated from the shadowy woods. Randy quietly cut into the undergrowth, doing his best to keep from being seen.

The voice chuckled in his head.

"Tatsu? You there?" Still no reply.

With all the dead leaves on the ground, Randy felt like each of his footsteps could be heard a mile away. Peering through the shadows, he spotted bare flesh between a pair of trees. Creeping closer, Tatsu's black hair came into view and pale skin shining back at him in the moonlight. She lay on the ground, her head propped against a large trunk.

She must be sleeping, he told himself. *I've been gone for hours. She must be exhausted.*

The tingling sensation spread up his arms and across his back, but he ignored it and rushed over to her. He knelt, and gently took her by the shoulders. "Tatsu. Wake up. I've got your clothes. Tatsu?"

Then he saw it. A dart—about four inches long with a feathered end—sticking out of her left thigh. At first, Randy couldn't make sense of what he was seeing. How had she gotten herself shot with one of those? But then the realization struck him. He sprang to his feet, grabbing Tatsu by the forearm. But it was too late.

The voice in his head rolled with laughter. Fool! You're a fool!

A sharp pain sprang up, all at once, on his right side. He looked down. A metal dart, similar to the one in Tatsu's leg, jutted out from the bottom of his hip, still vibrating from the impact. Glancing back into the trees, Randy spotted a man with thick glasses crouched beneath a willow twenty yards away, holding a rifle and smiling out at him from under the drooping leaves. Then, from the shadows, a beautiful girl with red hair glided toward him, laughing, her arms stretched out to him. Though his vision was blurring, he recognized the girl immediately. It was Stephanie Caine.

"What's. . .what's happening?" Randy asked. His voice sounded like a vinyl record played on a dying turntable.

"You've been shot, you idiot. That's what's happening," Stephanie said as she took him in her arms. "And now we have you, Randy Wall. Isn't that *fun?*" Catching the back of his head with her hand, she smiled down at his face, her sharp canines flashing white in the icy moonlight.

"Oh, shit," Randy mumbled. His eyes slowly closed as the voice of Surgat laughed hysterically in his head.

21

THE HOUSE IN WRIGLEYVILLE

Bettie awoke briefly in the afternoon to find Ava staring out the glass wall of their Michigan Avenue hotel room at the city skyline. It was a breathtaking sight to be sure, but something about her posture gave the impression that Ava was not focused on the city at all. From the repeated heavy sighs, she seemed shaken by something.

"Is everything OK?" Bettie asked. She yawned and sat up slowly.

Startled, Ava turned to her then straightened herself. "I don't know. I hope so."

"What is it?"

"I'm not sure," Ava said. "But there's nothing to be done about it now. Jack must travel this path alone, though I do wish he'd waited for me to return. Maybe he had no choice."

"Is he in trouble? Should we go back to Bettendorf?"

"It's too late for that." Ava wiped her eye. "There's nothing we can do about it now. Go back to sleep. I'll wake you when it's time."

Sleep returned to Bettie quickly, and she didn't wake until the dazzling city lights shone into the hotel room like a thousand stars. Though Chicago was only a few hours from Bettendorf, her family had never taken her there. Her father was not fond of large crowds, and her mother found the thought of leaving the house almost too much to bear. An enormous cramped city, like Chicago, would have been torture for both her parents, but Bettie's heart raced as she gazed out the window in wonder.

"How do you like the big city?" Ava asked.

Bettie glanced at her, eyes wide. "Amazing. I love it."

"You've never been here before, I take it."

"Nope. And from the looks of it, I don't think I ever want to leave," Bettie said.

"Believe me; I come here as often as I can—New York, too. Maybe sometime when things aren't so crazy, I can take you to both cities. We can decide, once and for all which kind of pizza is better."

"You got it!" Bettie said. "Pizza sounds good. I'm starving!"

"Sorry, but unfortunately, we must pick up something quick tonight. The people we are meeting may not be here after tomorrow morning, so we'll need to make the most of every moment. Sad, the food here is excellent, but I'll make it up to you. Next time, I'll take you to the best pizza joint in Chicago."

"Promise?"

"Promise! Now, go clean up. I went shopping while you slept and got us some proper clothes to wear. Halloween is over, after all."

They were soon driving the streets of downtown Chicago. Bettie stared up at the tall buildings hovering over their heads like metal and glass giants. Needing to eat something fast, they ran through a White Castle drive-through, which Bettie loved, and eventually headed up Lake Shore Drive to an area called Wrigleyville. Bettie had never been much for sports, especially baseball, but living this close to Chicago, it was impossible not to know about Wrigley Field and its beloved team, the Cubs. Everyone in her school seemed to be enamored with them lately, though she could not be bothered even to wonder why. However, as they drove through the city, the team's colors and logos were everywhere.

Before long, they were off Lakeshore and onto Addison street, cruising past Wrigley field. "Wow, there's a whole stadium right here in the middle of a neighborhood."

"Yep," Ava said. "Maybe we'll go to a game next summer if you want."

"I don't know anything about baseball."

"Doesn't matter. It's fun to go for the crowd and the food."

Bettie smiled at her. "OK."

Soon, they had pulled Ava's car in front of an austere old house at the corner of Addison and Janssen. Essentially, it was a brownstone, with a dark brick exterior, though unlike most brownstones in the city, it was a single residence and had never been converted into apartments. The house was dark and gothic, with a steep pointed roof rising high into the Chicago night and a small turret on the southeast corner that came to a sharp wrought iron spire.

"Dramatic, isn't it?" Ava asked as they sat in the car.

"Yeah. Looks spooky," Bettie said.

"Oh, it is quite haunted and not only by ghosts," Ava said.

Bettie frowned at her. "Then why are we here?"

Ava patted her on the arm. "Not to worry, dear. You've got me with you, and though I wouldn't say the people you'll meet tonight are exactly *good*, I wouldn't call them exactly *bad*, either. Regardless, we need their help."

"Will they help us?" Bettie asked.

"I doubt it. But we may learn some things, at any rate."

They approached the front steps of the old house and rang the doorbell several times before an old man in a black suit opened the door. "Lady von Tassen," he said, in a posh English accent. "How pleasant to see you. I am sorry, but I was in the kitchen when you rang."

"Hello, Gains, that's quite alright. I trust Lord Carmichael has not yet left for Europe."

"Oh, no, it seems you are just in time. We won't depart before tomorrow evening, at the earliest. Won't you come in?" Gains opened the door wide and stepped aside, motioning for them to enter. "And who is your young friend?"

"Ah, this is Bettie Stone. Bettie, this is Gains, Lord Carmichael's butler."

Gains laughed, adding, "And valet, and accountant, and footman, and gardener it seems these days. The only occupations I steadfastly refuse are cooking and driving, mostly due to my inability to perform either without casualties."

"Are times so hard?" Ava asked, laughing.

"In a way, yes. Oh, the fortune is quite well-protected and indeed thrives, thanks mostly to me. But the trustworthiness of *people*—that is another story altogether. I'm afraid the master does not have the patience for them he once did."

A gravelly voice called down from the upstairs, "Gains! Are you planning to bring my guests up the stairs, or do you wish to keep them as prisoners down there, talking them to death?"

"What were those choices again, sir?" Gains maintained a dry expression.

"God almighty, man, bring them up!"

"Oh, hush, you!" Gains called up the stairs with a dismissive wave of the hand. "There's no crime in a bit of small talk along the way!"

"Along the way? Have you even begun leading them up the stairs, or have you remained in the vestibule, feeding them all my private information?"

Gains started up the stairs, motioning for Ava and Bettie to follow. "Vestibule? The entryway to this modest dwelling can hardly be described in such lofty terms."

Ava followed behind Gains and winked back at Bettie as they climbed the old wooden stairs. It was hard not to chuckle at the banter, and Bettie found herself loving the old butler already.

Lord Carmichael scoffed. "Ah, yes, I'm sorry this is not

Stradlowe, but it seems America is in short supply of large country estates."

Bettie and Ava laughed openly as the old butler led them to the top of the stair and, turning right, into a small but well-stocked library. At the far end were two large chairs. In one of them sat a man, who looked nothing like his voice. He was young, perhaps in his thirties, with dark clean-cut hair and bright green eyes that positively glowed in the dimly lit room. He wore a tweed suit with a brown bow tie and reading glasses pulled down almost to the end of his nose. Though his appearance was that of a younger man, Bettie sensed that, like Ava, he was much older than he looked.

"I present to you Lord Henry Carmichael the third," Gains said.

Standing, Lord Carmichael smiled and said, "Hello, Ava, my dear! It has been such a long time since we last met. Three years? Longer?"

"No, three is about right. This is my friend, Bettie Stone. Bettie, this is Lord Carmichael."

"Hello, Lord Carmichael," Bettie said. Not knowing what to do in such a situation, she bowed her head slightly.

"Oh, please, call me Henry. You Americans aren't interested in titles or such things, so let's do away with the formalities, shall we? Can Gains get you anything? Coffee or tea?"

"No thank you," Bettie said, and Ava shook her head to Gains, who took his place near the door.

Returning to his chair and sitting, Henry asked, "So, what brings you to the windy city? By the look of you, things have taken a turn, I'm guessing."

"By the look of me?"

"Yes, your clothes are new; I can tell from the creasing, and I see from the cut it's a Maggie Asbury—a brand they do not carry in Iowa, not Bettendorf, anyway. I see traces of makeup behind the girl's left ear. She's only recently changed out of her Halloween costume, a witch, if I'm not mistaken. Since you are there posing as a teenager, I can only assume you were in costume, as well, though I cannot say for certain which. From the faint traces of perfume, which you failed to erase in your recent shower, you're more than likely attempting to seduce some young man for whatever purpose. If so, it would not be a stretch to assume you'd dress as whatever character the boys find titillating these days—perhaps a character from one of the popular movies. If only my knowledge were more current on such things, I'd have the name in an instant."

"Wow," Bettie said. "Are you Sherlock Holmes?"

"No, no, dear. Sherlock Holmes was not a real person but a creation of my good friend, Sir Arthur." Henry pulled out a cigar with a flourish and lit it, giving Bettie a small wink and a smile as he drew in the flame.

"That's awesome! Ava, he's amazing!"

"Yes, yes, he's annoyingly good at figuring things out," Ava said. "But stick around for a while, and you'll see it gets quite tiresome." This produced an unexpected chuckle from Gains, who did an intentionally poor job of covering it with a cough.

"Are you alright, Gains?" Henry asked. "Do you require a drink of water? Some syrup, perhaps? A lozenge?"

"Oh, no, my Lord. Quite alright, sir."

"You're certain?"

"Oh, yes, indeed. Quite well, thank you."

Henry sat back and scanned Ava's face. It seemed to Bettie that he was reading every line, every pore. At one point, he raised an eyebrow and made a grunt that sounded like a surprise. His eyes ran across Ava's features over and over, like he was reading and rereading a long letter from a friend. Finally, he said to her, "I see you have been a busy woman. Quite busy, indeed."

"I have," Ava said.

"You've seen things."

"Yes."

"Impossible things."

"No longer impossible."

"Perhaps not. But in this physical world, they were things that should not have been. And your coming here to this house is a breeze before the storm, I think. Devilry is afoot—chicanery. Troubled times are ahead."

"To be honest, Henry, I think they're here."

Lord Carmichael rubbed his forehead. "Gains, I'm afraid we must put off our trip for a time."

"Yes, my Lord," Gains said and stepped out of the room. Bettie heard the old man's footsteps descending the stairs and passing into another room on the first floor then the sound of a door closing.

Henry considered Bettie for several moments, and it seemed as if a dark shadow passed over the room. The air chilled, and the lights dimmed. Finally, Henry looked back at Ava and said in a measured tone, "You're in love."

Ava smiled, then glanced at the wood floor.

Raising his hands together in front of his face, Henry nodded and said, "Tell me everything. All of it. Leaving nothing out, no matter how small the detail. But first, we shall have tea. This night will be long."

22

THE LADY OF THE LAGOON

"We've got to find my clothes! I can't meet this lady of the lake—or whatever she's called—in nothing but my boxers! And that Cubs hoodie was brand new!"

Faelith laughed and sat on the grass next to him. "We're not going back into those woods looking for anything, not while you're as helpless as a lamb. Who knows what came and took your clothes? I'm sure you can get another—*whatever* it was you called it."

"Cubs hoodie!"

Faelith shook her head. "Sorry, but nope, you're just gonna have to go meet the lady in your panties."

"They're undies, not *panties*," Jack said. "Jesus. Hopefully, she at least has a blanket. Talk about being in a vulnerable position—and with you naked. It's a friggin' nightmare."

"Oh, I won't be naked, not in man-form, anyway," Faelith said.

"What do you mean?"

"I don't know this lady at all. I don't know how she'll feel about my kind, you know? So, I'll turn coyote; that way, I can sniff out any danger and maybe have a look around. I'll have your back." She giggled again as Jack fully blushed.

Faelith immediately dropped onto her hands and feet. At first, nothing seemed to happen; she simply stood there, frozen on all fours. But then her skin rippled and rolled slowly across her back as her muscles flexed and relaxed. All at once, hair grew out from seemingly every pore on her skin, and the entire shape of her body morphed from human to a coyote something more animal-like. The bones popped and rolled, as some lengthened and others seemed to shrink. Through all the cracking of bones and snapping of skin and popping of cartilage, Faelith made barely a sound. Her face elongated and sharp canines jutted from her jaw. Her tongue stretched out to lick the air and her mouth opened wide in a massive yawn. Though the entire process took less than a minute, Jack was astounded that the girl could handle the pain of it all.

"Wow, that's crazy! You didn't even scream." Jack stared at her with eyes wide.

"*Well, I have been doing it for quite some time,*" she said, her voice once again projecting into his mind as it had before. "*Your body gets used to the change when you're young, and after some years, you barely feel it at all.*"

"How does this communication work?" he asked as they walked. "How can I hear your voice in my head like that?"

"*I must say it is a bit strange. I've never met anyone who could speak with me this way, who wasn't of my kind. It was a bit of a shock when I realized you could hear me; I wondered if you were a shifter. Try speaking to me through your mind. Don't use your voice, just your thoughts. Direct your mind towards me, like you're sending a message to me with your brain, instead of your mouth.*"

"OK." Jack concentrated on Faelith's face and thought the words, "*I'm cold.*"

"*Wimp! Ha!*" Faelith said, delighted.

"Wow, it worked!" he said aloud. "Wait—does that mean you can read my mind?"

"Oh, no, unfortunately. I would so love to know what's going on in there, but alas, you must direct your thoughts for me to hear them, just as I must direct my thoughts toward you."

"Wow, that's crazy! But hope you don't mind if I just keep talking like normal. I'm not sure I'm ready to do that all the time. Nice to know if we're ever in trouble, though."

"Yes, indeed it is. Must be another of your peregrinating skills—a handy one, I might add. I'm sure it must be useful to have the ability to speak to anyone and anything when you're traveling to different worlds and dimensions."

Jack snorted. "I guess so, not that I would know. Just another thing to chock up to all the things I don't know about myself."

"Don't be so down on yourself. You aren't supposed to know everything about yourself, not at your age. You're young, even for one of your kind. I think you'll be amazed by what you discover, Jack Davies, before all is said and done. Isn't that exciting?"

"Yeah, it's a riot," he said.

Faelith stopped and turned to him with narrowed eyes. *"I tell you this, Jack. Your quest isn't only about finding your sister, important as that is to you, I'm sure. My heart tells me this is also about finding yourself—some aspects of yourself that have long been missing. Though I barely know you, even I can see you have parts missing, parts of your soul and your memories. There is much light, but I think there is also some darkness in you. You may discover many things, but you will not be unchanged by this journey, I fear."*

With that, she padded ahead some distance into the fog until Jack could see no sign of her. He followed along as best he could, cutting back and forth between the trees and undergrowth, trying his best to avoid the numerous branches and brambles growing haphazardly throughout the island.

As he emerged from the thicket, Jack found himself in the midst of a copse of pines so tall they seemed to reach into the sky as far as he could see, their thick branches spanning out in all directions like an endlessly intricate spider's web. A pair of squirrels chased each other across the forest floor, circling up and around the trunk of one of the trees not only a few yards away, utterly unfazed by Jack's presence.

Peering through the trees, Jack whispered, "Faelith?"

He stood there for several minutes and almost turned to go back to the lake, when he finally heard the soft sound of coyote paws padding over the needles followed by the sleek dark shape of Faelith's shifted form, cutting back and forth through the trees.

"I found the house," she said. *"It's just ahead in a small clearing on the other side of these evergreens."*

Eventually, they emerged from the woods onto a finely manicured Kentucky bluegrass lawn, with flowers and vines growing all around the front path and subtle landscaping throughout the front yard, not unlike what you would find in the front yard of any Iowa home. The house was a ranch-style midcentury design. Jack noticed there was a screen door, and just past it, the main entrance was ajar as if someone had left it open for them. They looked at the door for a moment then to each other.

From inside, came a woman's voice. "Don't stand there like a pair of idiots. Come in, young man—you and your dog."

"Um. OK," Jack said. Faelith gave a slight whine.

The interior was just like the exterior—adorned in midcentury decor, as if it had been yanked out of 1961 and plopped right into this strange world, down to the little black and white television with the smallest screen Jack had seen on a TV, sitting on a small stand in the living room. The couch, tables, lamps, and wallpaper were all similarly retro but authentic and lived-in. This was no recreation.

"Keep coming. I'm past the living room, down the hall in the kitchen."

Jack proceeded into a small hallway beyond which he could see the light green cabinets and the white and black tiled floor of a kitchen of yesteryear. The appliances, counters, glasses, and knick-knacks all around spoke of a simpler era, when technology was still primitive, and women always wore dresses while cooking. There was a small breakfast table pushed against one wall with three chairs around it, and a lime green phone hung on the wall near a doorway just beyond. Sitting in the far chair, facing them, was a woman smoking a cigarette. Her blond hair was set into a beehive-like up-do, and she wore a white and light blue flower printed dress, cut to her knees. She looked like she might be in her late twenties, perhaps, though it was hard to tell from her face, and her demeanor hinted at a woman far older. Though she was seated, she looked to be above average height, given her long shapely legs, which were crossed and turned out to the side of her chair. Jack immediately thought the woman looked exactly like Betty Draper from Madmen, right down to her bored yet subtly suggestive stare as she watched him step into the kitchen. When Faelith followed behind him, the woman called her over with a snap of her fingers and patted the girl on the head.

"My, I haven't had a coyote visit in many years. What a pleasant surprise this is," the woman said, stroking Faelith's head lightly, then turned to Jack. "And you. My goodness, you are a handsome young man, aren't you?"

"Thank you. . .uh. . .ma'am," Jack said.

"Please call me June." The woman held out her hand to him, palm down.

Not sure whether he was meant to shake it or kiss it, Jack clumsily accomplished a mixed version of both. "Nice to meet you too, uh, June," he said. "I'm Jack Davies."

She watched him as she took a light drag from her cigarette, her eyes roaming down his body. "Now, what's happened to your clothes?"

"Someone stole them," he said.

"Hm. I imagine that's uncomfortable." She absently ran the butt of her cigarette across her lower lip and bounced her crossed leg absently as she rubbed Faelith behind the ears.

"Yes, ma'am, it is."

"It's June, sweetie. I hate being called 'ma'am.'"

"Yes, ma—I mean, June. Sorry. Look, I don't mean to be a bother, but do you have any clothes I could borrow?"

June smiled. "Is that why you trespassed onto my island? Yes, I believe some of my ex-husband's clothes are still boxed up in the attic. Never did get around to throwing out those things. He was about your build—maybe a little bigger—but they should fit, I think. And I have a cute dress for your dog here, too. That is if she's ready to stop hiding."

Immediately, Faelith stood on her hind legs and shifted back to her human body, standing there defiantly with her hands on her hips. "I am not hiding! I never hide," she said.

"Of *course*. Oh wait, you're not a *lady*, are you?" June ran her eyes across Faelith's waist, smiling.

Faelith growled in response.

June reached out and took her hand, saying, "I'm sorry. I don't mean to offend. You are quite lovely as you are, and I mean that. You are most welcome here, especially as you have decided to help our young hero, here. Though I must admit you are quite the odd couple."

"Oh, we're not a couple," Jack said, quickly. "We just met actually—"

Faelith cut him off with a sharp look that seemed equal parts anger and hurt.

"Ha! Well, how about the both of you go upstairs and find something to wear, maybe take a nap if you need one, and then come back down here as soon as you're ready. And then we will begin."

Jack narrowed his eyes. "Begin?"

"Why, yes, sweetie. That's why you're here, isn't it? To begin?"

"Begin what?" Jack asked. Faelith rolled her eyes.

"He is a slow one, isn't he?" June said.

Faelith smirked, saying, "He catches on quick enough—with some guidance."

"What are you two talking about?" Jack asked.

June put out the cigarette, blowing twin streams of smoke through her nose. "If I'm not mistaken, you need to begin your training. That is why you're here in my home, isn't it?"

"Yes, but how do you know that? I haven't said a word about anything but clothes."

"Ah, sweetie, why else would you be here? Unfortunately, no one visits me anymore without reason, but don't worry! I'm not offended, not at all. I completely understand your need and why you're here, so I'm most happy to help you in your quest."

"My *quest*?"

June lit another cigarette. "Why yes, silly boy. Your quest to find your sister."

23

OF FLYING ON A LARGE LEATHER CHAIR

Jack exited the bedroom at the end of the hall, just as Faelith emerged from the room opposite him. They both stopped immediately and checked each other out. Jack wore a slim 1960's style midnight blue suit with black tie and a pair of shiny Florsheim dress shoes, while Faelith had found a yellow sundress with white flowers.

"*That* was the best you could do?" she asked.

"Yeah, it was all I could find. I guess June's ex-husband liked to dress up," Jack said, failing to hear the light sarcasm.

"I'm *kidding*, idiot. You look good," she said.

Jack wasn't sure if her body language suggested he should return the compliment or if she was merely uncomfortable giving or receiving them. She was impossibly difficult to read, but he realized just how unusually beautiful she was. He had no idea which was her real form—the girl-boy before him or the coyote he first met in the woods. Or perhaps her natural form was something completely different, and he had yet to see it. Either way, he realized none of it mattered. She was who she was.

"You look. . .*beautiful*," he said.

She returned his gaze, and there was a light in her eyes, small at first, which grew into one of the only warm smiles he had seen on her face. There was sadness to this girl, of that there was no doubt. Jack had sensed it from the first moment they met. Some loss lay under her independent strength, like the shadow of a troubling memory.

Faelith bowed her head, holding the smile. "Well, then, I think we should find our host."

After making their way down the hall, they crossed through the kitchen and saw June standing in the den, a rectangular, wood-paneled room with a large desk at the far end, backed by a large bookcase that took up the whole wall behind it. She was at a wide bay window that looked out over the backyard with one arm across her waist and the other holding up a newly lit cigarette. A pack of Lucky Strikes lay on the side table next to a stately leather chair behind her. She turned and bit her lower lip with a smile as she looked Jack up and down. "Handsome. Of course, at your age, I imagine anything would look good. How old are you?"

"Uh. . .sixteen," he said awkwardly.

"My, you're going to be quite a lady killer once you figure out how to use your abilities. What will you be like on that day? And those eyes—"

Faelith stepped next to him with a quick intake of breath, the back of her hand brushing softly against Jack's. June noted her presence with a nod. "Oh, a jealous one, aren't you? Well, don't worry, pooch. I have no intention of stealing your boy. But a girl can look, can't she?"

"Of course," Faelith said. "*Look* all you like."

The threat in her voice did nothing to put June off. Instead, she only winked and returned her attention to Jack. She walked straight to him and stared into his eyes, searching. "Oh, they are as blue as the ocean, as blue as the sea. I can see why they like you, Jack. Yes, indeed, I can see what draws them to you."

"Who?" Jack asked.

"'Who,' he asks. Don't play coy, young man. You *know* who. This one here, for one," she said, motioning to Faelith. "She barely knows you, yet she would lay down her life right here on my carpet to keep you safe. And, of course, there is another one drawn to you, one you seem to have forgotten already. Funny, she was quite important to you only a day ago."

Jack cleared his throat. "Who?"

"Ava, of course—don't play dumb. Have you forgotten her?"

"Of course not," he said.

"Who's Ava?" Faelith asked.

"She's a friend," Jack said, perhaps a bit too sharply.

"Oh, a *friend*, that's right," June said. "I think she's more than that, isn't she?"

"Yes, she is more than a friend, I guess," Jack said, turning to Faelith. "I'm sorry I didn't tell you about her. It's been so crazy."

"Why would you be sorry? I've only just met you. What does it matter to me if you have a girlfriend or whatever?"

The fact was, Jack had hardly thought about her once since losing Anne. His mind had shifted focus almost entirely when he found himself in this world; everything just started moving too fast. "She's a friend, and I guess more than a friend; you're right, June. But Faelith is a friend too. And I care about her."

"I can see that. She's an excellent friend, by my eyes." Her words would have almost sounded sarcastic, if not for the earnest tone. "You are truly blessed to have found this one, strange though she may be."

Faelith smiled with what looked like a small tear barely held back in her left eye. Jack returned the smile and, taking her by the hand, said, "Yes, I am fortunate. You're right—I wouldn't be here without her."

June's eyes sparkled as she watched them. "Perhaps—though who can say? Still, you made it this far together—I think you'll make it a bit further before you part." June's eyes remained fixed on Faelith, and it seemed to Jack that darkness passed over her face, like a cloud crossing the sun. Then she shook her head and said, "However, this first step in your journey, Jack, you must make alone."

"Where am I going?" Jack asked.

"That depends entirely on you. However, before you begin your training, you must find something you've lost. There is a place you must go. I think—it's a place I'm sure you've journeyed to before—a place deep in your memories."

"Yes."

Faelith cleared her throat. "He has to go alone?"

"I'm afraid so," June said.

"Is it dangerous?" Faelith asked. Lines of worry crisscrossed her face, subtle but noticeable.

"Oh, yes, it's always dangerous to travel where you've hidden your darkest secrets. There are few places more dangerous than one's mind, especially for someone like our boy Jack. I fear he has hidden something there, something dark, something that will change him."

"What is it?" Jack asked.

"If I knew, there'd be no reason for you to go. I'd tell you what it is, and that would be that. No, it is hidden and buried—buried deep beneath the soft echoes of a hymn that forever plays in your soul. You must go there to discover it."

"The hymn of forgetting."

June's eyebrows raised ever so slightly. "Yes, indeed."

"How do I find it?"

"You see the chair behind you? The big leather one with the worn arms?" June asked as she opened one side of the window. "It was my ex-husband's favorite chair. He used to sit in it, smoking and reading—dreaming or listening to music. This was long ago, before the coming of the hag, and even before the devils infected the glen—before I was trapped here on this island. My husband sat in that grand seat and traveled to faraway places beyond this world, even beyond time. You see, he was like you, handsome Jack. He was a peregrinator with much power. He learned to control it; he mastered it over many years, which is what you should hope to do, though I think you will not have the time. Great could be your power if you only made the time to learn. However, there is nothing to be done for it, at least not now. So sit. Oh, there is one other thing."

"Yes?" Jack said, sitting in the soft chair.

"You may run into my ex on your travels, probably at the very beginning, if at all. If you do, just ignore him. He's little more than a nuisance, though he can be distracting. Tell him to go away, and you'll be rid of him."

Jack considered all she had told him, blinking at her for several moments as he processed her words. The chair was comfortable, almost too comfortable—the kind of chair a person could watch a movie in only to fall asleep before the opening credits had finished. The leather creaked slightly under his weight as he sank into it.

Jack looked up to say, "When do I begin?" but before he could say a word, he saw that no one was there—no Faelith, no June. The room was suddenly empty and Jack realized he had fallen asleep the minute he his butt hit the worn leather of the chair. A hymn played, Anne's hymn, and he wondered if it was part of a dream, or if it had always played in his mind. Jack's brain was swimming and not very well.

My brain needs water wings.

"Confusing, eh?" asked a baritone male voice, startling Jack.

"Huh?"

"I said, 'confusing, eh?'" A tall man with jet black, finely combed hair, dressed in a finely tailored business suit, stepped out of the shadows from the corner of the room. If June looked like the perfect fifties housewife, this guy was the very essence of the fifties TV dad, right down to his sharply tailored suit and perfectly groomed haired.

"Yeah, it is. Who are you?" Jack asked.

"I'm June's husband. Didn't she mention me?"

"Yeah, she said to ignore you. She said you're a nuisance. And that you're her *ex*-husband."

"Ha! She would say that. Women." The man stepped in front of Jack with his hands in his pockets, jingling some loose change. "Let me get a look at you. So, you're the peregrinator, eh?"

"Yeah."

"I see. I don't often get a chance to meet a fellow traveler." The man narrowed his eyes and sized Jack up for several moments.

"You're a peregrinator too," Jack said.

The man nodded. "She's got you flying the leather chair, huh? Already?" The man shook his head and sighed.

"What?" Jack asked.

"Too soon. Not ready for this kind of test. But that's June for ya. Always too quick to give the benefit of the doubt—with everyone but *me*, that is. You've got some power; I can tell by looking at you—the cut of your jib as they say. But ready to fly the chair? Nah. Big mistake." He pressed his lips together, making a clicking sound.

Jack sighed. "Sorry, but I don't have time for this. I'm starting to understand why June finds you annoying. It's clear you have nothing to contribute, so I'm gonna have to say it—"

"No, no, wait!"

"Go away." And with that, the handsome man lowered his head with a sigh and stepped out of the room, humming an old song as he ambled down the hall.

Satisfied, Jack lay back his head as he felt the leather chair lift from the carpet of June's den. It floated above the floor for a moment or two then drifted lightly out the large bay windows and into a white cloud of nothingness.

24

LORD CARMICHAEL'S WHISPER

Henry sat there staring out the library window into the Chicago night sky. His hands had been gripping the arms of his chair throughout most of Ava's story, especially the coming of the wolves, Opus and Maximus, which drew from him a resounding, "Ahhh!"

When Ava spoke of Bettie's parents and the cult that had forced her to draw all the figures and symbols throughout her life, he gazed at her in wonder. He questioned them the most about the creature they had run from at Ava's house, and he repeatedly asked about everything they knew of Brother Jones. Oddly, he asked very few questions about Jack Davies, the person Bettie thought was at the center of it all.

When Ava finally finished recounting the events of the previous forty-eight hours, Lord Carmichael lay back his head and stared at the ceiling. After some time he said, "Opus and Maximus. Did they say where they were going?"

"No," Ava said.

"And this Davies boy. He's the *one*, correct?"

Ava nodded. "Obviously."

"Of Welsh descent?"

"Apparently."

"Mhm," Henry said as if checking off a box in his mind. "Where is he now?"

Ava shook her head and said, "Earlier today, I felt him leave our world—or rather, I felt his sudden absence. I think he peregrinated. I need to get back to Bettendorf and find the spot where he left to be sure."

"Yes, you should." Henry looked at Bettie. "Your drawings were obviously part of some powerful spell—no doubt an ancient one. Do you have any of them with you now?"

Bettie shook her head. "The cult burned them during the ritual."

"Of course, they did. Would you happen to remember any of the symbols you drew?" Henry asked, leaning forward. "Could you recreate them for me?"

"I guess. I drew a some of them so many times I could probably do it in my sleep."

"Good," Henry said, pointing across the room. "Go to my desk and look in the bottom right drawer—the big one. You'll find an old sketchpad and some pencils. Fetch them, dear, if you wouldn't mind." Bettie did as she asked, and Henry motioned for her to sit in the chair opposite him. "Now, draw each of the symbols in as much detail as you can remember. Would you do that for me?"

"Yes, of course."

Bettie found the supplies in Lord Carmichael's big dusty desk and immediately set about sketching all the symbols she could remember from all the years in her room. To her astonishment, she remembered quite a number of the drawings. Her hand glided effortlessly across the old paper as the figures, familiar to her as her own parents, came to life in her mind. Starting with the most significant symbols, she produced three, then six, then ten. One symbol would remind her of another until an hour had passed, and she was still drawing away.

She glanced up at one point and found Ava watching her with loving admiration, while Henry just stared. His eyes seemed to be glowing green. When a second hour had passed, she paused to stretch her hand and saw that Gains had returned to his position just inside the doorway. He was staring at her with an aloof curiosity.

She turned to Henry and said, "I don't know when I'll stop. There were thousands of images I drew over the years, maybe more than that. We might be here a while if you want me to draw them all."

"I think that won't be necessary. Let me look at what you've done," Henry said, gently taking the pad from her hands.

"The first few pages were the larger drawings I drew over and over throughout most of my life. The last few pages are more recent."

A smile slowly grew on his face as he carefully searched each symbol and each figure, running over them with his finger. He said little as he paged through the drawings, though he did mutter the occasional "hm" or "Isn't that interesting?" Ava seemed equally enthralled with the pictures as she stared over Henry's shoulder.

Soon, however, Henry's expression lost its wonder, and a shadow seemed to cloud his visage. His little exclamations of delight were silenced as he stared at the drawings with increasing intensity. His hand rose to his chin, and he glanced up at Bettie once or twice with unspoken questions written across his face. Finally, he set the pad on his lap and asked, "You say you didn't know what the symbols meant, even as you were drawing them?"

"That's right. I still don't know what they mean. From what I figured out, I believe the images were fed to me by members of the cult—my parents' friends." Bettie cleared her throat and bit her nails.

Henry's eyes narrowed, and Bettie almost thought he was going to ask another question, but instead, he continued leafing through the pages, studying the symbols with precision, until he came to the end of the drawings. "These last few pages with smaller symbols and words. You say you drew them recently?"

"Yes."

"How recently?"

"This past week. The ones on the last page, I think I did some of them yesterday afternoon, right before the ceremony at the Bennett mansion."

"I see," he sighed as he stood and looked around the room. "I wish we were in London, and I had my full library with me, but these will have to do. I may have a few that will be of some use. I may have to glean the rest from memory."

"What is it?" Ava asked.

"I'm not one hundred percent certain, and there is still much I can only discover through research, so I shall refrain from speaking in detail, now. However, I am reasonably confident your victory against the devils last night was only partial. I fear many consequences have come and will come because of their—*devilry*."

"Such as?" Ava asked.

"I think you know as well as I do. But since you asked—that man, the one who was waiting for you in your home last night, do you know what it was?" Henry asked.

"I can guess."

"And if you guessed it was a demon, you'd be correct. Though the gates were not open long enough for any of the greater powers to come through, some smaller beings, no doubt, slipped in. A victory, to be sure, but still a breach unlike any I have seen in a great while. Perhaps you remember something similar happening, but I would guess it has been a great many years, hundreds, at least. And such a thing—this physical world would be ill-prepared for it."

Bettie's heart raced at Henry's words. Ava, perhaps sensing her anxiety, stepped behind her chair and placed a steadying hand on her shoulder. "But it isn't the first time something has gotten through, and I'm positive it won't be the last. Like every other time, we will simply have to drive them out."

"You included?" Henry asked, abruptly, and he looked like he regretted it immediately.

Ava paused for a moment and nodded. "If need be, yes."

"I'm sorry, Ava. I didn't mean that. It's just that this world is not ready to face the supernatural. Perhaps a hundred years ago, they would have had a better chance, but now? Science changed everything, made it all so bound to—*physics*. The whole dimension has changed too dramatically to comprehend such things as demons and spirits. An incursion like this would rock the very fabric of the place. Who could predict the consequences of such a happening?"

"You forget one thing—Jack Davies. He is a weapon unlike any this world has had in centuries. Or do you doubt him, too?" Ava asked. Bettie sensed a great tension rising between them, and it seemed the mentioning of the Davies boy brought it to a head.

"No, I do not exactly *doubt* the boy, though I cannot say I believe in him just yet, either. He's not anywhere close to his potential, Ava. You must know that. He isn't trained yet, and there's no time for that. We are forced to take him as he is and hope he doesn't destroy us. Or are you too blinded?"

Gains let out a clicking sound from the other side of the room, cutting through the tension.

"Quiet you!" Henry called to him. Gains mumbled something unintelligible in response.

Ava took a deep breath. "No, Henry. I am not blind to the boy's inexperience. I've seen it first-hand. But I believe in him. I believe he can learn. We can teach him if you'll only give him a chance. I swear to you he is the strongest human I've seen since the darkness."

"Ha! And we know how well that went."

"The world is here, isn't it? It survived, did it not?"

Henry bowed his head and walked across the room to a large stained-glass window, his hands in his pockets. "Yes, it survived.

But something's missing. I believe there is something you don't know, Ava, something you don't understand. There's something wrong with the boy."

A flash of lightning lit up the windows briefly, followed by the low rumble of thunder in the distance. The storm promised in the weather was now fast approaching.

Ava asked, "What are you saying?"

Still staring out the window, as more flashes of lightning brightened the sky, he said, "I'm saying—he has a long way to go before he's ready for what's coming. And what's coming is on its way, or it's already here. I'm afraid there isn't enough time."

Ava walked across the small library to Henry's side, the wood floors creaking under her steps. She stood next to him and said, "Tell me."

Hesitating briefly, Henry finally turned, stepped close to Ava's ear, and whispered into it. Bettie watched as Ava's head bowed, and her hand came to her forehead. Once, she glanced back at Bettie but quickly returned to staring at the floor, her focus remaining there until Henry had finished his words.

When he finished, Henry came to Bettie, extending his hand to her and said, "It was a great pleasure to meet you, Miss Stone. I hope you will forgive me if I take my leave of you now. I'm afraid it's been a most tiring evening with many revelations upon which I must set my mind for a while. Though I may appear to you as a young man, I am far from it, and rest is a necessity. Gains will see both of you out. Would you be so kind as to leave your drawings here with me, Bettie? I believe they will be of some use in the coming days."

"Of course. And it was nice to meet you too, Lord Carmichael—"

"Tut, tut—*Henry*, if you please."

"Yes, Henry. Thank you," Bettie said.

And with that, Lord Henry Carmichael tucked the sketchpad under his arm, exited the library, and walked to his chambers, where he would spend many hours thinking about all he had learned and all he had yet to discover.

Ava, still staring at the floor in front of her, turned to Bettie when Henry had left and said quietly, "We must go now, Bettie. There is much work to be done."

"Where are we going?" Bettie asked, standing.

"Bettendorf, of course," Ava said with a shaky smile, overshadowed by a flash of lightning.

And in the distance, rolling thunder rumbled across the farms and fields of Illinois as it slowly advanced toward the city of Chicago.

25

LIVING DEAD GIRL

Shaun stood in a small patch of Farmer Dawson's field that had been cleared out by a few dozen undead minions. Lucy had supervised their work, now and again glancing back at Shaun with a look that might have passed for worry. Though her white-gray eyes gave the impression of blindness, she could see perfectly well. A line of drool slowly dripped over her lower lip, which she wiped away with the back of her hand as she returned her attention to the workers.

She's their queen, Shaun thought. *But what does she want from me?*

Once the minions had finished their work, they slowly backed away, encircling the outside of the clearing like a wall of living dead. Lucy stepped to the center and stared at Shaun, and he wondered if he might be the dead girl's next meal. Shaun shifted his weight and prepared himself for an attack. However, Lucy contorted her face into what might almost have passed for a smile—granted a slightly repulsive and alarming one, but a smile nonetheless. She raised her hands above her head and let out a guttural scream that sent a small flock of pheasants flying into the sky behind them.

As she screamed, Shaun felt something—not physically but emotionally. It wasn't anger or fear, both of which would have made sense under the circumstances, but rather something altogether unexpected. Was it love? He couldn't be sure. But a strange sensation grew in his stomach, one that thrilled him while it unsettled him at the same time. It began slowly at first but quickly rose in his chest until he thought he might explode with the feeling. Shaun was too young to have experienced real romantic love, so to him, this felt like the most potent crush ever.

Then, it seemed to Shaun that every slowed as the sun set further in the November sky, darkening the whole world, except for the clearing, which somehow remained illuminated by a light he could not see.

Lucy's voice spoke in his mind, *After tonight, we'll be joined. You and me. Us.*

Her heart lurched once with a random beat, loud enough for Shaun to hear it. Or did he hear it in his mind? Shaun tried to speak but found himself unable to form a single syllable. In fact, he could not do so much as move his lips. He looked at Lucy, and she tilted her head slightly to him.

Not with your voice, love, she said in his mind. *Use your thoughts—direct them to me. I'll hear your every word. Just think the words.*

Think the words? He thought to himself, then he directed them to her. *Think the words?*

Yes, think them, she said, startling him. *Think them, and I will understand, no matter where you are.*

Can you read all my thoughts? He asked.

Only those you direct to me, but after tonight, we will be as connected as any two beings can be.

Can the others read my mind, too? Shaun asked, motioning to the minions.

If we want them to hear us, yes.

How is this possible?

Lucy stepped closer to him. *They are ours. I am their queen, and you will be their king. They will do as we please. Our own army. Living for us, fighting for us. Killing for us. We'll be gods—they will worship us. I promise you. All of them.*

Gods. Us.

Yes. Us. Gods.

The thought was beautiful and it filled him with lust and joy. Lucy watched him, smiling wickedly. In the blink of an eye, she was on him, wrapping her arms around his shoulders, one knee running slowly up his thigh, and she breathed in the aroma of his flesh. Another animal-like growl rumbled from deep within her chest, and she lowered her head so that her lips were resting lightly on his shoulder, almost tickling him. Goosebumps rose across his body as he felt the electricity of her touch and anticipation—of what, he did not know.

This will hurt, she said. A *lot.*

I'm ready, he said.

I can tell, she said, looking down at his body.

With no further hesitation, Lucy clamped her mouth tightly and bit into his shoulder. Her teeth were not at all sharp. Unlike vampires, the undead have normal human teeth, unaccustomed to tearing living flesh. However, these creatures did possess inhuman strength. The girl clenched her teeth with all her undead strength to break through Shaun's skin, and when she did, blood flowed from the wound down his back. But she did not stop, for blood was not what she needed—she required flesh. She shook her head violently from side to side, growling with savage fury while holding tightly to his scapular muscle. She tightened her grip on Shaun's shoulders as more blood flowed through the widening hole, rushing down his back and over his chest. Finally, with one hideous scream, she flung her head back and tore away a mouth-sized piece of Shaun's shoulder. Lucy pushed the warm flesh into her mouth with one hand and chewed it in ecstasy.

Through it all, Shaun stood there feeling a mixture of agony and exhilaration, for though the pain was worse anything he had ever been through in his life, there was a pleasure in it to match. As Lucy devoured the last bits of the chunk of his shoulder, her lustful eyes were locked on his. She wiped her face with the back of her hand, unbuttoned her blouse, and pulled open one side, exposing her left breast, covered only by a sheer bra. However, her chest was not what drew his attention—it was her shoulder—her gloriously delicious shoulder.

The girl nodded. He stepped closer to her and leaned down until his lips grazed her cold skin. A smell of rot and decay permeated his senses, though he did not retch. Instead, he bit down on it as she had done to him. Though his jaws were not yet as strong as hers, his desire for her had grown so that an animal instinct had awoken in his soul. She pressed the back of his head with her hand and pushed it down harder to help him gain leverage. Finally, he felt his front teeth pop through the skin, and a glorious rush of metallic-tasting putrid fluid sprayed into his mouth. To Shaun's surprise, he did not flinch or recoil from the gore but, instead, sunk his teeth deeper into her flesh, shaking his head violently as she had done to him. Soon, with great effort, he had torn off a small chunk of her flesh and was savoring the taste of it, as wild sensations raced throughout his body.

They stood there, legs spread wide, heads down, eyes locked, mirror images of each other, each feasting upon the flesh of the other. Shaun stayed focused on her eyes as his body begin to change. At first, he tried to fight through the convulsions that rocked his entire being. His vision faded, and the world seemed to change before his eyes. Sounds became clearer—not louder, just sharper, like turning the knob of an old car radio to catch a station's elusive sweet spot. However, he could not remain standing for long, as the tremors became too violent for him to keep his balance. Slowly, he slumped onto his back on a bed of dead and drying corn stalks, looking up at the sky as the first stars shone through the last vestiges of daylight above.

Lucy came to him and knelt, pressing her wound to let what was left of her blood trickle out and down into his open mouth. Then she lay on top of him, her mouth finding his wound, licking and sucking all the blood from him that she could find, as Shaun Porter slowly died.

Then, some minutes later, he closed his eyes for the last time as a living teenage boy and let the ghostly dreams of undeath wash over him like a cold mountain stream.

26

THE THING UNDER THE FLOOR

Something is scratching at the floor. What is that? What's doing that?

Jack sits in the oversized leather chair as he passes beyond the realm of June's house, away from the strange alternate reality version of Bettendorf. He enters the whiteness of the in-between, the place without worlds, without end. He flies in the chair into memory. A memory.

A memory of his childhood. Jack floats above a small room in an old house—a familiar house—his house. Yes, it is the house he grew up in, and it is morning. He is hovering above his room, looking down at the multi-colored shag carpet, a leftover from the previous occupants, which his parents had refused to replace.

"It's still great carpet. Straight out of the eighties!" His dad had said numerous times to his brothers over the years as if carpet from the eighties was somehow desirable to a teenager.

"It's retro!" his dad would say, but again, such things matter little when you're a kid.

But the carpet is not the focus of Jack's attention; it is the least part. Something is scratching on the floor. . .it's been scratching for some time now, though Jack can't see it. Scratching and scratching and scratching. . .

. . .until it stops.

The whole scene is familiar, something he should remember. Something important happened here. The scratching. It's important, but Jack can't remember why. So he sits in the leather chair, floating near the ceiling, and waits for the scene to unfold.

A small boy enters. He has brown hair that sweeps across his forehead just over his large blue eyes. He is wearing Star Wars pajamas with alternating pictures of R2D2 and C-3PO. In his hand, the boy is carrying a Han Solo action figure. He is no more than five or six. The boy sets his figure inside a toy box at the foot of the bed then turns back to the door and is about to leave the room when the scratching sound returns, stopping the boy in his tracks. He turns slowly toward the sound of the scratching, both of his eyes clamped shut.

"Hello?" the boy says.

"Leave!" Jack yells down to the boy from his floating chair. "Get out of there!"

But the boy cannot hear Jack. He cannot see him. Instead, he remains in the doorway of the room with his eyes clamped shut. Quickly, he opens one eye for only a moment before he snaps it closed again. Eventually, the tension releases from the boy, and he lets out a sigh of relief. The boy opens both eyes and looks around the room. The scratching returns.

"Johnny?" the boy whispers. He goes to the closet and looks inside. "Johnny? You in there?"

More scratching.

He creeps back to the foot of his bed, staring down at the floor in the area between his toy box and his dresser. The boy gets down on his hands and knees and presses his ear to the floor.

When the scratching returns, he jumps back up to his feet and calls out louder this time. "Johnny! Come here!"

A second boy enters the room, this one from the closet. He is about the same age as the other boy, but he is slightly taller. "You called?" the second boy says.

The first boy wraps his arms around him and tells him about the scratching at the floor, pointing to the area where he heard it. "Make it go away, Johnny."

Jack's mind clears and he realizes what he's seeing. The boy in the room; it's him. A young Jack Davies, still hanging around his imaginary friend, Johnny Raynis. A lump forms in his through and he leans forward in the leather chair to get a better view.

"No problem!" says Johnny. "I'm here for you, Jacky-boy. I'm always here for you, no matter what."

"Thanks, Johnny," says young Jack Davies. "What's making that sound? I don't like it. Is it another ghost?"

"I'm not sure. But I think we should check it out, just to be safe. We might need to pull up the floor," Johnny says.

Young Jack shakes his head vehemently. "Oh, no, Johnny, we can't do that. I'll get in trouble, *big* trouble."

"True. Well, I think you should tell your dad about the sound. Let him investigate. That might solve our probably right there. Or, you can deal with this annoying scratching sound for the rest of your life," Johnny says, and he skulks back into the closet.

The scene shifts suddenly out of focus then, in a moment, returns. Time has passed. Hours? Days? It's hard to tell. Night has fallen on the room, and the boy named Jack is lying in his bed with the covers pulled up just under his nose. He is staring in the direction of his window, perhaps trying to get up the nerve to rush over and pull down the blinds. He calls out toward the closet for Johnny, but his friend does not respond.

Then the scratching.

This time, it is slow and quiet—long scratches over and over. The boy lifts the covers up to his eyes, both wide with terror as the sound shifts and seems to be moving closer to the side of the bed. He can hear the sound moving. Young Jack lets out a small whimper as he hears the sound continue to run under the bed until finally, it is directly under him. The boy's chest rises and falls faster now as panic begins to set in. Jack's heart goes out to his younger self, though he has no memory of the scene at all.

Finally, young Jack takes two deep breaths, whispers a quick prayer, throws off his covers, and runs screaming out of his bedroom. It is silent in the room for several minutes, and Jack can hear his father's tired voice downstairs. Soon, Mr. Davies stumbles into the room, appearing half-asleep and disheveled. He searches the floor, the closet, and under the bed but finds nothing. Just as he crosses the doorway to go back downstairs and reassure his frightened child, Mr. Davies is stopped by a sudden scratching sound coming from under Jack's bed. He slowly turns to look, probably wondering if his son's overactive imagination was getting the best of him, too.

But there it is again, the scratching at the floor.

The scene fades then changes again, and now, it is daytime—morning to be precise. Jack sees his younger self, standing next to his dad who is watching a pair of handymen pull back the carpet from the nearest corner of the room. All the furniture is moved into the hallway, except for the bed, which is turned diagonally to accommodate the workers.

"Don't worry, Jack," Mr. Davies says. "I'll bet it's nothing more than some mice or, at worst, a rat. It happens all the time in old houses like these. We'll put a trap in there, and you'll get your sleep back. Ok, Jackman?"

"OK, Dad," young Jack says.

From the closet, Johnny emerges and quietly steps behind Jack. "Sh," whispers Johnny. "Don't say anything, but it's not mice or a rat. You know that."

Young Jack, already aware no one can see Johnny and that he shouldn't talk to him with people around, gives a confused look over his shoulder and lifts his hands, pleading for information.

Johnny pats him on the back and says, "It's something else, Jack. But don't be scared, no matter what you see. It can't hurt you while I'm around. I'll handle it like I always do."

When his dad steps over to a worker to discuss how to proceed, Jack whispers, "What is it?"

His dad turns and asks, "What'd ya say?"

"Oh nothing, Dad," Jack says.

"Don't worry. It's probably mice," his dad says and turns back to the workers.

Johnny whispers, "I told you not to say anything. It's down there, under the floor. You'll see when they pull up those floorboards but don't be scared. It can't hurt you."

After ten minutes of careful prying and pulling, the sweaty workers carefully remove several parallel slabs of wood from the floor, exposing three slats spaced a foot apart. The lead worker, a large Mexican man, named German—pronounced Herman—gets onto his knees and peers between the slats, pointing his flashlight under the floorboards.

"Mr. Davies, I don't see anything," German says.

"Really?" Mr. Davies says. "I heard it last night and this morning, scratching like a son of a gun. You sure?"

"Yeah, nothing there. You want to look?"

Mr. Davies takes the flashlight and searches back and forth in the area but stands back up, shaking his head. "I don't get it. Where could the dang thing have gone?"

Something moves at the side of the hole nearest the window, but Jack's dad and the workers are oblivious to it. At first, Jack can't make out what it is, but then long gray fingers emerge from the darkness. Soon, a hand has reached out from under the floor, grasping the sides of the hole. Young Jack sees it, too. He backs away, his eyes wide and his mouth open.

"Jack, don't say anything," Johnny says to him. "Your dad and the workers—they can't see it. But don't worry. It won't hurt you."

Another dark gray hand reaches out, and ten fingers grab hold of the tops of two slats. The long, lean forearm muscles bulge as the creature pulls its head just under the edge of the opening. Its face is gaunt with narrow eyes glowing from the shadows. It silently stares out from its hole, its eyes filled with hatred. Young Jack gasps for air.

A gurgling voice calls out from the creature. "Jack. . .Davies! I'm coming to get you. Yes, I am. I'm coming to get you tonight. Tonight, when your parents are asleep, I'm going to crawl out of this hole and steal you from your bed. Yes, I will grab you, Jack, and pull you out of your bed and drag you down here under the floor with me, where they'll never find you. They'll seal up the hole, and you'll *stay* down here with me forever."

"Oh, no you won't!" yells Johnny. "You won't touch this boy; you hear me?"

The creature lets out a hideous laugh. "Your friend can't help you, Jack. I *will* crawl out of this hole tonight, and I *will* drag you down here under the floor with me. What fun we'll have down here in the darkest corner of the dark—just you and me—forever!"

With that, the creature withdraws back under the floor, its fingers the last things seen as they slither back into the shadows.

The scene fades and returns again. It is night.

Young Jack is in his bed. The carpet is still torn up, and the hole in the floor remains open. The dresser and other furniture are still in the hall. The gap remains open, and a few sticky mouse traps are set up between the slats. Young Jack is weeping as Johnny stands over him, doing what he can to console the boy. Johnny pats young Jack's head and says, "Shh. Don't worry. I told you I wouldn't let him hurt you, and I meant it. You believe me, don't you, Jack?"

"I don't want to be here, Johnny. Why can't I go downstairs and sleep with Mom and Dad?" young Jack asks.

"Oh, Jack, you don't want to do that. It won't do you any good—this thing will find you no matter where you hide. You don't want this creature to think you're scared—you never want any of them to believe you're afraid, or they'll never leave you alone," says Johnny. Before young Jack can respond, Johnny covers the boy's mouth with one hand. "Sh!"

The scratching returns and young Jack pulls the covers up just under his chin. "Johnny, make it go away."

"I will. You wait here."

Johnny walks around the side of the bed and stands above the hole in the floor, looking down to see the creature's dark gray face looking up at him through the gap between the floorboards. It hisses and gurgles at him with uncertainty.

"Stand aside, you," the creature says. "I am here for the other. I have no quarrel with you, so be on your way and haunt someone else, you nasty boy."

Johnny waggled a finger. "Tut! Tut! If you quarrel with him, then you have a quarrel with me, demon. You will not leave this hole, not while I'm here guarding him."

The creature blinks several times as more guttural noises spill forth. It pulls itself out of the hole just past its shoulders and rests his elbows on the wood flooring. Johnny does not retreat but, instead, steps forward a pace—his hands clenched at his sides. The creature pauses, blinking its large eyes again. "You do not know what I am capable of, young fool. If you did, you would step aside and let me take my prize."

"Oh, I think you don't know what *I'm* capable of," Johnny replies. "In fact, if you don't leave now, I'll have to crawl down there and make you leave, myself."

"No, Johnny," young Jack says.

The creature pauses for a moment, and then his eyes widen with a smile. "Yes, why don't you come down here with me, and we shall see just what you are."

Johnny shifts on his feet, glancing at young Jack and then back at the creature. "I think it's time to do just that and take care of you, once and for all." Johnny steps forward and hops into the hole as the creature retreats into the shadows, a wide smile sparkling in the moonlight.

"No, Johnny!" yells young Jack. "Don't go down there!"

"Don't worry, Jacky-boy. I'll be back soon and everything will be fine. Trust me."

And with that, Johnny dives onto all fours and squeezes his

entire body under the floor as the smiling creature backs away from his advance. Johnny struggles momentarily to pull himself into the small opening under the floorboards, but with some effort, he wiggles himself further into the hole, and soon, he is gone from sight.

Hours pass and young Jack hardly moves, save for periodic tremors of anxiety. He has pulled the covers up to his chin, which he lowers only occasionally to steal a quick glance into the floor. Every few minutes or so, he whispers, "Johnny," but there is no reply.

Then, suddenly, a boy's hand shoots out of the floor and into the moonlight streaming in through the window. Young Jack springs out of bed. He runs his little legs over to the hole, grabs the hand, and pulls back, leaning with all his weight to drag his friend out of danger. Johnny emerges and scrambles out onto the bedroom floor. He scrambles to the wall, heaving, and panting. Johnny pats young Jack on the back. "Thank you, Jacky boy."

"Is he gone, Johnny? Did you make it go away? Are you hurt?" young Jack asks.

"I'm all right, Jack," Johnny says. He sounds far away, like the other end of a long-distance phone call.

"You sure? You look hurt."

Johnny stares out the window for a time before he closes his eyes and shudders. Then, slowly pulling himself to his feet, he drags himself into the closet without saying another word. Young Jack remains on the bedroom floor until his mom comes in to wake him for breakfast.

The scene fades. It changes once again, but this time it's different.

Jack is outside. Snow is falling slowly in sheets of giant flakes. He is in the leather chair, hovering above a path that leads into a small wooded area, much like the woods at Sunnycrest Park. A teenage boy is walking toward the woods on the path, his hands tucked into the pockets of his winter coat.

Just as he arrives at the entrance to the woods, he stops and waits. In a few moments, the sound of crackling leaves can be heard from somewhere not far away, and then a pair of enormous wolves, one dark, and one light emerges from the trees. The boy pats each on the head and follows them into the small forest as the light flakes of an early winter storm dance toward the earth below.

The scene fades.

The leather chair floats over the Woodland of Weird, just above the treetops. Peering over the worn arm of the chair, Jack sees several figures moving through the trees below, all robed in gray. They make no sound as they pass across the leafy ground. Though Jack can't be sure, it seems the boy and the wolves are searching for someone.

The scene fades one last time, as the leather chair falls into nothingness.

27

TOO LATE

Jack opened his eyes to see the wood paneling of June's den. As his mind adjusted to the change in dimensions, he heard voices coming from the kitchen—women's voices. Jack considered going back and traveling again. He knew there was more to the story than what he had just seen. However, a thirst was clawing its way up his throat, so he made his way toward the conversation.

As he expected, June and Faelith were sitting at the small breakfast table. Laughter echoed from the pristine walls, counters, and cabinets as Jack entered and took a seat opposite June. She looked at him with curious eyes.

Faelith, seated to his right, reached out her hand and took his, asking, "How did it go?"

"Uh. OK, I guess," Jack muttered. "I'm not sure what to make of it. I need to think."

"What's there to think about?" June asked.

"There's a lot to think about!"

Faelith patted his hand. "Don't get testy, Jack."

"You're on *her* side now?"

"What are you—" Faelith began but was quickly cut off by June.

"There are no *sides*, young man. Not here, anyway. There is what's best and what's—other than best. You have seen what you must. If you're to learn how to use the power you've only just rediscovered, you must first understand why you hid it."

"I didn't hide it," Jack said.

June paused then asked, "How do you know?"

"Because I don't remember hiding it." The reasoning of the statement fell flat, even for him.

June shrugged. "Let me ask you. Did you remember the creature scratching under your floor?"

"How did you know about—"

"Never you mind that. How much *do* you remember from your childhood? I would guess you remember little to nothing, and what you do remember is probably shaded a particular color of rose. Oh Jack, by now, you must be past depending on your memory. You know why your memory is gone. Your sister hid it, Jack. There is so much you don't know about yourself."

"Yeah, I'm pretty effing aware of that!"

"Did you know you can see the future?"

"The future?"

"Yes, that last vision you had of yourself, with the snow and the trees and the wolves, it hasn't happened yet, Jack."

"The kid in the snow—that wasn't me. . .was it?"

"Yes."

"And that was the *future?*"

June lit another cigarette. "Afraid so."

Jack stood and paced back and forth in the small kitchen.

"Stay calm," Faelith said, taking his arm.

Jack shook it off and pointed at June. "I can't see the future!"

"And yet, you did."

"Bullshit! No one can predict the future. And how are you reading my mind?"

June pushed herself back from the table and glared at him silently. Faelith swallowed as she glanced back and forth between them, but Jack stayed focused as if he were trying to slice through the woman's head with his eyes. Anger rose in him, and the red vision filled his sight as he felt the power flow across his skin and through his veins. This time, Jack didn't let it master him. This time, he held it, and to him, it felt like a gigantic sword—one at least twice his weight. But he kept his grip on it.

"Good. Hold it. And don't let go," June said. "Hold it there, Jack. You're right. It is very much like holding a sword, though one that carries the weight of the entire world within it. I know you're angry, and you'd very much like to lash out at me or flee, but you won't do either. You will stand there and feel the energy of it, get used to holding it. Go on; feel it, Jack."

"Feel it? I don't know what you mean." Jack's eyes began to water.

"Bullshit. You know exactly what I mean. Manipulate it with your mind."

His perception changed—it sharpened. The house seemed to shiver and bow with an odd elasticity as if it were at the center of an event horizon, almost like a Salvador Dali painting. Jack Davies stood in June's kitchen, but his core, his power, was the center of the galaxy. Through it nothing could pass—neither light nor dark, good nor evil. Riding waves of energy and light, Jack raised his hands above his head on either side and imagined an enormous ball of flame between them, like a small star burning for the better part of eternity.

Then Jack felt something else, *someone* else. Another entity. It's hands stretched out to seize him. It was holding onto him, trying to take control of his mind. It was familiar, this force, though Jack couldn't quite place it.

Though June's face betrayed no hint of emotion, an aura of surprise glowed around her body as if she were burning with it. Faelith started at him, eyes as wide as saucers. Jack involuntarily reached out into her thoughts and felt Faelith's emotions. Terror filled her mind. The poor creature, strange as she was, had never known any power like what now stood next to him. Anxiety hit and he gasped for air, grabbing his chest.

"Jack, you must stay in control. Do not take too much of the power—you're not strong enough for it. Resist the desire," June said.

"Strong enough?" Jack managed to spit out with a laugh, though the words were his and yet not his. They came from his mouth but did not come from his mind. It was as if he were a puppet. "Has anyone ever been stronger than me? Tell me, witch, have you ever seen my like before?"

Faelith raised her hand as if to slap him across the face, but June stopped her with a wave of the hand.

"Do not fret, Faelith. This is not Jack. Good, now we have it. I did wonder, but now I see it is true. And to whom am I speaking, now?" June asked.

"Jack."

"You're not Jack Davies," June said.

"Shut up, lying bitch!" The words were flying out now, but Jack had no idea how he was saying them. They were not at all what he was thinking. Something else was inside him, speaking to June.

"To whom am I speaking?" June asked, calmly, then she took one long drag off her cigarette and blew it in Jack's face. He coughed several times and glared at her. "Again, I will ask, and I expect an honest answer. To whom am I speaking?"

"I am Dreadman."

"Ha! What a silly name to give yourself. It is nothing more than a cheap disguise, a masquerade." June smiled, though there was a hint of pity in her eyes. "I suppose that's close enough for now. Why did you come here, *Mr. Dreadman*?"

"To bring the one."

"And you think Jack is this *one*?"

"I do not think it. He is. But you already know that, witch."

June took another drag from her cigarette, her eyes running over every pore of Jack's face. "And how did you bring him here, exactly? He came here by his own power, did he not?"

"Yes. But he came here to find something I have."

"His sister? Anne?"

Jack screamed out in his mind but was silenced by the entity controlling him. However, at the same time, uncertainty rippled across Johnny's essence.

"You know much," Dreadman said. "I wonder how much I might discover when I have you on my rack, spreading your limbs apart. How much will I learn when you're begging to die?" And with that, a picture flashed into Jack's mind of June, naked and beaten, tied to a wooden table in a dark room with her wrists and ankles bound, as a black hand reached out from the shadows to turn a large crank—each click of the wheel followed by screams of agony.

"Get behind me, evil one!" June called out with a voice of command that shook Jack and rattled the entity.

He felt a stabbing pain in his chest, and the entity shuddered from the impact of the words. For a brief second, Jack caught a flash of memory from Johnny's mind.

In the vision, a girl sat on a wooden chair in a small bedroom with one door and one window. She had her head in her hands, and she seemed to be crying—then she looked up. Jack shuddered at the sight of her. It was Anne. She paused for a moment, appearing to be shocked, then yelled something at him, making the vision go black.

"You will not win this. I warn you now," June said. "You would be wise to leave these two behind and seek out some other. When the dark meets the light and the two are one, you'll be cast into the Forevernever, where you should have been sent long ago. This I proclaim, and so it shall be."

A gurgling issued from Jack's mouth and a coughing fit overtook him. Bending at the knees to keep himself steady, he heaved and heaved until a great river of black ran from his mouth down onto the pristine kitchen floor. As he heaved, again and again, Johnny's mind flashed another vision into Jack's head. It was like a picture—a picture of a house in the woods, old peeling white paint across its walls and broken shutters hanging loosely on its windows. There was something hidden in this house. For a moment, Jack thought he could almost hear a familiar hymn coming from the upstairs window.

Jack recognized the song.

Rage filled him once again, and a red hue filled his eyes like a glass filled with crimson water. He reached out with all his strength and retook control of his mind and body. With great effort, once again, Jack held the power above his head and stood there struggling against the desire to drink in more of the light.

"Perfect, young man," June said. "Push the other away. Your temple is no longer his."

Jack stood there for a time, fighting with all his mind to push away any trace of the Dreadman's presence. Finally, he looked at June and said, "He is gone."

"Good. Now search yourself. Feel the power in you and remember it. Remember every molecule, every atom of it. Name each one if you can."

"Name them? How in the world can I do that?"

"It's not so hard when you remember they are as much a part of you as you are of them. They move at your word and bend at your will—they come to life and die with but a word from you. When you learn to wield them, your mind will name each and rename them again within the blink of an eye. They will live and die and rise again all at a snap of your fingers but only when you understand what you are."

For a while, he remained there, feeling the power flow through him, directed by June with subtle but direct words. She guided him across what felt like the entire expanse of the universe. After a time, Jack sensed the power subsiding.

"Begin to let it go now, Jack, a little at a time. But remember it! Remember how it feels and where it goes. Take note of the area of your mind where you last see it. That will be where you find it when you need it. Set it there like a watch on a nightstand. It bows to your command, young Jack. It is there for you and you alone—no one can ever keep it from you unless you let them."

"What is this power?" Jack asked.

"Who can say? Everyone believes what they believe, but no one will know until their final day has come."

"The afterlife? Isn't that where we are?"

"Oh no, this is not the afterlife. It's a different plane of existence from your own, yes, but afterlife it is not. The afterlife comes eventually for all of us, but some of us live many lives in many places between now and then."

Finally, the power was gone. Anger and urgency had replaced the power, and his vision, though no longer red, was crystal clear with purpose. There was nothing to be done for it.

"We must go," he said.

"Go? Where?" Faelith asked.

June put out her cigarette, shaking her head as she exhaled one last puff of smoke. "This is a mistake, but you already know that."

"Mistake or not, I have to go. I have to find her."

"I suppose I could go through the motions and tell you that you're not dead, which you aren't, and that you could be killed, which you might, or pay dearly for your trouble, which you almost certainly will. But I think saying all that would be a waste of my breath, and I'm not accustomed to wasting anything. So instead, I will walk over to you, kiss you softly on the lips, pat you on the back, and tell you to be safe and to come see me again when you're truly ready."

Faelith stared at him. "If you're not ready to use your power, Jack, we shouldn't be leaving. Don't be a fool. Do as June says."

"I'm not a fool! Or if I am, it doesn't matter. I'm going to save my sister, and I'm leaving right now. I've seen where she's imprisoned, and I know she's suffering. How can I stay here and do nothing?" Jack asked, gripping the back of the chair in front of him.

Faelith touched his arm. "But if you're not ready, you won't succeed. You should stay here and train. Wouldn't that give you a better chance to save her?"

Jack pointed at June. "Ask *her*. If I do that, she'll be dead before I'm finished. Won't she, June?"

"Probably," June said. "But I think you know what Anne would want. She'd rather die than have you take this risk. And you know why? Because she knows she isn't the important one. *If you* die, all will be for naught."

"I won't leave her to die, not after everything she's done for me. How many times has she saved my life? How many times did she chase away demons or ghosts? She sat with me and watched over me my whole life, and now, you want me to forget about that? I can't do it. I may be walking into a trap, but I can't just leave her to suffer. I can't."

June smiled sadly then stood and walked over to him, putting one hand on his cheek. "And into the woods you must go, Jack Davies," she said then stood on her toes and placed her lips upon his, holding a soft kiss for what felt to Jack like many minutes. Finally, she went back to her seat at the small kitchen table and lit another cigarette.

"I promise I will come back," Jack said.

June took one long drag and smiled. "I'm sure that's true. But, sadly, it will already be too late."

28

THE DREADMAN'S PRISONER

Lara pulled the head off a field mouse and, holding it over her mouth, squeezed until what little blood it had in its tiny veins trickled onto her outstretched tongue. She needed far more than the small bit of blood she could scavenge from little forest critters. Unfortunately, there had been precious few large animals to choose from, so she did her best to scoop up any critters she came across.

As she moved through the dense forest, she came upon a small hill overlooking a broad valley. At the top of the hill, the trees thinned out, giving a clear view of the surrounding area. She sprang up the slope with ease until she stood at its rounded peak. Less than a mile away, a slithering band of smoke twisted into the sky. Lara crept down the hill, careful not to draw attention to herself. There was not nearly as much cover here, so she tore into a dead run to the next copse of trees, moving as fast as her vampire legs would take her.

She darted from tree to tree until, at last, she found the source of the smoke, a small house nestled in a dark and misty hallow. It was a two-story home with chipped white wood siding. It was a simple home, not unlike any number of old houses she might have found in her own world. The windows were dark, and though she heard nothing stirring within, Lara sensed it was not empty. As she listened carefully, she heard muffled voices talking inside, perhaps arguing.

Suddenly, an alarm rang out in Lara's mind. Someone was nearby—more than one, by the sound of it. She sniffed the air instinctively and immediately recognized several distinct scents—at least five people, maybe more. Two were human, while the others smelled like herself.

Vampires? With humans?

A slight crackling sounded behind her, but before she had time to react, several things happened at once. She was hit in the back of the head with something heavy and grabbed from behind by someone, who covered her mouth with one large hand in a glove made of pure silver. The glove burned her skin and muffled her scream. Immediately, she lost all strength and collapsed to the ground on her back. Above her, a man with a dark face and piercing blue eyes stared down. His mouth was open in a snarl, exposing two sets of razor-sharp fangs. In a blink, three other vampire faces were on her as well—three females. One had hair as black as the night sky in a long black gown to match, the one closest to her had white, almost silver, hair down to her shoulders and wore a silver frock with thick leggings, and the third was bald with numerous primitive tattoos covering her scalp and clad in brown leather. She had eyes as black as coal.

"Why are you here?" the man asked in a gruff whisper as he lifted his hand from her mouth far enough for her to answer. "Do not cry out or you'll pay for it with your life. Who are you?"

"My name is Lara, and I'm looking for my friends," was all she could mutter before her mouth was covered again.

"Your friends?" the man asked. "And what are their names? Speak quickly!"

"Jennifer and Mark Warren. They're humans. They live not far from here, I think. I mean you no harm. I only want to find them."

The man's eyes narrowed.

"Wait," came a familiar voice from someplace behind him, and moments later, Jennifer Warren pushed her way through the vampire faces. "It's Lara—this is our Lara!" Jennifer fell on top of Lara, wrapping her arms around her shoulders. "Oh, thank God you're alive."

Mark Warren followed soon after, and the vampires cleared back to make room. "This is her," Mark said. "This is the one we told you about—the girl who saved Jennifer from Griselda."

"Bless you, Lara—let's help you up. I'm sorry for the scare, but we didn't know who you were," said Jennifer.

"It's OK, but who are they?" Lara asked, motioning to the vampires when she had gotten to her feet.

"Yes, of course. This is Alexis," Jennifer said, touching the dark-skinned man's shoulder. "He saved us from Griselda when we were out searching for you. He's protected us ever since. He was helping us find you."

"Hello, Lara," Alexis said in an unusual accent. "We have heard much of you."

"Hello. Thank you. What are you doing out here?" Lara asked.

Alexis said, "We are here to rescue the girl imprisoned in this house."

"Wait. . .what?" Lara asked. "Who's imprisoned?"

Right then, the white-haired woman motioned for everyone to be silent and closed her eyes. She seemed to be listening to something or reaching out with some other sense. Finally, she opened her eyes and said, "I can feel the girl—she is frightened and confused. There are several creatures in the house, including one who is unlike the others. He might be human, but I'm not certain. There is something. . .*wrong* about him. Alexis—"

"Yes, Laurel?"

"I think it is Dreadman."

"The Dreadman?" Lara asked.

"You know this creature?" Alexis looked at her with another confused expression.

"I ran into him a day or two ago. Maybe longer—I don't know. I've lost all track of time since I was in the Muert's house."

The vampires stared at her like she had pulled a frog from her nostril.

"Muert?" the raven-haired woman asked. "You were with Muert?"

"Yes. She took me to her house."

The bald vampire climbed onto a nearby tree, scoffed, and said, "You mean the Autumn King's house."

Alexis gently took Lara by the arm. "You were in the house of the Autumn King?"

"Yes, for a while. I left a few hours ago. Why are you all looking at me like that?"

The raven-haired woman said to the others, "This is a strange omen. A stranger in the house of the King of Autumn."

Laurel nodded, staring at Lara. "Yes, Avenya. Change is coming—it is coming soon."

Olga hopped down from her perch and said to Lara, "This one smells new. Does she even know how to fight?"

"Yeah, I can fight. I kicked a vampire's ass the other night, and I wasn't too bad with my fists, even when I was human. But who the hell is the girl in that house?"

Jennifer said, "It's Jack Davies' sister. Her name is Anne."

Lara's mouth dropped open, and she glanced back in the direction of the house. "Anne?"

"You know her?" Mark asked.

"Yes. Well, I met her once in our world, the night Jack Davies was kidnapped and taken by the devils. The night you brought me here, Jennifer. I went looking for Jack but I found her in his room and he was gone. She was a ghost in our world. How did they bring her here?" Lara asked.

"We don't know," Jennifer said. "But the gates were open for a while. Maybe just enough time for the Dreadman's henchmen to sneak in and take her."

Alexis considered Lara for a moment, his white-blue eyes reading every random freckle on her face. Though she felt exposed and vulnerable, she sensed no hostility coming from his dark brown face. "We should withdraw from this area and make a plan," he said. "I sense there are more creatures here than just Dreadman."

The group retreated to a small grove a hundred yards away. They sat in a small circle as the Alexis, Laurel, Avenya, and Olga held hands with eyes closed. They sat there together silently and it seemed to Lara that the group was communicating telepathically. She could see their eyes moving behind their lids, almost like they had each fallen into REM sleep. In fact, if one of them had begun snoring, it wouldn't have surprised her at all. Lara glanced at Mark, who simply shrugged and waited.

Finally, the four opened their eyes together and Avenya spoke. "We are in agreement."

"Agreed," Olga, Laurel, and Alexis said as one.

Lara glanced around the room and said, "Okaaay. What does that mean, exactly?"

Alexis cleared his throat. "We agree you are not an enemy. You may join us on this task."

Lara stared at them, not sure what to say. "Well. . .thank you, I guess. I'm glad you didn't take me for an enemy."

"I'm sorry, Lara," Laurel said. "But Vampyr do not mingle easily and once a house has formed, it is difficult to accept a stranger. Our decision meant more to us than it would to you."

Mark said, "So, what do we do about Anne?"

In the end, a simple plan was set. Three of them—Laurel, Avenya, and Alexis—would enter the house from the back, while Lara and Olga would search from the front and try to find Anne. Jennifer and Mark, neither of whom possessed any supernatural power, would remain outside and attend to the girl once they had her.

"This Dreadman," Mark said with some hesitation, "none of us know his true power. He can move through the air by some dark magic, and his touch is deadly, but we know little else. It would be best not to engage him directly, and most importantly, do not allow yourselves to be touched by him. Do not break group."

"Yes," Olga said. "Stick together with mind of steel. Heed not words of Dreadman. They poison the soul."

"He must be powerful. Even Meurt was afraid of him," Lara said.

Alexis dismissed the notion. "I doubt Meurthanasa was *afraid* of Dreadman. I would think he matters very little to her. Meurthanasa's reasons for evading him were most likely something else entirely—reasons all her own. At any rate, we must distract the creature and remove the girl, then escape with all the speed we possess. His minions do not have much power, but anyone with a stake can be a problem."

The group returned to where they had found Lara and assembled in the trees to the side of the Dreadman's house. Olga rounded up as many small animals as she could find and the vampires fed. Jennifer and Mark turned their heads in disgust as the bodies of small woodland creatures piled up at the edge of the trees.

Lara whispered, "I think we should scout the inside first and get an idea of the layout."

"Good idea," Alexis said. "Avenya and Laurel will come with me around the back. Lara, you and Olga check out the windows on the near side—but be silent and do not be seen."

In an instant, the three of them were gone, with only a black and white blur marking their passing. Lara and Olga crept to the front corner of the house and crouched under one of the side windows. Lara slowly rose and peered into the nearest window. Several figures stood in what appeared to be a small living room, empty save for a fireplace and a few random pieces of furniture. The creatures were small and thin with bald heads and bent backs. These were obviously the Dreadman's henchmen the others had talked about.

Olga whispered, "Do you see girl? You see Dreadman?"

Lara squatted down and crept over to her, shaking her head. "No, just his toadies."

"I go around house and see if I can find her over there," Olga said.

Lara looked at the window above them. "OK, I'm gonna go check out the second floor."

"No! They hear you climbing walls."

Lara smirked. "I don't need to *climb*."

"You fly?" Olga's eyes were wide with surprise, like two black eggs.

"Yeah, but I'm not good at it—I can't land, for one thing. I'll probably wind up breaking my neck on the way back down. But I don't think we have any other choice."

"Good luck." Olga awkwardly patted her shoulder and took off around the front corner of the house.

Looking back at the upstairs window, Lara noticed something she hadn't seen before. A blue light glowed from it, reminding her of the aura she had seen when Jack Davies entered the cafeteria. In fact, the more she looked, the more she realized it was exactly what she saw that day.

Now, to get up there.

She gathered her thoughts and focused them on the window pane, its white paint chipping away from years of weather. Then she quietly whispered to herself, *Float.* And suddenly, she lifted off the ground, hovering there awkwardly. At first, she kicked and jerked, trying to keep her balance. Lara calmed herself and soon had the hang of it, at least enough to keep from flailing like an idiot. Then she looked again at the window. *There*, she said to herself and began to slowly rise. Fortunately, it was not far to go, and within a few seconds, she was at the window, willing herself to remain floating there.

She cupped her hands on the glass and peered inside. As her vampire eyes adjusted to the light, Lara saw a girl in a dirty white gown huddled in the corner, exactly where the blue aura was most intense. Suddenly, an alarm rang out from behind the house, followed by the sounds of battle. The vampires were discovered. Lara had to move fast.

She called to the girl. "Anne? Anne Davies?" The girl's head shot up, her face frozen in shock. Finally, she nodded. Lara kicked her foot through the upstairs window.

"Hurry," Anne yelled. "He's coming!"

Without hesitation, Lara concentrated on the wall opposite her and suddenly shot like a bullet directly at it, crashing into the wood paneling hard enough to break her collarbone. "Crap," she said. "I'm not very good at this."

"It's OK! Just get me out of this house!"

"Your chains," Lara sighed. "Those aren't made of silver, are they?"

Anne nodded. "I'm sorry, but yes they are."

"Shit." Lara looked down at her dress, realizing she was still wearing her Halloween costume, Sally from Nightmare Before Christmas. "Well, I guess I won't be wearing this one next year." She tore two long strips from the bottom, effectively turning it into a very short skirt, and proceeded to wrap the pieces around her hands for protection. "God, I hope this works."

Taking a deep breath, Lara seized the metal clasp around Anne's left wrist and immediately felt the searing pain of the silver shot through her hands and up her arms. However, the strips of fabric seemed to help dull the intensity, making the pain manageable. Small blisters bubbled on her palms as she pulled the clasp apart. Without pausing, she grabbed the other clasp and did the same. When she was done she stared at her palms, which were red with angry sores, like they'd been held over an open flame. However, within moments, her vampire skin had already begun to heal itself

Lara grabbed Anne, slinging the girl over her back and ran back to the broken bedroom window. Just as she had pulled Anne through the window and was readying herself for the descent, the door to the bedroom burst open and a word of command roared out to her. The Dreadman stood in the frame, his hands clenched at his sides. Frozen still, fear swept over Lara and she lost her balance for a moment. Pain rushed through her mind, and she dug her nails into the windowsill. The Dreadman's orange eyes glared at her across the room.

Lara hovered there, unable to move—her hands shaking, her teeth chattering. Images rushed through her mind—her mother tied to a post, being whipped by a large woman in a black hood; dead bodies piled up all over the streets of Bettendorf; an enormous winged-beast, soaring across sky, chilling the hearts of any who fell within its shadow; hundreds of people tied together, naked and terrified, walking toward a vast lake of fire. Lara's heart darkened, and she felt an intense desire to climb back in through the window and give herself to the creature. The Dreadman's mouth curled into a sickening smile, exposing rows of sharp white teeth, and he stepped into the room, reaching out one hand toward her.

A desire grew in her heart. She longed to go to the Dreadman, to give herself to him. The desire felt like the only choice, the only thing she could do. Lara was alone, a silly teenage vampire babysitter, without any house or family. No boyfriend, no way to get back home. His voice, deep and silky, dripping with spoiled sweetness, spoke in her mind. "Wouldn't you love to go back home? See your mother again, young vampire? Your friends? These are not your friends; they are not your family. Come to me and I will send you back to your world."

Her heart lurched once, sending a wave of adrenaline through her body and she leaned herself against the edge of the windowsill. Then, as Lara lifted her left leg to swing it into the opening, she heard a strange music in her mind—a soft hymn that cut through the gloom like beams of sunlight through a cloudy sky. The song swept over her and the terror that had gripped her slowly began to fade. The Dreadman faltered for a moment; he too seemed transfixed by the sound.

"Ignore him, Lara," Anne said, her voice weaving together with the palliative notes of the melody. "He's using fear. Push it from your mind! Push it away now, before he touches you. We must leave, or die!"

Summoning all her will, Lara pried her thoughts away from the images the Dreadman was showing her. Looking out at the edge of the forest, where Mark and Jennifer were hiding, she launched herself away from the house toward them, just as the Dreadman's hands reached out through the broken window to grab hold of her, missing only by inches. Lara flipped over in mid-air to land on her back, cushioning Anne from the impact.

Jennifer and Mark were at their side, helping Anne up, as Alexis and the other vampires rushed out to meet them, blood dripping from their bodies. Lara looked back at the house and saw the Dreadman still standing in the upstairs window, staring down at them. Then, without a word, he leaped out the window and climbed onto the roof above. Once there, he glanced down at them again, his eyes filled with bloodlust. Then he blinked out of sight and was gone.

29

THE HOUSE IN
THE WOODS

1.

Jack and Faelith made it back across the lagoon with little
difficulty—a welcome relief after the incident with their clothes
on the previous trip. June had sealed their garments into a small
plastic bag, taped shut to keep out the water. Jack kept the suit,
thinking the jacket might come in handy with the cold air
blowing through the forest—it was November, after all. He did
manage to find an old pair of hiking boots in June's basement.
They were slightly large on his feet but close enough to do the
job.

June made each of them a sandwich, cut diagonally, on a plate
with a generous dollop of potato salad and a bowl of fresh fruit.
Jack wondered where she had gotten the food, but she only
hushed him with a wave of the hand and told him to finish his
lunch.

Of course, June had no swimwear, so they had to make the trip
across the water once again in the nude, which delighted Faelith,

if for no other reason than it made Jack blush. When they finally reached the shore and put on their clothes, Jack led them to a small, but fast-moving, creek not far away.

"Yep, that's just like Duck Creek in Bettendorf. I have a feeling this place is kind of like home—*my* home, I mean. Just a bit different."

"How are they different?" Faelith asked, taking his hand in hers.

Jack looked down at their hands and then back at her. "Are there others like you? Where did your people go?"

"I don't know. They went away long ago, chased away by the Host, and my pack was one of the few that chose to stay behind."

"So, what happened to your pack?"

Faelith stared at the ground and then looked up at him, with one tear creeping across her lower eyelid. Then she said, "My sister Faelyn and I had a. . .*disagreement*. One that took on a life of its own. The cause escapes me now—stupid and insignificant it was, I'm sure. She was stubborn and smart, like me. And when we fought we spared no insult, softened no blow, avoided no injury. It became impossible for us to be near each other, so after some time, our parents separated us from the rest of the family. Banished each of us from the pack for one year, a terrible punishment for our kind. When at last I returned, I found my family dead, frozen like statues by some evil spell."

"And your sister too?"

"No. Though our year had passed, Faelyn did not return and I haven't found her in all my travels since." Faelith stared out into the trees as Jack rubbed her hand.

"I'm sorry, Faelith. After we find Anne, I promise you, I will do everything in my power to help you find your sister."

Shaking her head and wiping a tear from her eye, she said, "It's OK. I don't know if Faelyn wants to be found. But thank you. Anyway, I think your path will lead you elsewhere, though I appreciate the offer." She leaned into him and kissed his cheek once, softly. "We should begin our journey."

"Yes," Jack agreed. "I suppose we should."

"And you know where we're going?" Faelith asked as she put on a pair of black Chuck Taylor's.

Jack looked at Faelith's shoes and laughed, which brought a soft smile to her face.

"Hey, I'm not walking through those woods barefoot."

"They look good. But yeah, I know where we're going. Or, at least I have a good idea if I'm not wrong about this place being like an alternate Bettendorf. The dimensions are a little off, so it might be a longer walk than it would be in my world, but I think that creek over there should keep us headed in the right direction. We'll need to cross at some point."

They followed the lazily flowing water as it wound through what looked like a tunnel formed by rows upon rows of enormous oak trees, their thick and twisted branches looming ominously above. A light breeze cut through the pathway, running against the current of the stream.

On the other side of the creek, they heard twigs cracking and dry leaves crunching. Jack hoped it was nothing more than squirrels running about in the trees. But whatever was making the sounds seemed to be shadowing them. Faelith's face was alert, and her eyes scanned the area as she sniffed the air.

"Damn. This breeze is wreaking havoc with my senses. I'll need to shift to my animal form to get a good whiff. Hold my clothes," Faelith said as she pulled June's dress over her head and flipped the high tops off her feet. She then dropped to her hands and feet and quickly morphed into her coyote form.

"I'm never gonna get used to seeing that," Jack said out loud.

"Don't speak," Faelith said in his mind. *"Remember, we can talk through our minds."*

Jack knelt and stroked her back with his hand, feeling the same affection he had felt for every dog he had ever owned growing up. As he looked at her form, he realized something he had not noticed before when she was in feral form. In coyote form, Faelith was entirely female.

"Hey, you don't have a penis!" Jack said.

"Wow, you're quite the observant one," Faelith said.

"Sorry, but why is that? I mean, what's the difference? Why don't you have both parts like you do when you're human?"

"Is this the most important thing on your mind, right now?"

"I'm just wondering."

"I told you—I am both, and I am neither. But the thought of having sex as a coyote seems a bit gross to me, so that's where the 'neither' part comes in."

Kneeling there and scratching behind her ears, Jack thought about this new information. "So, what happens when you pee? Do you change into your human form?"

"Yes!"

"OK, OK! Sorry, I'm just learning about you. And I'm impressed."

"By what?" Faelith's ears flicked as she looked at him.

"You're so comfortable with yourself, so confident."

"Why wouldn't I be?" Faelith asked.

"No reason. I'm just not very confident, myself. It's like I can't get comfortable in my own skin. But you don't seem to mind being exactly who you are, even when you're so different. I've always lived my life trying to fit in, trying to be something I'm not, just to impress the other kids or my teachers or my parents."

"Why would you do that?"

"I have no idea. I guess that's what happens in my world—when you're a teenager, anyway."

Faelith stepped to him and licked his face. "Your world sounds dumb."

Jack laughed. "I guess it is."

"Well, I'm not accepted by everyone in this world, either. The Host? They do not tolerate my kind, which is why I try my best to avoid them. Funny I should run into you, a damn magnet to them. But you can't live your life worried about what others think of you, Jack. At some point, you have to say 'screw you' to the ones who won't accept you. It's their loss." Faelith glanced back at him then trotted down the path. "Wait there; I'll be back."

When she returned, she accepted a hug, leaning into it, and said, "OK, the wind is making it difficult for me to tell for certain, but I think the coast is clear. I picked up a scent, and it's clear the Host have *been near here recently, but I'm not sure whether they're following us or if they were just searching the area. We should keep our eyes peeled, either way."*

"OK."

"Where is this place you want to cross?" she asked.

"If this place is like it is in my world, there should be some large stones just ahead, maybe a quarter mile or so. We can use them to cross."

As Jack had hoped, the stones were right where he had expected them to be, only they were larger than they were in his world, and there were more of them. Even so, the rocks were slippery enough to make the crossing difficult. It took some time for Jack to make it to the other side. Faelith, however, returned to her human form and sprang across with little to no effort—even barefoot.

"Show off," Jack said. Faelith laughed, and it seemed to him that the sound rang throughout the forest for several seconds after she had gone quiet.

They found no obvious path, so Jack did his best to keep them going in the right direction based only on his intuition. However, he soon realized he had no idea whether they were going in the right direction.

The whole way, Faelith was on high alert. Her head darted back and forth, and her ears were up, twitching at every sound. Now and again, she ran ahead to check on a sound or a feeling that didn't seem right, and once or twice, she doubled back behind them. She ranged out to their sides, staring off into the dark woods as if she heard something she didn't like.

"Are we OK?" Jack asked when she returned to his side.

"We're being followed. This is dangerous country," she said. *"We need to find the house or take cover soon.*

"Have you been here before?"

"No, but I can feel it. Danger warnings are sounding in my head, like drums, and I can feel it in the air and the rocks and the dirt. There is a threat ahead, though I can't tell what it is."

"Is it the Host?" Jack asked, his nerves beginning to feel somewhat frayed.

"Maybe. I think I can sense them somewhere near. But there is something else ahead too, a nameless malevolence I've not felt before," Faelith said.

Faelith trotted ahead, and as she did, once again, Jack noticed a strange familiarity about the place. The trees around them had grown thicker, and he realized they had begun up a long, gradual slope some ways back and were now coming to the crest of a hill. When they reached it, Jack saw they were standing atop a tall hill overlooking a broad valley at the center of which ran an enormous river, too wide to see across. He immediately realized he was looking at this world's version of the Mississippi. It was at least double the size of the real-world river, and he would almost have thought that, perhaps, it was a lake, except for the ripples of current running across it.

"Would you look at that? We made it," he said aloud.

"Quiet! We're close to the house, aren't we?"

"Sorry. Yes, we are close. If I'm not out of my mind, we're at the top of the hill near my street—or at least where my street would be in my world. The old house, if it's the one I'm thinking of, is to our left less than a half-mile away, maybe closer."

"Then it's no coincidence I feel the malevolence stronger here, growing ever stronger the further we walk. I would warn you against this if I thought it would do any good. I think June may be right about what you're going to face. You may not be ready for this test, Jack."

"If it were just a test, I'd go back to June right now, but it's not—it's my sister. What am I supposed to do, waste a bunch of time training, when my sister could be dead? I can't do it, Faelith. You know that."

"Yes, I do. But if you fail because you aren't ready, Anne will die anyway. Still, I can feel your determination, and I won't stand in the way of your quest. It's a noble one, and I respect it. I just worry you're making the wrong choice."

"I won't leave Anne to live one more day in that house. You don't have to come with me, Faelith. In fact, I think maybe you shouldn't. It's my sister—my job."

"That's great. And I'm going too."

Jack smiled at her, and though he did worry about her safety, he was glad for her help. He did not know what he would face inside the old house in the woods, but he had some idea it would test his limits. Now that he was this close, his focus narrowed, and Jack began to feel like it didn't matter what happened to him. Anne was the only thing that mattered. He knew he could not survive long without her—every part of him screamed it.

As they began down the hill, they soon came to a clearing covered in waist-high grass and weeds. At the center of the clearing was a small oasis of trees, and beyond that stood the edge of what appeared to be the Sunnycrest woods, the very woods in which he had played through most of the summers of his life. They were also the same woods in which he had found and saved Ava from the bottom of an old cellar.

They crossed the small clearing and entered woods. Sure enough, they quickly came upon an old pathway leading toward the center of the forest, which wound through the thick undergrowth and numerous trees. Then, as they quietly crept around a slight bend in the path, a small white two-story house came into view. Just like his vision, its windows were black as the night, giving off no light or any reflection at all. The front porch steps needed repair, and the entire place looked like it had been left uninhabited for several years.

"What did you want to do?" Faelith asked. *"Knock on the door?"*

"I don't know. Let's go around the side and see if we can look in one of the windows. Maybe we'll see something if we're closer. It's too dark to tell much from here."

"Wait while I sniff the area, first. I'm not getting anything from this far back. I feel like the malevolence I was sensing earlier is gone."

Faelith trotted around the side of the house, pausing to sniff the ground around the place. Once she stopped in her tracks, her ears straight up, listening to something. But she went back to smelling and looking and was soon out of sight as she circled around the back. She remained behind the house for several minutes, and Jack was almost going to check on her when she came galloping at full speed from the other side of the house. Her hackles stood on end, and her tail drooped down between her hind legs.

"There's blood in the backyard," she called.

"Human blood?" Jack asked, standing.

"Yes, a little of it was human or human-like. I smell it inside the house, too. But there was something else as well—a strange scent."

"What do you mean?"

"I'm not sure. There was something odd about it, Jack. It scared me. And stranger still, in the trees behind the house, there was a pile of dead critters."

"A pile of what?*"*

"Dead animals, like squirrels and maybe a couple rabbits, it was hard to tell because this other scent was mixed in with it. I think there were vampires here... vampires! Very strange. And there were footprints too—a barefoot girl, I think. Too bad my sister isn't here. She was the tracker. She could have told the whole story of what happened back there, right down to the smallest detail. Oh! And there were other tracks too, but everything was too trampled to see much of what happened. I think a battle was fought back there, which would explain the blood. And the evil is gone, and recently, too. Whatever happened here, I think we just missed it."

"But no bodies?" Jack asked.

"Other than the critters, no." Suddenly, Faelith's head jerked up, and she looked behind them, her ears once again at attention.

"What is it? You're freaking me out!" Jack said.

"I'm sorry. But I'm getting a bad feeling, Jack. We need to make a decision or keep moving because I'm afraid this place won't be safe soon."

"Anne! Anne!" Jack called out to the house.

"No, Jack! She's not here. You must be quiet! Something is coming!"

"She can't be gone. Anne! Anne! It's me, Jack!"

"Jack, please! Be quiet!"

Jack barely heard her—his focus remained on the house in front of him. Without saying a word, he took off at a full run, the red vision once again filling his eyes. Anger boiled within him, rising red in his vision, and opening the doorway to his power. As he had done in June's house, he held it above his head, like a ball of fire. The soft sound of footsteps behind him told that Faelith was following.

He ran up the porch steps and reached out with his mind, lashing out with a burst of power, breaking the front door from its hinges. Leaping into the entryway, Jack saw a staircase ahead, rooms to either side and a narrow hall in front leading to a closed door at the end and another on the right. Blood and flesh were splattered all over the walls and floor of the abandoned house. Jack ran upstairs, while Faelith searched the downstairs rooms and the basement. Minutes later, they met back in the entryway.

"*Anything?*" Jack asked.

"*Nothing,*" Faelith said, staring out the opening where the front door had stood.

"*I found empty shackles chained to the wall of one of the upstairs rooms. We're too late!*" The red vision was now a deep crimson like it had been dipped in a pool of blood. The fury in his veins was white hot, and he stood there shaking from it. When he spoke, it was more to himself than to Faelith. "*We need to find the scent!*"

"*We don't have time for that now. Jack? Do you hear me? They're coming! We must go! Now!*"

Jack, hearing little of what she said to him, ran out the front door and down the steps, looking for any sign of Anne or her captors. "*They have to be around here somewhere. They were just here. Anne! Anne! I can. . .feel. . .I can—*"

Suddenly, his head felt cloudy, like someone had given him a strong sedative. His words slurred, and the world looked fuzzy. Jack looked at Faelith, who stood there naked and frightened. She too seemed to be feeling the anesthetic of a powerful spell. Without realizing it, he had fallen to his knees. He tried to stand, getting to a squatting position, but wavered there and fell onto his back. He stared up at the sky as he felt waves of sleep rushing over him. He tried to reach out for the power, but all of his anger had left him.

Jack lifted his head and saw six very tall figures, all robed in gray and hooded, striding out of the forest. He tried to call out for help, hoping perhaps they were friendly, but they only stood there looking down at him, their blond hair pouring down from under their darkened hoods.

"Who are you?" he managed to ask, but he felt like the words didn't sound right–like they were slurred.

Anesthetic waves of warmth passed over him, and he heard Faelith screaming his name from somewhere behind him. He tried to answer, but words were now impossible for him to form. Then, gradually, Faelith's voice weakened, too, until it sounded like she was talking through a yawn.

Jack let his head fall back and looked up at the gray sky through the twisted fingers of dead branches. His vision grew dark, but before he closed his eyes, Jack saw what appeared to be a raven-haired man descending from the sky above him, singing a solemn hymn and smiling a wide grin, exposing a lovely set of perfectly white teeth. Then Jack lost consciousness as his mind floated off into a tide of nothingness.

2.

"Jack," called a voice from somewhere nearby.

He was floating through the ether of time and space, searching for something or someone. Jack couldn't remember where he had been or where he was going and his power sat beyond his reach. Something was blocking him, keeping him tethered to the white nothingness. Searching for family, searching for a friend—for a way out. Try as he might, he could not pierce through the invisible barrier. No matter how hard he flung himself at the boundary, he could not penetrate its force.

"Jack," came the voice again.

This voice sounded urgent, panicked even. It was a familiar voice, a woman or maybe a girl. Or was it the voice of a boy? It wasn't Anne or Ava or his mother, and it didn't sound like Randy or Shaun or Joe. But nonetheless he knew it, and he had a keen idea it was someone he should remember. Jack tried to think, but the cloudiness in his mind slowed his thoughts to a crawl.

"Jack, wake up! You have to wake up now!"

Finally, with herculean effort, Jack opened his eyes and slowly his surroundings came into view. He lay on a bed, his wrists and ankles shackled to each of the four corner posts. The room was stone, human-made and old, like the inside of an abandoned prison cell. The only light came from a torch on the wall opposite him. To his left was a wood door, and to his right was another bed with a metal frame, like a hospital bed from the fifties. A girl lay on it.

"Hello?" he said. "Faelith? Is that you?"

"Oh, thank God. You're awake." Her voice was weak but desperate.

"Where are we?" Jack asked. "Where's Randy and Ava?"

"Jack, we aren't in your world. Remember?"

"Yeah. We're looking for something." Jack's head felt like his mom's famous mashed potatoes.

"Good. Do you remember what we're looking for?"

"Uh, I think so. We're looking for. . .my *sister*?"

"Yes, that's right! Anne, your sister. We're looking for her. She was kidnapped."

"Anne! That's right—we have to find her," he said groggily. He tried to get up from his bed, but his restraints were far too strong to budge an inch, and even if he could have broken through them, his head felt like it weighed a thousand pounds.

"Yes, that's right. But you need to get out of here, Jack. You must get away from here as soon as you get the chance. They might even let you go. They don't seem concerned with you very much, which is good."

Jack noticed the bruises on her face again. "Hey, are you OK?" he asked. "Did they hurt you? Who are they?"

"We're with the Host. They have a *unique* way of looking at things and a particular disliking for my kind. But don't worry about me. June was right—you must save yourself."

Jack struggled to reach out for the power with his mind, but he could barely think straight. He knew he should be angry, but something was keeping him calm. Given his circumstances, he should be livid. "I think someone drugged me. I can't feel anything. I can't find my power. I can't get angry. I should be furious, right now. I only feel tired."

"They've put a spell on you—on both of us. I can't shift, and it's blocking your powers, too. We're helpless, right now."

"Who are these people?" Jack asked, feeling like he might doze off again.

"They aren't people."

"They're not human?"

"No."

"Vampires?"

"No, much, much worse."

"Are they demons or devils? Ghosts?" Jack was starting to run out of monster categories.

"No, Jack, they aren't any of those things."

"What in hell are they?"

"Hell has nothing to do with them," Faelith said as her voice started to fade from hearing.

"Faelith, what are they?"

"They're angels."

30

IN THE COMPANY
OF THE HOST

"Young man, awaken. Awaken and be glad, for you are blessed to be in the company of the Host."

The voice was light, like a hint of a breeze passing over a grassland in the afternoon of a mild summer's day. When Jack opened his eyes, the face he saw looking down at him took his breath. It was an absolute beauty—her skin, peach-colored and soft, glowing with a radiance both natural and ethereal. When she smiled, Jack's heart burned with longing. He felt an overwhelming desire to reach out and touch the woman. He lifted his hands to do so and realized they were no longer bound to the bed. In fact, he was not on a bed at all but a hammock in the middle of a forest.

"How did I get here?" he asked as she took his outstretched hand in hers.

"My brothers brought you down. We thought you might enjoy some fresh air while you recover."

"Where is Faelith?" he mumbled, feeling energy flow from the woman's hand to his. A sense of joy, unlike anything he had ever felt, filled him. He laughed for a moment, overcome by the sensation. "What *is* that?"

"The sensation you're feeling? It is the power of the Host flowing through you from me. It is but a measure of the awesome power bestowed upon us by the Almighty. It can be overwhelming for those who have never felt it before. I can remove my hand if you would rather—"

"No, please don't! It's incredible," he said, and they stayed like that, his hand in hers, for many minutes before he remembered his previous question. "Where is Faelith?"

"Who is Faelith?" she asked.

"My friend. The girl who was with me."

"You had no girl with you," the woman said.

"Well, she wasn't exactly a *girl*, I guess. She was a lot of things."

"You mean your companion? No, she is not a girl at all. But worry not, young Jack. We're attending to it."

"When can I see her?" he asked.

"Soon, I should think. It won't be long."

Jack closed his eyes. He was confused, partly by the spell cast upon him, but mostly by the distractingly electric power flowing from the woman's hands. There was something he was forgetting. An alarm sounded in his mind, but he could not place it.

As if sensing his inner struggle, she placed her hand on his head and said, "Go back to sleep, Jack. Do not bother your mind with thoughts like these. Rest easy. You are blessed to be in the company of The Host."

And with that, Jack fell once again into a deep sleep.

He was floating again in his impenetrable bubble, unable to move further than ten yards in any direction. Though he could still not think entirely straight, and the only emotion he could feel was something akin to joy, he sensed danger all around him. The warning alarms sounded in his mind, but he was powerless to respond appropriately. Something didn't make sense. If these people were angels, as Faelith had said, why were they using a spell on him? Why were they unwilling to let him walk freely among them? And why had they separated him from Faelith? He wasn't injured. He didn't need to rest.

Then, without warning, a voice rang out in his mind. It was not his own, nor was it Faelith's. It was a woman's voice, and it said, *"Jack! Wake up!"*

"Who is this?" he asked as he floated in the nothingness.

"Wake, you idiot! You must find a way out. It's too dangerous for you to stay there. Get out while you can!"

"What do you mean? They're angels. They're going to help me get Anne back. Angels are good."

"Nothing is always good, Jack. When you get the chance, you must leave. Do not hesitate for even one moment! You must flee!"

"I don't understand!"

June's voice began to fade, but before he lost it altogether, Jack heard her say one last time, *"Leave, Jack. Do not hesitate for even one moment. You must go now!"*

And then he was alone, once again, floating in his bubble of clouds.

Jack awoke, still in the hammock, staring up at a multitude of stars. The clouds were breaking up, and he was finally able to see what was above them. It was a sky just like the sky in his own world, and he even thought he saw part of the big dipper. The woods around him were dark, but not far away stood an old tower made of stone with several open windows illuminated in the darkness by flickering torchlight. Jack sat up, blinking his eyes, feeling refreshed.

A voice, June's voice, faintly cried out in his head, but he dismissed it, pushing it into a hidden pocket of his consciousness. He felt happy and safe for the first time since he peregrinated to this place. Nothing but serenity and contentment existed within him at this moment, and he thought he might stay here with these angels for a while. He remembered Anne, but the urgency was gone.

Why is that? Jack thought. *Why am I so content? Is this where I belong? They did offer to help me find Anne, didn't they? I think I remember that much.*

With friends like these—

Jack strolled up a small stone staircase and into the tower. As he entered, the woman who had talked to him earlier at the hammock emerged from one of the doors. She was tall, well over six feet, with golden hair and crystal blue eyes, in the same light gray robe. Her ivory skin glistened in the candlelight.

A bell clanged loudly in his mind like an alarm clock, but he pushed it aside just as he had June's voice.

"Well, hello, my young friend," she said. She had an unusual accent, almost British but with something else mixed in as well. The sound of it, like everything else about her, mesmerized him. "I am so pleased to see you up and about. I imagine you are anxious to get started."

She took Jack by the hand, and he closed his eyes in ecstasy from her touch. Like an intense surge of emotional warmth, pushing his adrenaline through his chest, the feeling made him gasp for air.

"I'm sorry," he said with some effort. "This feeling is incredible. What is your name?"

"I told you before, but I think you were not awake. I am called Versaundra, and I am wife to Thedeus the Righteous."

"Is he here, too?" Jack asked. He didn't want her husband to see him enjoying Versaundra's touch so much.

"Not at this moment. He and his brethren were called away, but they will return before long."

Jack wavered there for several moments before he remembered why he had come into the tower. "I would like to talk about how to find Anne."

"Excellent, I do have some information about her. We believe she was held captive by a malevolent being—one that has terrorized this place for many years," Versaundra said.

Jack nodded slowly, his eyes still closed as he continued to drink in the sensations. "Yes, but I don't think she's there anymore. It was holding Anne captive in that house in the woods where we met you, but they were gone when Faelith and I got there. The house was empty."

"Someone else has her now. A group of beings just as dark, though perhaps not as malevolent. Still, they are quite dangerous and evil at heart. Fortunately, one of my brethren found their hiding place while you were sleeping and confirmed the creature's prisoner, your sister, is with them. They are not far away."

The ringing returned, and Jack pushed it away again, thrilled at the good news, though it took some effort this time.

"Yes, if they have Anne, we must find them as soon as possible. But I'd like to see Faelith now," Jack said, withdrawing his hand from hers.

"Well then, you're in luck. I was coming to take you to her. Follow me," she said, leading him out the door and into the woods.

June's voice echoed in his mind.

A coldness passed over him as they walked the small path that wound down the hill from the tower through a thick patch of trees and bushes. There was a strangeness to her tone when she offered to take him to Faelith. His unease grew the further they walked. The trees were silent, but Jack sensed them watching him anxiously.

"This Faelith. What do you know about her?" Versaundra asked, placing a hand on his shoulder, once again, flooding him with emotions, this time, doubled in power. Lustful thoughts raced through his mind, and he pictured Versaundra naked in his arms, her long legs wrapped around him as he made love to her. He recognized what she was doing, but he was powerless to stop it. The woman played on every adolescent urge in his body.

The alarm rang in his mind again, but this time, Jack did not push it away. Instead, he tried to shrug away Versaundra's hand, but her grip tightened sharply, almost to the point of pain. Panic rose up through the desire.

"I know very little about her. We just met," he said at last. "She is a shapeshifter, I guess, but that's about it."

"Jack, you are very powerful. But you are also young and easily influenced. Indeed, even my simplest of spells play upon your youthful desires with ease. If I were a thing of darkness, I could use your weaknesses against you, doing great evil to the world in the process. I could control you so easily—make you do things for me. You would be a most delightful weapon. You are a blessing—a blessing to The Host. You will be a great hero, and songs will be sung of you, not just in this world, but in your own as well. And countless civilizations throughout the many universes will hail you as the greatest champion of the light. Is that not a beautiful thing?"

The alarm rang louder now, resounding through his mind so loudly Jack wondered if Versaundra could hear it too. A thought entered his mind, one that he had not considered until now. Perhaps, he was not supposed to find his sister, not yet. "Yes, I agree I'm meant to stop evil. It's true. But first, I have to find my sister."

"Of course, of course. Though your sister matters little, I see she means much to you. As a show of good faith, we will help you find her and send her back to your world."

As they continued down the path, Jack could see the light of several flickering torches burning through the trees ahead. They were coming upon a small clearing. "Are your. . .people. . .here?" he asked, the ringing in his head now rising to a fever pitch.

"They are waiting for us."

"And Faelith. . .is with. . .them?"

"Yes."

"Is she. . .OK?" the ringing seemed to be slowing, taking on an almost melancholy tone if such an emotion were possible in an alarm.

"She is free."

Jack looked up at Versaundra, who kept her eyes solemnly fixed ahead. "What... does that mean?"

"Jack, when you have a gift such as yours, you must use it to drive out the darkness of the world. Too long has it lived here, growing unabated. It has become strong, almost as strong as the light. Soon, it will be stronger, and there will be nothing even the Host can do to stop it. We must, all of us, find a way to drive it back—send it into hiding again, or it will spread from here to your world and all the worlds of eternity."

"What does that have to do with Faelith? She's not evil. I know it." Jack's senses were coming back to him as the alarm steadied in rhythm.

They came around a gigantic elm tree, covered in parasitic vines, and into a small clearing encircled with torches. Several of Versaundra's brethren stood in a semi-circle before two large oak trees. The Host did not turn to them but kept their focus on something hanging between the oaks.

"You see, young Jack. Not every evil is darkness—some are *different*. They are not dark or light, man or woman, human or animal, saint or sinner. But they are an abomination, all of them, and must be rooted from our world. It is hard. I understand, but it must be done."

At first, Jack couldn't register what he was seeing. Two ropes hung from the trunks of the two giant oaks, each of them attached to a girl. The girl's head hung toward the ground—her long wild hair drooped down, covering her face. Spatters of red had soaked through the gown, and just below her waist was one large dark red patch of half-dried blood. Streams of blood ran from under her dress and down her legs, dripping from her toes. She had been killed only recently here in this clearing. On the ground directly below her, something small was on fire. The smell of burning flesh hit Jack all at once.

Versaundra took her hand from his shoulder.

"What. . .is. . .this?" he asked, falling to his knees as recognition crashed into him like a tidal wave. "What. . .have you. . .done?"

"Only what had to be done, and it pained us to do it. It is what you must do if we're to be saved. These are hard things, Jack. We know it; such is our burden. This thing was a friend to you of sorts, or so you believed, but I assure you it was nothing more than an *abomination*." Somehow through all of it, Versaundra managed to sound sympathetic.

"Faelith was NOT an abomination! She was loyal. She was kind. She was good. She. . .was. . .my *friend*!"

"Not *she*, Jack. There was nothing *she* about her. It was leading you astray. Someday, you will see. We, the Host, will help you see, and you will understand. It is why we are here, why we found you, why you were delivered unto us! This thing was tempting you, leading you down a degenerate path, but providence saw to it that we should find you just in time. We have protected you from it." One sparkling tear ran down Versaundra's face.

"She was not leading me anywhere. She was my *friend*, why don't you see that? Don't you know what a friend is? How can you not see that?"

The blood-red rage swept quickly over his vision, and Jack reached out boldly to seize it and destroy the Host, every one of them. But before he could grab hold of it, the brethren joined together in song. The hymn washed over him, like a river breaking through a dam, casting him onto his back.

Jack began to lose consciousness. He kept his eyes open for as long as he could, fighting against the anesthetic hymn, to stare at Faelith's body hanging dead above him. Jack prayed she would wake up and run away in her coyote form. He would join her, and together, they'd escape the Host and fight their way to safety.

But her body remained still. She was gone.

As his vision faded, he heard Versaundra speak. "Fear not, young peregrinator, your life is spared and much will you learn. We will teach you to use your power for good. You now belong to the Host."

And with one last moment of consciousness, Jack lifted his head and managed to whisper, "Goodbye, sweet Faelith. Goodbye."

31

DIVERGENCES

1.

Shaun stared around him. His undead eyes focused on everything and nothing all at once. Though his mind now processed thoughts quickly, it did so only one at a time. He felt unmoored and perpetually distracted. As he looked at the ground, a blade of grass seemed to be waving at him. All he could do was stare at it. He tried to return the gesture but forgot what he was doing the moment he caught sight of his hand in the corner of his eye.

I know it's confusing. Lucy's voice drifted into his brain. *You'll get used to it. Your mind needs to adjust. Soon, you'll control your thoughts. Soon, my love, you will be more powerful than any of them. I promise.*

He looked at her and grimaced in a half-smile. Her voice washed through his thoughts, knocking them over like a line of dominoes. *These others are so dumb. Why are you different?* Shaun asked. *They don't think. How can you? How can I?*

After I left the preacher's church, as I walked down the road toward Whitey's, a man came to me. He was handsome and dressed in a business suit, not cheap like the preacher, but new and elegant. Though

I hungered for flesh, something about him made me wary. He stared into my eyes and told me I was different from the others. He asked if I wanted to ascend. Though I didn't know the word or what it meant, I sensed the power of the word. His voice made me feel alive again like I had woken from a dream. I nodded to him. He touched my forehead and whispered words, quietly but intensely. And like that, I was changed, though still undead.

Who was this man? Shaun asked.

I don't know. He didn't say, and I didn't ask, but I think we must find him.

Shaun looked at the minions stumbling along behind them. *Will I be like them?*

No, you'll be like me. You ate from my body, so you have ascended as well. You were different. I saw it the first moment our eyes met in the ice cream shop. There are others like us as well—others who can ascend, and we must find them.

A lumbering army of undead—maybe fifty strong—followed them through the endless field of corn, drawn like a herd of hypnotized cattle by Lucy's power. Her jaw was set, and her pale, dead eyes focused ahead of her. More undead had gathered around her in the past day, though not all that Jones had created. Shaun glanced back and grunted with satisfaction. *A lot*, he thought.

It's still not enough, Lucy said.

For whatever reason, Jones's undead had divided into two camps—those who followed the preacher and those who followed Lucy. As far as Shaun could tell, Lucy's side was winning the war of recruitment, but Lucy said they were still outnumbered by Jones's horde of undead, not to mention whatever others he may have drawn to him in the past day.

Suddenly, Lucy stopped and clamped her eyes shut. She did this whenever a vision came to her. Shaun waited, watching her.

What is it? Shaun asked.

Lucy wore a worried expression, her cloudy dead eyes

searching his face in a way that seemed apprehensive. *Something has happened*, she said finally.

What?

I must show.

Show me? Where?

Close your eyes.

OK, Shaun said. *What is it?*

You'll see. Relax and take my hands.

Shaun did as she said. A scene popped into his mind, startling him at first. It was the inside of a small church, dimly lit by hundreds of candles lining the walls and pews. A tall man robed in deep black stood at the front of the church near the pulpit. At his feet were two people, teens, bound by silver chains and rope. They were gagged and listening to the preacher. Then, doors opened on both sides of the vestibule and in stumbled dozens of the undead, filing around the pews on either side until they encircled the two teenagers.

Oh my God! It's Randy, Shaun said. He opened his eyes from the shock, and the scene faced. *They're in trouble.*

Lucy squeezed his hand and said, *Yes, they are with Jones.*

Jones? The Jones who made all the undead? The one who kidnapped Jack?

Yes, the very same, Lucy said, *the one who made me what I am.*

We have to help them! Shaun looked in the direction of the church, struggling to make his mind work.

We will, my companion, Lucy said. *But we must build our army. You and I. We will be Queen and King of the Dead, and none shall challenge us.*

Lucy's voice echoed in Shaun's mind, as together they proceeded across Middle Road and through a ditch into another cornfield behind the same Whitey's Ice Cream, where the undead had made their first attack two days earlier. Lightning flashed, illuminating the whole world in a ghostly light as a storm gathered above.

2.

"Dreadman's henchmen are dead. We should pursue him and finish this," Alexis said. He wiped the blood from his mouth with the back of his sleeve.

"No," Anne said. "I'm afraid he won't follow us. He's saving himself for his real battle."

Olga shook her head. "But it so close. We kill it, once and for all. You know not the damage he cause."

"No," Anne repeated. "If we pursue him, some of us will die. And if he wanted me back so badly, he would have pursued us. I'm worried about why he didn't."

"What do you mean?" Lara asked.

Anne paused for a while and then said, "I think he kidnapped me to lure my brother Jack. The fact that he didn't pursue us says a lot. Jack must be here in this world, looking for me. We can't waste time looking for this Dreadman. I have to find my brother."

Alexis frowned. "I'm sorry, young one, but we will need a better explanation than that if you expect us to let this creature go. He has caused much mischief in his time here, and more to come if we do nothing, I fear."

Anne clasped her hands and touched them to her chin, thinking. "You don't understand. He won't be found unless he wants to be found. Besides, this Dreadman act is only a disguise. I know his real name."

Laurel's eyebrows raised. "What do you mean?"

"He's Johnny, Jack's childhood imaginary friend."

"Imaginary, you say?" Laurel asked. "How is he imaginary? He is quite real, I would say. Ask any of the many souls he has stolen."

Anne wiped a tear from her eye. "I'm not sure I understand. But you're right; he isn't imaginary any more than I am. I have to tell Jack. We have to find him before Johnny does."

Everyone stared at Anne, silently, for several minutes. Finally, Jennifer interrupted the silence saying, "Look, I don't think any of us understands what's happened here. But we do need to rest and come up with a plan. As do you, I'm sure, Anne." Jennifer took Mark by the arm. "Our home is not far from here. Let's go there and decide what to do next. We've done what we came for—we've saved Anne. Now let's figure out how to find her brother."

Avenya, who had been staring into the woods, turned to the others and said, "I sense something else in these woods, my friends. We should not wait here long. Something is coming."

"What is it?" Alexis asked.

"I'm not certain, but I'm afraid we've been spotted. We need to leave this place at once. I sense hostility and greater numbers than we have."

"Yes, we should leave. If we are all in agreement, we will make for Warren's home. Anne has given us much to discuss and much to decide.," Alexis said. "Such things require clear minds."

As the group made their way through the woods toward Alexis's home, Lara glanced back toward the Dreadman's house, and for a moment, she thought she spotted a pair of hooded figures hovering in the air just above the ground with great wings thrashing against the cool air.

3.

"Can you *feel* them, Mr. Wall. Can you?" Brother Jones stood over Randy. A flash of lightning lit the interior of the little church in blinding white.

"Who?" Randy asked, squinting from the flash of light as the dull rumble of thunder quaked above them.

"The devils, of course. Surgat and his brothers. You feel them, don't you, young Randy?"

"I don't know what you're talking about." Randy was bound head to toe, wrapped in strange rope with a silver metal chain laced around it. He glanced to his right and saw Tatsu, still sleeping and tied in the same. They were in the sanctuary of a small church, lying on the floor next to an altar, just below the pulpit. A man with thick glasses stood in the back corner of the church, and a great many people, who looked like zombies, were standing around them, staring with hunger.

"Oh, my young friend, I do not believe you're at all honest

with me. In fact, I am almost one hundred percent certain you're lying—and I ain't the kinda man who labels a man a liar without reason. I am quite certain, as I stand here today in this house of my Lord, that you do indeed feel them—one of them, anyway."

Randy struggled with his bindings for a moment, his anger rising. "So? What of it?"

"What of it?" Jones laughed. "What of it? Well, now isn't that something, Carl? Isn't that just amazing? This here old boy has a devil in him, and he says, 'what of it!' Oh, that is something else, I tell you."

The man at the back of the church did not reply but stood there, staring at Randy with a blank, expressionless face. His eyes were cold, and he looked like the type of man who might kidnap and dismember a nun without a second thought.

"My friends will be here. You know my friend Jack? Jack Davies? You remember him, don't you? He'll be here soon—he's gonna kill you and everyone you know if you do a thing to me."

"Oh, I don't doubt it, Mr. Wall. In fact, you might say I'm counting on it. My time here on this earth is limited, unfortunately. I had my chance ya see, and I blew it. And I have *you* to thank for that—you and your dirty friends. So, you won't mind if I take this moment to have a little revenge, will you?"

Jones knelt next to him, removing the leather glove from his right hand, and held it above Randy's face. "Do you have any last words?"

"Yeah. Opus and Maximus!" Randy screamed.

Jones recoiled. He stared at the walls and ceiling, his eyes wide and his mouth trembling. But when no sound came, no rumbling, no growling, or breaking of doors, he breathed a sigh. "Ah, now isn't that just a shame? I guess them pups don't afford you the same respect they do Mr. Davies. Such a shame. I may have enjoyed going out like that! Alas, it's just you and me. Don't worry, Randy. When you wake up from this, you'll be good as new—and a lot more useful; that's a fact."

Randy closed his eyes as Brother Jones brought his hand down to his face, and a searing pain shot throughout his body like white-hot iron. Though the pain was excruciating, Randy realized he was not dying. The burning on his face crackled and popped like a piece of meat on a skillet, but aside from the pain, he was not harmed. He opened his eyes and saw Jones staring down at him, once again, eyes wide. Great beads of sweat popped out on the preacher's forehead as he pressed down harder on Randy's face.

"ICH BENT ILTU FORNA!" Jones screamed. "ICH IM FRENT!"

But no matter the words, no matter their order, all he could do was cause pain, nothing more. The preacher pulled back his hand, frustration twisting his face into a look of horror, and balling up his fist, he began to hit Randy in the head. "If nothing else will work, I'll beat you to death!"

The preacher's blows rained down. Randy, unable to defend himself, took the beating as he lay there bound in the enchanted rope and silver chains. His head snapped left and right. Blood splattered on the preacher's face as a shower of punches rained down upon him. Surgat howled with laughter inside Randy's head, praising the preacher and cheering him on. Then, just as Randy was about to slip away from consciousness, the front doors of the church burst open, shattering into a thousand pieces.

Randy turned and saw an enormous man standing in the doorway, rain pouring down in sheets behind him. The man wore a long black coat, his bald head covered in dark tattoos. As Randy slipped into unconsciousness, he heard Brother Jones laughing above him, and saying, "Well, now isn't this just the nicest surprise—"

4.

Jack awoke in darkness, being jostled back and forth. He reached out his hands to steady himself and found he was inside a wooden coffin-like box. His hands and feet were bound tightly. As his eyes adjusted, he saw slivers of light cutting through the wood slats of the box. He could barely make out leaves and branches moving across the light. They were on the move.

He remembered Faelith, what the Host had done to her, and the pain of it returned. It felt like a knife to the heart. He reached out for his power like June had taught him, but could not find it. When he tried to get angry, attempting to seize it through the rage, he found himself unable to find any emotions but sadness. June was right. He had not been ready.

Little shafts of light flashed here and there on the inside of the box. Jack rolled himself from his back to his side and pressed his face against the box to get a look. There was just enough space between the slats to see flashes of passing forest in the dim light. He was indeed riding on a flatbed wagon pulled by two brilliantly white, almost glowing, horses. Some of Versaundra's brethren rode next to the team with their hoods pulled over their heads.

"Ah, Jack, you are awake," Versaundra's voice sounded from above the box. "I know you must be upset with us, so we have placed a calming spell on you until you can bring yourself to understand and accept your fate. You are blocked from your power by Versamuel's spell. You will not reach it until we allow you to do so."

Jack reached out for it. He felt something holding him back, blocking him. Rolling on his back, he let out a sigh and said, "Couldn't you at least find a bigger box?"

"I am truly sorry, my young friend, but worry not. Your power is going to be used for so much good! With it, we can finally rid this land of so much darkness, so much pain, so much evil. You will see, young Jack. With *our* guidance, your power will free the land from death and darkness. You are blessed to be in the company of the Host."

A voice called to the horses, and the wagon lurched to a stop. Jack listened as he heard Versaundra calling out commands in a strange tongue. The sound of the language was beautiful, but Jack sensed evil in the words.

Then Versaundra said to him, "We will begin here, Jack, by ridding the land of a most dangerous witch."

Jack rolled to his side and peered through the wood slats, once again. His heart sank. The Host had gathered at the shore of a quiet lagoon—one with a small wooded island at its middle. Jack searched desperately for a way to break the spell, as June's last words to him played over and over in his mind.

". . .*it will already be too late.*"

Matthew Speak grew up in Bettendorf, Iowa, within sight of the Mississippi River. He moved to Chicago after college, performing in and directing several plays around the Midwest. Eventually, he moved to California where he appeared on stage and in a few short films before seeking his teaching credential. When he isn't writing novels, Matthew is a special education teacher at Northpoint School in Northridge, CA. He lives in Burbank, CA, with his family.